T0113935

APOCALYPSE

Book 1

THE QUEST

PAUL OSHIRO

WESTBOW
PRESS®
A DIVISION OF THOMAS NELSON
& ZONDERVAN

WestBow Press books may be ordered through booksellers or by contacting:

WestBow Press
A Division of Thomas Nelson & Zondervan
1663 Liberty Drive
Bloomington, IN 47403
www.westbowpress.com
844-714-3454

All Scripture quotations are taken from The Holy Bible, New International Version®, NIV® Copyright © 1973, 1978, 1984, 2011 by Biblica, Inc.® Used by permission. All rights reserved worldwide.

ISBN: 978-1-6642-5016-1 (sc)
ISBN: 978-1-6642-5017-8 (hc)
ISBN: 978-1-6642-5015-4 (e)

Library of Congress Control Number: 2021923387

Print information available on the last page.

WestBow Press rev. date: 11/18/2021

When you hear of wars and uprisings, do not be frightened. These things must happen first, but the end will not come right away." Then he said to them: "Nation will rise against nation, and kingdom against kingdom. There will be great earthquakes, famines and pestilences in various places, and fearful events and great signs from heaven. (Luke 21: 9–11 NIV)

When he opened the seventh seal, there was silence in heaven for about half an hour. (Revelation 8:1 NIV)

CONTENTS

PROLOGUE

Dom's heart was pounding through his chest, and sweat rolled down his face as he raced forward through the narrow tunnel. Just a few lights along the long tube illuminated the way forward. His prey was just ahead. It had taken so long to get this far, and he had abandoned and forsaken all to apprehend his foe. Dom was the hunter chasing his prize, getting closer, and no one would stop him now. He yelled at the top of his lungs. "Stop where you are! Or I will blast you two out of sight!"

No answer, and the two fugitives ahead kept on running. Dom did not actually intend to shoot them. He needed his prey alive. He needed to interrogate them to find out the answers to the questions he had. All the answers Dom needed were in his adversaries' heads. Dom's partner, Jack, fell behind as Dom picked up the pace. He could hear Jack yell, "Dom! Wait up! Don't go it alone! They may have reinforcements!" Dom picked up speed. He was close—so close he could hear his prey's footsteps ahead. Their boots made a rhythmic thumping noise; they were in synch with each other in a military marching cadence at high speed. Dom's thumping footsteps matched their beat. The two were almost within his reach.

The heat was unbearable. They were in a small utility tunnel. The humidity must have been one hundred percent and the temperature over a hundred degrees Fahrenheit. The tunnel walls were lined with pipes that radiated more heat, adding to the already unbearable temperature. Dom's clothes were soaked with so much sweat it looked as if he had been caught in a thunderstorm. Just a little more. He was just within arm's length of the two fugitives when a bright light shattered the darkness, bathing the tunnel in pure white with the intensity of the sun's light. Raising his hands to his eyes, he was blinded, but he continued to run at full speed. Dom veered slightly to the left and brushed against one of the super-heated pipes. "Arrrghhhh!" Losing his balance and falling face first, Dom tumbled for about fifteen feet before he skidded to a stop. Dazed, he squinted his eyes. The tunnel still reverberated with the blinding white light. He called out to his partner who should be just behind him now, "Jack! Jack! Where are you?" No answer. Did they somehow get his partner from behind?

Dom no longer heard the footsteps of his prey ahead or his partner behind him. There was just an eerie silence. The light was blinding, yet warm and comfortable. An intense feeling of peace and calm came over Dom. Then a loud voice seemed to come from everywhere all at once. It was a male voice, deep and resonating with strength, and something else—an emotion filled with a pang of sorrow. Dom couldn't make out the sound; it was muffled somehow. The words were spoken clearly, but his mind could not process them to make any sense. The light intensity grew stronger and stronger as it blazed through Dom's closed eyelids. Then, from a state of pure blinding white, everything went black. Dom descended into cold, dark, blackness void of light, sound, and smell. His sense of touch was even rendered useless. All of his senses were gone, and he was floating in a sea of nothingness. A fear came over him that was like nothing he had ever felt before in his life. It was as if all the world had disappeared, and he was left alone in darkness. Madness, despair, and hopelessness came crashing over him.

Dom woke up yelling, "Aaaargh! Make it stop!" His face was dripping wet, and his blanket lay crumpled on the floor, thrown off during his nightmare. It had seemed so real. Dom sat at the side of his bed, his hands shaking from the dream. He said to himself, as he had on many occasions when he'd had this same nightmare, "It's just a dream, Dom. It's just a dream."

Dom's mind wandered. *How did it all come to this? The way we live now like robots. Is this all life will be for me? Born and raised to a predetermined position in life.* And what a life he lived. Simon Christopher Halos (also known as Dom), catcher of criminals— judge, jury, and executioner.

Dom levered himself up from his bed a bit more slowly than usual that morning. His forty-year-old body wasn't what it used to be. Standing nearly six feet tall with two hundred pounds of toned muscle, Dom was still fit like an athlete just after his prime—only with a few extra pounds around his waist. But his years of hard living were starting to take a toll. While brushing his teeth, he looked in the mirror. His face was fair in complexion with European and a touch of Middle Eastern features. A few winkles had formed around his eyes, and his wavy, dark-brown hair had started to show a few grays around the edges. Mumbling to himself, he said, "Getting old, Dom." He thought of how he had got to this point in his life, living alone in a small apartment. Every day was either mind-numbingly boring or potentially his last day alive. Being a detective in these times was 98 percent routine boring work chasing down leads, and the rest was total life-or-death action.

Dom jumped into the shower and let the steaming hot water rain down on him. His mind drifted to the far past, what little past he knew. He thought about what had been taught, and what he had learned from others during his years on the streets. He thought about how the old world had come to an end and how the new world—the world he now lived in—had risen.

CHAPTER 1

Background

The world population had reached ten billion in the year 2050. From there, the numbers kept growing much faster than predicted due to advances in technology and medicine. The previous estimate that ten billion people was the upper limit of what the planet could sustain was proved wrong. Advances in technology that provided cheap power, clean water, and sanitation to developing countries were blessings to all. At least in the beginning, they were blessings. People were living longer, healthier, and happier lives. The developing nations continued to have good birth rates, and the reduction in working hours and better lifestyles in the West and across Europe gave the people a boost. Birth rates climbed in those countries as well.

Despite all the benefits to society, the few at the top grew richer, and the divide between the rich and the masses grew wider. The elite did not see the equality, prosperity, and the better living conditions; they saw the numbers climbing—eight billion, nine billion, ten billion. In fact, the numbers kept climbing ever faster. They remembered the studies and predictions of the scientists on overpopulation and the resultant strain on the earth's resources.

The developed world was using clean power, which allowed the developing nations to use the excess oil reserves at a low cost. Their vehicles and machines polluted the air without regard as they strove to catch up with the rest of the world.

After a population of ten billion was reached in 2050, the original prediction of reaching eleven billion by the year 2100 became a gross underestimation. The world teetered at fifteen billion people by the year 2100, pushing the limits of technology to feed and house the sea of humanity.

It was then that climate change also hit hard. No amount of clean energy or environmental sustainability could stop the natural forces of change. Twelve thousand years ago, the world was at the end of the last ice age. The theory that the ice age started because of melting polar ice stopping Earth's warm-water Atlantic Gulf Stream from circulating—a major part of the ocean's global conveyor belt—was correct. Predictions that it took thousands of years for the warm water circulation to slow and stop were incorrect. The minority of scientists who theorized that this would be a sudden event were more accurate in their predictions.

The already-changing climate was accelerated by human impact from years of stripping the earth of its resources and belching out carbon dioxide and waste fumes. The weather patterns became more erratic. Instead of a steady warming due to increased carbon dioxide that helped to retain the sun's warmth, Earth grew cooler. The scientists knew what was happening, but no one could reverse it. The polar ice had melted, and as a result, the Gulf Stream's warm water engine was slowing.

It didn't take much to ignite the end of all things. A few seasons of crop failures and reduced solar radiation to solar panels that powered most of the developed world's electricity was all it took. The northern world leaders looked to the African, Middle Eastern, Asian, and South American nations who were still bathed in warmth. Muslim radicals ratcheted up the rhetoric that it was God's punishment to the Western and northern powers. Russia, Europe, and the Americas, desperate, began to take by force that which was not given to them through diplomacy. As the northern countries turned and took land to the south, the world order went into chaos. The fighting was conventional and devastating—years of slow, painful battles. It was World War I and World War II all over again. This time, though, there was no thought of surrender or peace. The northern countries were starving for food and power; to lose the war was to condemn their nations to utter oblivion from the new ice age.

It was inevitable that the Middle East would fall in the conventional fight. The powerful troops of the northern countries overran Iraq, Syria, Kuwait, Iran, and even Saudi Arabia. Faced with the reality of losing, Saudi Arabia was the first to launch a nuclear missile. China and India saw it as their chance and let go all their formidable nuclear arsenals as well. They had to launch then or else fall to the same fate as the Middle Eastern countries. In the exchange, the Russian arsenal let loose its warheads, directing them to predetermined locations. With only minutes of notice, there had been no time to change any of the preset locations. The targets were global including the Americas. The response was also automatic, as the United States released all its missiles and sent its bombers to drop their nuclear arsenals on predetermined targets. The end had come in the blink of an eye. From an overpopulation of fifteen billion, the population of the planet was reduced to just under one billion from climate change, years of conventional war, and full nuclear war. The radiation fallout killed many instantly, and then many more died slow deaths from hunger and disease. Life in once-proud countries reverted to life as it had been long ago, filled with tribal wars for scarce resources.

Out of the ashes, a savior rose from a little country in West Africa. He proposed an alliance between the remaining nations. Theirs was one of the few countries untouched by the madness of war and climate change. A charismatic and extremely intelligent leader, Shoa Khad, opened the doors to the other devastated nations, offering a new way to live. He was African but had white skin and blue eyes. Some say he was from the lost tribe of Israel. No one knew and no one asked because he had all the answers the world was so desperately looking for, and the remaining remnants of people were willing to trade their freedom for necessities and safety. A grand covenant was struck with the most powerful tribal leaders.

Ten empires—kingdoms—ruled by ten absolute rulers were formed out of the covenant to restore the world from the ashes of what came to be known as the Great Conflict and the depths of the ice age. The world was reunited the traditional way. There were two choices: absolute allegiance to Shoa and his ten kings or death. Millions more died in what would come to be known as the Great Enlightenment.

The Great Enlightenment began in 2118. Shoa declared that history was to begin anew to erase the differences and horrors of a civilization that tied its calendar to religious beliefs. The year 2118 became the new year zero, and the new era was known as the Enlightened Era (EE). No more BC, AD, CE, or other religion-based calendar references.

Over the next several hundred years, Shoa's empire was realized as resources were consolidated and concentrated into ten mega cities, the ten kingdoms, protected by environmental domes.

CHAPTER 2

Current Day: 420 EE

Today, 420 years later, in the year 420 EE (old date: 2538), civilization had stabilized after centuries of consolidation. The ten kingdoms were spread evenly throughout the world in the Middle East (Iraq), Southeast Europe (Turkey), India, China, Malaysia, Australia, South Africa, Central Africa (Nigeria), South America (Brazil), and Central America (Mexico). Absolute power in each of the kingdoms was held by a few with a heavy security force to maintain order. The center of all power for the ten kingdoms resided in the Middle Eastern Kingdom.

Laws in the kingdoms were few but absolute: Do what you are told, when you are told, and ask no questions. Break any of the rules, and the price was instant and severe.

Just as in previous times, technology enabled people to live to old age. Now, with limited usable land, the world population had to be set at a manageable number. A comprise had to be made. It was declared that six hundred and sixty-six million was the maximum population that the world's resources could support.

The ultimate compromise was that no one could work after the age of forty-four years and four months. This was considered a good, long productive life by current standards from what the world had gone through after the Great Conflict. At forty-four years and four months, each person was retired by the Authority (the government).

Citizens' ages were tracked from birth to the very second. The number of living people—from newborns to retirement-aged people—was exactly tracked across the ten kingdoms for the purpose of maintaining the total world population. Some said retirees were sent to another planet to help foster a new world. The place where everyone went for retirement was a mystery, but everyone knew. Society was paying for the excesses of the previous generations. Some tried to run away and escape "retirement."

An identification chip was embedded in every citizen's right wrist. It was used to track age, wages, purchases, and location at all times. The chip regulated purchases to ensure everyone had just enough clothing, food, and living necessities. Some people—designated as criminals—tried to manipulate their chips to roll back the years, and some tried to manipulate their chips to enable them to obtain "more."

Dom's job was to catch those criminals, and he was one of the best at it. His superiors often asked how he was so successful at catching the outlaws. Dom pushed them off by simply saying that it was a genetic gift. As everyone was a genetic manipulation, who could know for sure? But inside, Dom knew why he was the best. Deep down, Dom had a burning desire to be free, and he had dreamed up a thousand ways to do it.

Dom understood the passion for freedom and therefore knew how to go about attaining it. And there was something else—an empty hole in his life. A void that no food, no drink, no woman could fill. He had no idea what it was that he was missing from his life, and he hid his void deep down inside lest anyone notice. He did not want to be sent for "treatment." Dom was a robot in his zeal, and he displayed precision in finding the enemy.

Hunched down and concentrating on the digital screen, Dom reviewed the latest movements and information about a runaway. He didn't notice the man standing next to him. "Dom." Nothing. A bit louder. "Dom!" It was the hand on his shoulder that made Dom jump. Startled, his natural instincts took over. He flipped up and turned at the same time, moving forward with speed. His hands came up as he drew his weapon with a fluid move borne from a lifetime of training. Jack jumped back. "Whoa, fella! Ease up! It's just me."

Recognizing his patrol partner, Jack, Dom eased up. "Sorry, man. I'm just a bit jumpy today. Tracking our mystery man. Thought I saw some information of interest on him." This particular runaway was Dom's Achilles heel, his white whale. Dom had been tracking him for some time now and was embarrassed that his quarry kept eluding him. The man popped up on radar, somehow reset his identification, and then vanished again. He was so good at manipulating his chip so that no one even knew his age or his real name.

Jack strained to look at Dom's screen. His eyebrows lifted. "The white whale?"

Dom replied without turning his head. "I think that's him. Been tracking some unusual purchases this morning, and although they might seem random, they do seem to fit his pattern."

"Well, keep that bloodhound nose on him, and we'll get him soon, my man."

Dom's reply was a simple "Yep." Nothing more to say. Just had to dive into the details, and the whale would slip up sometime. They just needed to be right there when he slipped.

Jack was a good cop and a good partner. The two had been partners on the street beat for over fifteen years, and Jack went about his job as well as anyone in the force. Jack had a wife, and they were raising two children. Natural pregnancy was outlawed, and all births originated from test tubes. The vast majority of children were raised by the Authority, but under special request, children were provided to couples to raise. Jack and his wife were thankful to have been given the opportunity to be selected to raise children. Two was almost unheard of, and Jack took the responsibility seriously. He also did not want to do anything to rock his perfect world. Being with Dom was not easy. When Dom went after someone, nothing stood between him and his prize. Having no family and relatively few friends, Dom considered work his life, and his target for the day was all he had. Bending the rules was something that didn't make him blink twice. Dom did what he had to do, and that got him and Jack in hot water with the higher ups on many occasions. But their loyalty and success rate tended to make their supervisors look the other way while they doled out only minor punishment—reduced food rations for a week or something like that. It was no problem for Dom to go hungry a night or two, but Jack had a family, and seeing them go hungry for his nonacceptable methods made Dom feel bad. Even though Jack did not agree with all of Dom's methods, he never asked for a transfer. They got results in the end, and Jack was a true believer in upholding the laws and serving the supreme leader who gave him so much.

Dom didn't know why the higher ups got so angry when he bent some of the rules to catch his targets. He firmly believed that, to catch the target, he had to do some of the same (illegal) things they did. So, on occasion, Dom felt obliged to hack into the Authority's secure systems to find alternate methods to track elusive targets. A lot of information, tracking programs, and software were off limits, and the Authority was very strict about granting access. The reasoning behind this was beyond knowing, and everyone grew up learning not to question the rules. Dom's supervisors were nervous over the ease with which he obtained information, but success had a way of giving Dom and Jack room to work. There were rumors of some Authority officials getting special privileges as a result of the duo's success. But rumors they remained. That would upset the balanced order of the utopian society and restart the have-or-have-not, more-is-better mentality.

CHAPTER 3

The Favor

T he bellow came from down the hall, and the tapping of footsteps made by hard-sole shoes echoing off the hard-surfaced floor was all too familiar. "What are you two yahoos up to now?" Dom was about to reply when the retort came back. "Don't tell me! I don't want to know. I'm still paying the price for the last time you two messed up and detained the governor's daughter for manipulating her chip for more cosmetic rations.

Jack jumped in. "A crime is a crime, chief."

Don't give me that Boy Scout junk, Jack! Hey that kind of rhymes—junk Jack!" He laughed.

Dom replied to save Jack. "Wow that's a funny one, chief! Are you sure you were supposed to be a police captain and not a comedian?"

On the captain's desk was a vintage bottle, empty of course, that had once held Captain Morgan's spiced rum, a fairly tasty drink. It was the source of the captain's nickname, Pirate. Someone had called him that long ago at the police academy, and it had stuck. Only his friends called him Pirate to his face of course. To Dom and Jack, he was just Captain or sir, or if they wanted to be friendly, Morgan.

Moving toward them in just a few strides of his long legs, the captain motioned them to join him in the conference room. Once there, he did something unusual—he locked the door, took a small device from his pocket, placed it on the table, and turned it on. It was a scanner that disabled any electronic device within a twenty-foot radius, making electronic eavesdropping impossible. This was getting serious.

"I just got a call from the governor himself, asking for a favor. There's been an incident at his office, and he needs someone to check it out. I can't stress enough how confidential this is. I need you two to go to the governor's office now, find out what's happened, and report back directly only to me. No recordings, no photos, no notes, no calls, and absolutely no discussions with other officers."

They got the message. Jack turned to Dom. Dom shrugged his shoulders and waved his arm as he levered himself up from his chair. "Let's go, Jack. Time's a-wastin'." And off they went. The duo had done this type of drill before. Anytime something sensitive—some "misfortune"—happened at the office or home of a high-ranking official, Dom and Jack were called in to assess the issue for the department. It usually meant a slap on the wrist to the offender. The usual white-collar crime was stealing products and bartering them on the black market. With the ID chip system and no cash, there was a significant underworld of high-level bartering for services and goods. Almost anything could be bartered for if a person had something of value that others wanted. There was always a way to work around the system. Everyone knew there were issues, but no one knew what the full magnitude was because the vast majority of people—the masses—obeyed the laws and lived out their lives as required; otherwise, they faced brutal punishment.

Dom and Jack hopped into their aero car for the fifteen-minute flight to the governor's office. They expected someone to greet them when they arrived; typically, it would be the governor's personal aide, but the aero pad was eerily deserted and silent. No one around. Dom motioned to Jack in a silent signal to grab his weapon. Dom didn't need to ask him twice; Jack sensed that there was something wrong as well. They slowly got out and made their way to the front entrance, their heads swiveling as they scanned all around as they approached. Still, there was no one around. Dom checked the door and found it open, which was not a good sign; unlocked doors at government offices meant trouble. Dom opened the door. Holding his pistol in front of him clasped in both hands, he pushed the door with his right foot. He crouched down and moved to his right. Jack followed, moving to his left. They scanned around looking high and low. Nothing amiss. The front entrance opened into a large foyer. A spiral staircase led up to the second level where the governor's main office was located. Next to the staircase there was a reception desk, which was normally manned by two security guards twenty-four hours a day, seven days a week. Today it was deserted. Nothing seemed out of place—no papers or anything else toppled over, no scuff marks, blood, or signs of a struggle. People had apparently just walked off. Maybe they'd been forced at gunpoint.

Creeping slowly, the duo made their way to the staircase, and they made their way cautiously to the next level. When they opened the door to the governor's office, a stench hit them immediately. Foul play for sure. All bodily functions let loose when a person dies, causing a sewage-type odor to fill the air. Moving into the room, at first they found nothing amiss. But … there near the desk! Jack closed the door and locked it to prevent whoever had done this from barging back in as they examined the room more thoroughly. Closing in, they examined the body, which was slumped over on the chair, the head resting on the desk. No obvious signs of struggle or gunshot wound. The deceased was a woman; her hair was covered in a veil. She was wearing a professional-looking suit that must have cost a lot of credits. This lady had to be high up in the government order to rate that kind of clothes. It was Jack who reacted first after looking closely at the victim. Her face was beautiful, but there was something startling about her. There were wrinkles around her eyes and mouth. Jack took the veil off, exposing her full head. She was wearing a dark-brown wig, hair flowing down to about shoulder length. It was one of those easy-on wigs held with only pins, so it was quick to remove. Jack exposed her real hair, which was faded blond with a bit of gray. It was a bit thin, but he could imagine that, in her youth, she had beautiful, long, flowing blond hair. This woman was well beyond forty-four years old.

Dom stood next to his partner. "Jack, I can see why the governor wanted this one to be confidential." No one was allowed past forty-four years and four months—retirement age—no matter who they were from the governor to senior Authority leaders. Anyone caught harboring someone over the age of retirement—what they called a runner—would receive the same punishment as the runner, which was total and final.

Dom called the chief and gave him a short report. The chief's only question was, "So it doesn't look like foul play?"

"Yeah," Dom responded. "I've been to enough domestic violence crime scenes, shootings, and other violent crimes to know that this woman most likely simply decided it was time and quit living. Because of her age, it could have been from any number of natural causes."

The chief replied, "Okay then. Wrap up the body, clean the place up as best you can, and get the body to the City West Hospital. There's a central morgue facility there. Go around to the back entrance. Someone will be there waiting to take the bag."

"Okay chief. Under one condition."

"What's that?"

"I want to be there when the doctor examines the body to make sure there was no foul play." The call went silent, and Dom thought maybe they had lost connection. "Chief, are you there?" More silence. "Chief?"

"I'm here. Okay. Just get the body to the morgue as soon as possible." And he cut the line.

"What now, Dom?"

"Jack, the chief said, since there is no apparent foul play, we clean it up and keep it under wraps for now."

Jack just stared at Dom. "You've got to be kidding me."

"I'm not kidding, and I'm going to find a body bag. You look around for towels and cleaning material." It took a good couple of smelly hours, but Dom and Jack got the place halfway decent. By the time they were finished, no one could tell what had happened.

"Dom, this had better not come back to us. I have a family to take care of now. I can't get involved with some cover-up that will get me fired. Or worse."

"We follow orders, Jack. That's what we do. I am sure the chief will be there for us to catch our back if we get any blowback." Dom's voice wasn't very convincing. "Let's roll, Jack. We're wasting time."

In less than an hour, they were on their way—Jack, Dom, and the old lady in a body bag. It took them only fifteen minutes to rocket over to the hospital in their aero car. Dom and Jack's previous aero car had been a beater vehicle and had seen its fair share of action chasing runners, illegal traders, and other criminals. It had even sported multiple dents and blaster holes that they hadn't bothered to fix. Having a dented-up aero car was a bit of a badge of honor that showed that they were the go-to guys who had seen more action than anyone else on the force. The duo's aero car was nicknamed "Hutch" from the old 1970s police TV show *Starsky and Hutch*. Jack liked the old TV shows and had acquired from the black market the whole *Starsky and Hutch* series. Dom always told Jack he'd been born in the wrong period of history, and Jack would also respond with a knowing, "Yup."

The vehicle they were flying in now was the latest and greatest in the police aero car technology with military-grade hardware and software including all the armory bells and whistles. Definitely not the Hutch aero car; it was more like a flying tank in disguise.

Approaching the hospital, they circled around the building a couple of times to make sure no one was around. By this time, it was three in the morning, so there wasn't much action in the area. Dom and Jack wanted to make sure no one would see them. The fewer eyes the better. They landed just short of the back entrance of the hospital. It was more of a wide, dark, back alley with enough room for access by larger aero transport vehicles as well as large ground-based transport.

Aero vehicles were common, but the newer models were used mainly by the government and for commercial passenger transport. Most of the people lived on basic credit wages and used ground vehicles with wheels. In their travels, they were stuck to two dimensions. The world had come so far in technology since the early twenty-first century, but the war and aftereffects had slowed down the pace of mass production of the newer aero vehicles. The older, traditional larger trucks with wheels were still used, mostly for commercial deliveries, trash pickup, and other tasks that required heavy transport. Limiting the use of aero cars was also cheaper and gave the upper advantage to the Authority law officials who had the modern aero fleet. The Authority didn't see it as a class distinction; they saw it as a way to control the general masses. Quite simply, the Authority got all the new technology, and the public had to live with technology from hundreds of years ago.

The buildings around the hospital were over fifty stories tall, and the area looked like old downtown Manhattan, New York, with tall buildings filling every block. Dom and Jack had seen New York in old photos.

Dom shut off the aero car engine. He and Jack waited for a minute, taking in the scene. Darkness covered most of the alley area. Just a few streetlights hovered overhead, and there was a bit of illumination from the ramp that led down into a cargo area where bodies were received, processed, and taken away. Silence. Not a person around. Even at three in the morning, this was a bit unusual. In a kingdom inhabited by sixty-six million people, there was always something happening everywhere.

As instructed, they continued to wait in silence. A drop of sweat formed on Dom's forehead. It wasn't hot. The shear concentration of trying to take everything in at once had raised his blood pressure and anxiety level. He felt as if he were experiencing the calm before the storm. It felt like an eternity, but it was just a few minutes until, anticlimactically breaking the silence, the double steel doors at the bottom of the ramp opened and a single person slowly appeared, looking around in both directions and saying something into his collar phone mike. Suddenly, from the alley on both sides of the duo and from above, lights flashed on and off. That's why they were alone. Someone had sealed off all access to the area. The figure at the door waved Dom and Jack in, and they slowly got out of their aero car.

Their contact wasn't imposing at all—slim in build, about five foot eight inches tall. Dom let out a whisper, "Let's do this, Jack." With Jack on one end and Dom on the other they started the short walk from the aero car, carrying the body bag to the door. Low-level lighting glowed behind the figure before them keeping him in a darkened shadow. The scene reminded Dom of an old spy movie. It was a bit over the top, but he could see the need to keep absolute secrecy. No one wanted to get captured on video with an illegal package. As far as Jack and Dom could tell, their faces would be nice and shiny for prying cameras.

Jack murmured, "I think we're being set up in case things go wrong. What did they used to say we are? Scapegoats? Fall guys?"

Grimacing, Dom whispered back, "Pick up the pace, buddy, and let's get this package delivered."

Jack knew what Dom was talking about. Less time in the open meant less time for anyone to see them. Jack immediately picked up speed and, in a few moments, they were at the door. Suddenly, from behind the man, another figure appeared and reached out to grab the package. At well over six feet tall and sporting over three hundred pounds of muscle, the giant man tossed the body bag over his shoulder as if it was a twenty-pound sack of potatoes. He quickly disappeared into the low glow. The smaller man at the door looked around nervously again and turned without a word, closing the door quickly.

Dom had but a split second to react. Quickly levering his right leg forward, he placed his boot between the door and the door jamb.

There was confusion on the shadow's face behind the crack in the door. Before he realized it was Dom's foot preventing the door from closing, Dom yanked at the handle and swung the door out and the man with it, his hand still gripping the inside handle. "What are you doing?" the shadow bellowed.

Not answering, Dom moved in past him with Jack right behind him, moving hesitantly. Obviously, Jack did not want to get caught in any compromising situation—not more than he had to—but Jack was a trooper and friend, and Dom knew his partner would always catch his back. Once they were inside, the small man closed the door. The giant man had seen the commotion and quickly came back to see what was going on. Dom turned to face the two. "I told the chief I wanted to be there when the doctor examines the body, and that's just what we are going to do." Dom moved closer to the Giant and slid his right hand down to his side arm just to heighten his point. The Giant stumbled back from Dom's quick move forward toward him. Gathering himself, he looked straight into Dom's eyes and gulped to clear his throat. Seeing Dom's hand next to his blaster gun had weakened the Giant's normal fearlessness. His brut size was no match for the weapon.

Stepping between Dom and the Giant, the smaller man directed, "Right this way, then, and make it quick. We do not want to draw suspicion by being seen together." Dom and Jack walked behind the others trying to look as if they belonged there. The four men moved quickly through the winding corridors. The place was a maze, and Dom was glad they were following behind the Giant and the smaller man. There were no identification plates on the doors they passed, and there were no signs along the corridors—just white walls, white doors, and sterile white lights recessed in the corridor ceilings. Certainly, a place not meant for anyone but those who belonged there.

After a few minutes, they arrived at another blank door at the end of the hallway. The Giant looked into a retinal eye scanner. A click followed, and the door opened, sliding sideways into the wall like the doors in the old Star Trek movies. Very high tech. Dom and Jack were used to old-fashioned doors that swung on hinges like the outer door to the building. This was definitely a restricted area. To their surprise, the door opened to reveal an elevator rather than the room they had expected. Instinctively, Jack and Dom hesitated to go through the door.

The Giant looked at them. "We have a special zone for 'sensitive' procedures in the lower levels." What could they do? It was either move forward or get out now. Like the old saying goes, in for a penny, in for a pound. Dom and Jack reluctantly went in. The door closed immediately and rapidly as if someone had been watching. Dom was sure there had been. He had noticed little spheres along the corridor ceilings, and in this elevator, there were no fewer than four spheres, one at each corner of the ceiling. There were no floor indicator buttons in the elevator; instead, there was a facial recognition screen that glowed with a soft blue light. The Giant looked at the blank screen. A green light flashed, and then a keypad appeared. After he punched a series of numbers and letters, a ping sounded, and a second later, Dom and Jack felt gravity disappear for a moment as the elevator dropped so fast it felt as if they might go to weightlessness. After a few seconds passed, the elevator slowed and came to a stop. Curiosity got the best of Jack. "How far down are we?"

The smaller man answered with a slight smile. "You are now exactly one hundred fifty feet below ground level."

Whoa! Jack thought. *This is one secure place, to get into—and, more spookily, to get out of!* Jack laughed half-jokingly. "I hope there's more than one way out of this place in an emergency." He was hoping for an answer, but he got none. The Giant and small man just gave him and Dom blank stares that said it all: *You asked for this. It wasn't my idea.*

CHAPTER 4

Secrets

The elevator door opened to a long, low-ceilinged corridor with spectacularly white tiled flooring, white walls, and white ceiling. The lights were so bright Jack and Dom had to squint or be blinded. Their well-prepared guides simply slipped on sunglasses. Walking briskly, Jack and Dom had to almost run to keep up with the Giant and the smaller man. Down the long corridor, every twenty feet or so, they noticed doors on either side. No handles. Just keypads. It took several minutes for them to reach the end of the corridor where they stopped at a door that looked more like a fort Knox bank door. It was made of shiny silver metal, and there were massive cylindrical bolts in all four corners. This door was meant to protect what was behind it.

The Giant's initial nervousness as he got close to the door made Jack and Dom look at each other. Was this door meant to protect what was inside or to keep what was inside from getting out? A bad feeling came over the duo. After years on the job, they naturally sensed danger. Together, that door and the look on the Giant's face projected Danger with a capital D. The Giant motioned Dom and Jack back as he approached a camera—another eye and face recognition scanner. There was also a pad scanner, and the Giant placed his right hand on it. He grimaced for a quick second as a small device pricked his finger. DNA test! This was some secure room! A light above the door flashed green, and the four equally spaced cylinders slid in unison with a smooth gear sound. The door cracked open, and a rush of air escaped from within with a loud sound. Positive pressure in the room ensured that no contaminants would get in.

Dom and Jack followed the Giant and small man into a room the size of the elevator they had just come from. The door silently closed behind them. The small man announced, "Close your eyes and hold your breath when you hear the siren. Don't open your eyes, don't breathe, and don't open your mouths until the sound stops. Don't move a muscle. Keep your arms at your sides. I will count to three, and then it will start."

Dom started to ask a question when the small man started counting. "One, two …" He obviously was not going to entertain any questions. "… three!" They closed their eyes and took deep breaths just as the man's hand stretched out to press a large red button. Through closed eyelids they could see that the light in the room had turned from bright white to a deep red. And a loud siren blasted, reminding them of an evacuation warning. The air pressure in the small room instantly increased, and their ears begin to hurt. A light mist filled the room. Time seemed to slow; it seemed as if an hour elapsed before the siren stopped.

"You can open your eyes and breathe now," the Giant said in a deadpan voice. A door slid open in front of them revealing a large room filled with medical instruments. It was a small auditorium with balcony seats behind glass walls that sealed the room from floor to ceiling. In the center of the room were two operating tables. The Giant gently placed the body bag on one of the tables and stepped back.

A phone on the wall rang, and the Giant moved to pick it up. "Yes, sir. Yes, sir. As you command, sir." After placing the phone back in the cradle, the guides moved toward a shiny steel door at the back of the room. The Giant typed a code into a keypad, and he and the small man both departed, leaving Dom and Jack without saying a word. The silence in the room that now held just Dom, Jack, and the dead woman was a bit eerie. Dom and Jack didn't attempt to go close to the body. They passed the time with idle chit chat, not speaking of anything of substance; they knew that cameras and audio recorders were probably everywhere in the room.

About twenty minutes later, two figures entered through the same door. They were both much smaller than the Giant, and one of them was even smaller than the smaller man who had departed. These two had to be the medical examiners. They were both wearing white medical gowns and, unusually, they also wore hoods to which were attached slightly tinted face shields that made it difficult for Dom and Jack to see their faces.

The two examiners ignored Dom and Jack; indeed, they did not even acknowledge their presence. They approached the body bag, unzipped it, and proceeded to perform their autopsy. It was a puzzling scene. Normally, examiners would scan the body with equipment that could ascertain how the woman had died. They would use instruments to inspect organs, draw blood for testing, and do whatever else medical examiners needed to do. These two, however, just visually inspected the woman's body, looking intently over her entire body with large magnifying lenses. They were looking for something on her skin.

After a few minutes one of them exclaimed, "There!" And the other rushed over to see what his partner had found. Curiosity got the better of Jack and Dom, and they also approached. "Step back!" the examiner on the right exclaimed in a surprisingly authoritative voice. It was a female voice! Dom stumbled back from her abrupt command. Recomposing himself, he looked to see if he could make out her face. The tinted face shield obscured her facial features, but her hair was black as coal. Oddly, her eyes glowed like bright green emeralds. Dom just froze at her intense gaze on him.

Jack was in front of Dom, and the forcefulness of her voice had stopped him in his tracks as well. After freezing for a few seconds, they looked at each other. Dom shrugged his shoulders and gave Jack "the look" as he jerked his head to get Jack moving forward. One lesson Jack and Dom had learned a long time ago was that looks can be deceiving. It's amazing what some people study. The two examiners may appear weak, but Dom and Jack had no idea what sort of training they had received—jujitsu, close combat training, karate, or some other self-defense art? Upon closer inspection, Dom and Jack realized that their flat-footed stance, feet planted wide apart, and hands at the hips were indicators that they were not trained in close combat. Now, if they stood with legs closer together, knees flexed, weight concentrated on their toes, and arms loose but raised, there would have been more concern.

With no apparent concern, Dom stepped forward and moved Emerald Eyes aside—not forcefully—and gazed at the point on the dead woman's body that held the interest of the two examiners. They were looking at the woman's right wrist. One of the examiners removed a small metallic band, revealing a tattoo that was so small it was hard to see. It was simple—nothing fancy. For such a woman of wealth it was oddly plain and simple. Two slightly arced lines, concave sides facing, touched at one end and crossed a bit at the other, creating a shape symbolic of a fish.

Dom was going to snap a photo of it with his clear pad device, but it was so simple even he could commit the image to memory for research later. Dom and Jack stepped back and let the two examiners move back to the body to look at the "fish" tattoo. Something changed in the air. In seconds, the facial expressions of the examiners went the full range from excitement at finding a mark, to interest at what they found, and finally to a somber realization of what they found. It was the end state that was most concerning. Normally, Dom would expect them to be either excited about the clue, fearful of the clue, or some other sort of emotion in company with some sort of chatter. From them it was just utter silence. They stood rock still in front of the dead woman, their eyes closed, their heads bowed, saying nothing. Just silence. It was just a moment, but it was the most bizarre thing to witness in an autopsy.

Saying nothing, the man went across the room, retrieved a gurney, and returned to the autopsy table. The two examiners gently moved the woman from the table to the gurney. They then rolled the body to a small steel door at the side of the room. Stopping just in front of it, Emerald Eyes typed a code into a keypad and the door opened, revealing a small rectangular box. They slid the woman into the box, and Emerald Eyes typed into the keypad again. A ping sounded, and a red light above the closing door illuminated. Quickly turning, their faces blank masks showing no emotion, they departed the room through the door through which they had entered, not saying a word to each other or to Dom and Jack. It was all very bizarre and weird.

Left alone in the room, Jack spoke first. "Dom, that was the fastest and strangest autopsy I have ever seen. No forensic examination. Nothing. They just checked out the body for marks and then slid the body back into the little freezer!" The two looked at the little door behind which the body was stored. The red light was still flashing. Jack walked to the door and put his hand on it. Instantly, he jerked his hand back and bellowed. "Ouch! Man, that door is blazing hot!" A bad feeling came over them. It wasn't a freezer meant to preserve the body. Quite the opposite—it was a furnace meant to cremate the body!

"Jack!" said Dom. "They're burning the body wiping out the evidence. We have to get out of here now!" Dom ran quickly to the door through which the two examiners left. Locked. He went to the main entrance to the auditorium. Also locked. No way out.

Again, time seemed to slow down as they passed the time in silence. Jack started to nervously pace the room. Nothing to do but wait. Dom's thoughts were lost on the female examiner—her jet-back hair and mesmerizing green eyes.

It felt like hours, but only fifteen minutes passed before the steel door at the back of the room reopened. Three men entered—the Giant, the smaller man, and one man Dom and Jack had yet to see. Blond and fit, and dressed in an expensive black suit, he looked like a lawyer from the old-time movies. Or did the trio look more like gangsters? Their anxious expressions turned expressions of confusion as they scanned the room and saw only Dom, Jack, and an empty table. The suited man, the obvious leader, bellowed, "Where is the body!" The Giant, wasting no time, moved forward and thrust out his enormous arms. He grabbed Dom and Jack by their shoulders and slammed them together side by side like they were toys. "Where is she?" he shouted.

It had been a clumsy move, and Dom could easily have disabled the Giant, but he decided to play the part of a typical detective, rattled and scared of the gargantuan. Jack caught on instantly, and his face too turned from rock-hard cop to scared kid. That was the result of partnering for over ten years. They were a team, each able to instantly read the other's thoughts in multiple situations. Dom stammered, "Wh– what do you mean where is she? Your two medical examiners already came, viewed the body, and then placed her into that little holding area." Dom raised his right arm and shakily pointed to the little door with the red light over it. "They put her in there."

Blondie ran quickly to the little door and typed into the keypad. The red light stayed on, and the door remained shut. "How long? How long has she been in here?"

The Giant squeezed Dom and Jack. "You heard the man! How long has the body been in there?"

Jack stammered "At least half an hour. Probably more."

"*Nooo!*" yelled Blondie. The other two stood rock solid showing no emotion at all. Like robots. The smaller man next to the Giant was black haired. Shorter in height and much thinner than the Giant, he was brown skinned and had Hispanic features. Fit and trim, he looked as if he was in his mid-twenties. Blondie slowly turned from the door. With a dejected look on his face, he approached Dom and Jack. He waved to the Giant, who reluctantly released the duo from his grasp, but he stayed very close, like a tiger ready, to pounce as Blondie came within arm's length of the two detectives. His cold blue eyes stared at Jack and then focused on Dom. "Those two examiners—what did they look like?"

As Dom thought back, realization came to him and he blurted, "They were wearing surgical gowns and masks, but they kind of looked like them." His hand shakily pointing to the two stone-faced goons.

Blondie's blazing eyes swiftly turned to his two associates. The two hard-faced men—the Hispanic-looking man (Dom nicknamed him the Spaniard) and the Giant—wilted under Blondie's gaze. Their eyebrows raised in a "who me?" sort of look. Obviously, neither of them wanted to get on Blondie's bad side. Disgusted, Blondie turned back to Dom and Jack. "How did they examine the body? What did they see? Did they say anything to you or to each other?" As he stared at them waiting for a reply, the Spaniard went to a monitor on a table along the wall and began to type into a keyboard. A video flashed up on the monitor.

Blondie looked at the screen as the Spaniard searched for the day's video recordings. Thinking quickly, Dom stammered. "We didn't see anything. The examiners kept us over in the corner of the room, and they didn't make a sound as they viewed the body." Jack's eyes widened just a bit as Dom spoke, but not enough for Blondie to catch it. It was a calculated risk. How thorough would the two examiners be at covering their tracks?

The Spaniard spoke up just as Dom finished stammering his words out. "There's no video log from today. Someone either disabled the recording feed or erased anything that was recorded."

The room erupted in noise as the coroner's table where the lady had been examined slammed against the wall. Blondie was in the midst of a temper tantrum, and the room whirled with equipment. Boom! Smash! All accompanied by profanity that would make a sailor blush. And the guttural screams! "*Aaaarrrrggggggg!*" The detectives both wondered if Blondie would have a heart attack.

Jack and Dom played their part by lowering their heads and whimpering during the tirade. The Spaniard and the Giant stood by not making a sound. Apparently, this was not the first time they had witnessed this sort of spectacle. After a few minutes, Blondie tired and stopped his rampage. He stared at Dom and Jack, seemingly intently looking for something—signs that they were lying. They knew the drill and cowered, doing their best to look frightened. Their acting was honed to perfection, and they revealed nothing.

Blondie straightened his ruffled suit out and composed himself. Looking to the Giant he barked, "Take them away. We are done with them." The pit of Dom's stomach tightened, and he was sure Jack was feeling the same way. It wasn't what Blondie had said but how he had said it—with such finality. And the Giant's expression— absolutely blank—was frightening as he turned to face Dom and Jack. No pity or remorse or excitement or fear or apprehension. His dark-black, cold, emotionless eyes stared at them as if Blondie had just told him to stomp on a fly. Unfortunately, Dom and Jack were the flies.

CHAPTER 5

Escape

As the Giant approached them, Jack took a quick look at Dom, and Dom gave Jack a quick response with a quick nod of his head. Dom then turned to the approaching monster, his face turning to a mask of fear. What came next was expected. As the Giant raised his right arm and his massive hand came down toward Dom's face, Dom lifted his feet and levered himself backward in the same direction as the blow. When it came, the impact sounded like a freight train, and Dom saw stars as he fell back. The trick was in the timing. If Dom fell backward at the same rate the Giant's massive hand moved, Dom's backward motion would soften the blow just enough to keep him from blacking out. Or at least that was the idea. On impact, the air rushed out of Dom's lungs, and he fell ungracefully to the ground with a thud! To say that it was all an act to satisfy the Giant was not completely accurate. Even with all that fancy footwork, Dom's head felt like it was going to explode. It wasn't hard to lie on the ground like the corpse they had seen earlier. The Giant must have been satisfied because he did not kick or hit Dom again, but moments later, Dom heard familiar sounds and knew that Jack had received the same treatment from the Giant. Dom hoped that Jack had understood his signal and would follow his plan.

While Dom acted like a log, the Spaniard and the Giant picked him up by his legs and shoulders and dumped him onto a gurney. As he lay on his stomach, they fastened his hands behind his back with a plastic zip tie, but carelessly, they didn't realize Dom was actually awake, and Dom was able to hold his hands apart a bit to provide a bit of slack. The Giant was used to his mighty handiwork resulting in his enemies being incapacitated for a few hours. Then a heavy weight landed on top of Dom. It was Jack. They laid him out face up right on top of Dom, his hands already secured behind his back. Jack's face was right next to Dom's but facing up. His hands were right next to Dom's hands. Finally, a bit of good fortune. With Jack covering his arms, Dom was able to move his left arm to the back of his belt. The gurney started to move, and Dom had to think fast. It would take them only about four minutes to get from the morgue to the elevator, and the elevator ride would take another few minutes. Once the elevator reached ground level, they would have another couple of minutes before they were back at the loading dock area behind the hospital. Dom and Jack had less than ten minutes tops to get themselves ready. They would have one chance—a split second—to decide on and launch a plan of action. It was all about timing and surprise.

One of the secrets of staying alive in the detective business is being prepared for any situation. And that includes having tools at the ready. Dom moved his right hand slowly to his belt and felt around until he found his pants belt loop in the middle of his back. Just to the right of the loop, a razor-sharp blade was imbedded in the top of the belt. Colored black, and just slightly protruding from the belt top, it was impossible to see. Dom slowly rubbed the plastic zip tie against the sharp edge. The sharp blade easily cut the tie. Jack's arm moved slightly as Dom's arm became free, which was a good sign. Jack was conscious, and he knew what Dom was doing. Dom used his free right arm to move Jack's tied wrists to his belt so he could cut Jack's tie as well. It was slow work because they dared not move too quickly. The weight of Jack's body on Dom, and angle of his wrists in relation to the blade made it hard to line the zip tie up to the blade. Dom felt Jack's left side tense up, and his left arm jerked slightly. *Ooops! Sorry, Jack.* The sharp edge of Dom's razor had cut into Jack's exposed skin. Dom would hear about that one later. If there was a later. Hopefully that would be the extent of their wounds. Finally, Jack's zip tie was in position over Dom's belt blade, and Dom slowly cut it. When Jack was free, he pressed his thumb into Dom's back. That was the best Dom would get for a thanks. They were ready now.

Time slowed down as they rolled down the corridor. It took just minutes, but it felt like hours. The bright lights illuminating the corridor must have been torture for Jack because he had to remain motionless with his head facing directly upward at the intense light. After a few minutes, the gurney came to a stop. The Giant and the Spaniard hadn't made a sound since they left the circular room. The silence and the stillness were maddening to Dom and Jack. Finally, the sound of the elevator bell echoed in the corridor followed by a soft woosh as the doors slid open. The elevator wasn't large enough for the gurney with Jack and Dom on it and the two goons. The only grouping that fit consisted of Dom, Jack, and the smaller Spaniard. The Giant—Dom and Jack assumed reluctantly—stayed behind. Blondie was still somewhere behind them, probably still in the autopsy room trying to figure out what had happened.

The door closed and the elevator surged upward. What would happen when they reached the top? Would the Spaniard push them into the hallway and then wait until the elevator went down to get the Giant? When should they make their move? If they did it now in the elevator, someone might be watching the security monitors and stop the elevator, trapping them in a disadvantageous location. Dom and Jack would have to wait until they reached the top and exited the elevator. If the Spaniard rolled them out and stopped, they'd have to make the move and overpower him and hope no one was watching the hallway cameras. It was a big risk either way, and the duo had only once chance to get it right.

The elevator slowed, the bell sounded, and the door opened with a woosh. Luckily, Dom's head, face down, was pointed toward the door. Tilting his head ever so slightly, he looked down the hall. There was no one there. They had to move now. Dom yelled, "Now, Jack! Now!" Instantly Jack jumped up. The surprised Spaniard stumbled backward. Jack hit him square in the face with his fist. It sounded like a baseball bat hitting a homerun. The Spaniard slumped into the corner of the elevator. Jack quickly took out his blaster and hit him one more time to make sure he was out. Probably not necessary, but seeing that they had played the "fake knockout trick," it made sense to make sure. The Spaniard was obviously a bad man anyway. "Let's go, Jack!" Dom pulled on Jack's shirtsleeve, and they raced out of the elevator, pausing to cram the gurney in the open elevator doorway to keep the door from closing. The Giant would have to remain deep under the earth, at least for now.

The detectives ran down the corridor until it branched off in different directions. The place was a maze of white—white doors, white ceiling, white floor tiles, white blending in everywhere with no signage. "Wow, Jack, I forgot how much of a maze this place is!" Dom unconsciously began to slow down, and Jack ran full speed into his back. "Keep going, Dom! We'll make it! Don't slow down now!"

Wise words, and Dom picked up the pace. "There!" Dom yelled as they raced down a randomly chosen side corridor. Straight ahead, at the end of the corridor, was a set of double doors. It looked like the exit to the back area of the hospital where they had entered. When they reached the doors, Dom opened them slowly. *Yes!* They were at the back entrance. The area lighting was much dimmer than it was in the corridor, and Dom blinked a few times trying to get his eyes adjusted. There was no one around, and Dom yelled, "Let's go, Jack!" They sprinted out and ran as fast as they could along the loading area, swiveling their heads trying to take everything in. *Where was it?* There, just to their right in the shadows, was their aero car! Luck was on their side tonight. Wasting no time for relief, the duo kept running at full pace to the aero car. They hopped in, and Dom powered her up. Like a bullet, they vanished into the night.

After a few minutes, Jack broke their silent thoughts. "Dom, easy on the speed. We're clear of the goons. I don't want to die now. This is the easy part of our escape."

"Yeah, yeah. You are right, my friend."

Dom eased up on the throttle until they reached a safe cruising speed.

"Where should we go now?"

"Good question, Jack. We need to lie low for a bit to think this through before we contact headquarters. This is an awful mess. How will we ever explain losing the body? The chief will have our heads for this one. We shouldn't go back to our places either. No telling who will be there to greet us. Jack, when we get into the underground tunnel system, turn off the transponder so we can't be traced. Let's disappear for a few hours."

"Roger that, Dom. We need to take a breather and slow down." A few minutes later, after some high-speed weaving, they entered a tunnel system that spread out with multiple branches. After flipping a couple of switches, Jack looked at Dom and gave him a thumbs up. "We are ghosts now!"

CHAPTER 6

Good Cop, Bad Cop

"What was all that about?" Jack said aloud.

It was the same question that Dom had been asking himself since their narrow escape. They had almost become another pair of corpses in the hospital morgue! "It's the strangest thing yet, Jack." What else was there to say? "One thing is for sure, my friend—that was no ordinary death, and it seems that the lengths people will go to find that old woman's secrets have no limits." It was one thing to kill one of the masses, but to have the guts to kill a pair of Authority cops? That was a whole other level of nefariousness, and only the most hardened of criminal elements with very high-up connections would even think of offing two high-level detectives. Dom's thoughts wandered. *Well, okay, maybe we aren't the cream of the crop, and we're not that high up in the department, but we aren't newbies in the force, and that should have commanded some respect!* Dom spoke, "We have to lie low for a bit. Not sure who we can trust. Who knew about the death of the woman and where we were taking her? It was a hush-hush operation. Senior officials ordered us to handle this matter quietly and discretely."

The duo had done this sort of thing before as favors to those above, and they had always been well compensated for their discretion and results. All they had to do was just keep quiet. Jack and Dom were two of the few who could be counted on to get the job done with no questions asked. Now that the body was gone, why were some goons after them? Just for seeing the body? Did the goons think that Dom and Jack knew something that they surely didn't know? One thing for sure was that there was a leak inside the department that had led the bad guys to them at the morgue. Dom and Jack knew they could not trust anyone. And what about those two medical examiners? If that's what they were. They acted more detectives—like Dom and Jack—looking for clues and searching for answers to questions. Questions and answers that Jack and Dom needed to find out.

After they'd been lost in their own thoughts for a few more minutes, Dom blurted out. "Jack, we need to unravel this mystery or we'll never be safe. Let's start with the two medical examiners and what they were looking for. Or, more aptly, what they found."

"The tattoo," Jack muttered.

"Yes, the tattoo, Jack. We need to find out more about its meaning. It must be some kind of gang symbol." There were so many faction groups, all trying to cheat the system. It was almost laughable that their fearless leaders spoke of unity, peace, and happiness while letting the world burn in murder, prostitution, hate crimes, and cyber wars. You name it, and there was a gang war for it. It almost seemed as if the more ruthless people were to each other, the more the leadership liked it—as long as the status quo didn't change: the same amount of production, the same number of people, the same anti-religion rules. Peace came at the forced retirement age of forty-four years and four months when citizens were taken to paradise. Or whatever that place was. Everyone knew that was just a good word for termination. When your time was up, you had to go to make way for others in the world.

"Dom?" Jack prodded Dom out of his momentary lapse.

"Yeh, Jack."

"Dom, we need to dig into this symbol that was on the woman's wrist. It's the only thing we have to go on."

"Jack, did you notice something odd about the two examiners?"

"Besides that woman's perfectly tan skin and eyes so green that you could get lost in them forever?"

"Yes, Jack, I did notice those eyes."

"Wait a minute! Dom, there was something else. Something else indeed!" Jack pulled Dom back to that most unusual scene. Just after finding the symbol, the two "examiners" bowed their head in silence for a moment. The man held his fingers intertwined together and the women held her hands together with fingers stretched out. This was something Dom and Jack had almost missed. Their minds struggled to remember the scene. It was so surreal. Peaceful almost.

Jack got it first. "Dom, remember the dead woman's wrist? The symbol?"

"That's it, Jack! You are a genius! I remember now. Both examiners also had that same symbol on their wrists! Two arcs coming together making a long oval and a sort of triangle. They were in the same gang! She must have been one of their leaders, and they bowed in silence to pay their final respects. We need to find the source of the symbol, Jack. Then we can track down our examiners." Inwardly Dom's heart skipped a beat as he thought of finding the mysterious emerald-eyed woman. "Jack, if we access the data system, those thugs will locate us instantly. If the symbol is even recorded. So much data was lost in the information purges. We'll need to do this the old-school way."

"What's that, Dom?"

"I remember one of our old contacts saying there was a secret building that housed a library—a library full of printed books dating back to before the Great Conflict."

"Whoa, Dom! Now that is way outside of the law. You know that the penalty for getting caught with a prewar book is death! And if it's a religious book, death would be a gift." It was no exaggeration. The leadership posted videos of the torture performed on those who were caught with religious books.

"Jack, we have three choices. One, we go back to headquarters and explain what happened. Whoever was on the inside and tipped us off will inform the goons, and we'll be captured, tortured, and killed. Two, we could continue to hide, and then headquarters will think we had something to do with the disappearance of the body, and we will end up fugitives. The goons will eventually find us, and then we will be tortured and killed."

"Well, Dom, those two options don't sound very appealing. What is the third option?"

"We dig into it, find the two examiners, and take them back to headquarters where they will confess what they did. The insiders will leave us alone and pound on the two examiners. Worst case, we get a slap on the wrist and live on reduce rations for a while." That option left a bitter taste in Dom's mouth. Just thinking of harm coming to Emerald Eyes raised his blood pressure. But the examiners were the offenders not Dom and Jack. The examiners had broken the law, and that was that. They had to pay for their misdeeds.

"I don't like the third option at all, but that is the only way."

"I don't like it either, but the two examiners are the only lead we have, and as far as I can see, they are our only option for getting us out of this mess. We need access to a good amount of ID credits." Jack mumbled. "I figured this would cost us. I don't have much in my account, Dom. You know honest cops don't live well."

"That's for sure, Jack. I don't have much either, and we'll need a lot more than we have combined. We also can't make any financial transactions without giving up our location."

The great leaders, in their infinite wisdom, had developed a totally cashless system. The entire world was tied to a single monetary system called The Credit. One credit was roughly worth one US dollar in the year two thousand (the old calendar system). All citizens were assigned identification (ID) numbers and were issued ID "chips" that kept track of their age along with wage balance and everything they bought or sold. The chip—actually a microchip— was implanted into citizens' wrists. The chip also enabled leadership to track, monitor, and record everyone's movements. Leadership said the monitoring was for the people's "safety" because government officials would be able to detect fraud and other nefarious activities by those who might try to steal or manipulate credits. That was definitely a possibility because nothing was truly safe. So, for safety's sake, citizens lost all freedom; they accepted the grand bargain. But was that all the ID chips were used for? Everyone knew that the chips kept tabs on citizens' locations, but some said that the chips even had audio capability so the government could listen to and record all conversations. Extremists said that the chips were tied into citizens' brains and recorded what they saw and even what they thought! Who knew what was true? The one great thing about being a police officer was that the leadership knew that, if they could monitor people using the ID chips, then so could their enemies—the groups in the shadows that still held on to freedom first before safety and those individuals who didn't agree to "retire" at the ripe old age of forty-four.

Years previously, Dom and Jack had found that their effectiveness at catching criminals was diminishing at a rapid pace. Their ID chip tracking system had been compromised! From then on, they did not have to get their ID chips embedded in their wrists. Instead, they had each been given a portable ID credit chip embedded on a plastic card. When they were on duty, they left their ID chips at the police station or at home.

"Jack, they'll track us down in a second if we use our personal chips. We need access to a black-market chip." This was aptly called in the underworld a black chip.

"Whoa, Dom. I've heard of those before but never seen one. It's a credit chip device that generates a random user Identification and location for every transaction, right? The number just gets lost in the system and is completely untraceable." Dom nodded. "Dom, if we can't get access to our ID chips, then how do we get access to any credits to buy a black chip that is loaded with credits?"

"Jack, I have just the idea. Let's go."

"This time I drive," said Jack. Jumping into the aero car, the duo flew off silently, undetectable, on manual pilot, with their location transponder off.

Dom loved their new aero car. She was a thing of beauty and able to seat four people plus the pilot and copilot. She had advanced flying navigation for all weather conditions, powerful engines, exterior shielding for high strength, and was equipped with the latest advanced weaponry. There was even a stealth cloaking mode in which the exterior car panels mirrored the surrounding environment, making the car seem to disappear. It was invisible to any observer! That was all amazing enough, but to add to all the bells and whistles, their ride—the newest version—was equipped with a mini no-maintenance nuclear reactor that could power the car for over a hundred years. Only the most trusted officers had been issued this model. Dom and Jack's car was even more unique. Because of their undercover operations, their aero car was also equipped with manual overrides on all tracking and location safeguards. This was the result of a previous experience when their navigation systems and transponders had been hacked by the bad guys. They needed to travel undetected during special operation works.

Dom and Jack were heading to the outskirts of ring five. The interior rings were packed with high-density new mega buildings. The older and smaller buildings were farthest away from the center of the ring. At the fringes were the warehouses, some of which were hundreds of years old. And they looked it too. People did not come to this part of town unless they were looking for something—something outside the law. Usually they got what they were looking for, and the results were bad for them. No rules out there.

Each of the ten kingdoms had been developed with a six-ring master plan. That's how the common term *ring kingdoms* arose. The innermost ring held the top Authority leadership and the elite class that ran the kingdom. The second ring held the high-technology sectors. The third ring comprised other professional services and lower-level government facilities. The fourth ring was primarily made up of general storage, warehousing, commercial business buildings, and housing for the general lower-level, white-collar citizens. The fifth ring housed the heavy production industries areas for fabrication, materials storage, and general housing for the lower-level citizens. And the sixth ring consisted of the agricultural farming and livestock farming that took up larger land areas. Generally, people worked, lived, socialized, and did everything in their assigned ring. Rarely were people allowed to venture outside of their ring. It was never admitted, but it was obvious that the kingdom layout had been established to control the masses and ensure the safety and security of the people and infrastructure of the innermost rings. The flow of goods from ring to ring was tightly controlled and seamless at the ring borders. The rings were separated by thirty-foot-high walls monitored by a sensor system that extended to the top of the dome. Anything that broke the plane between rings was immediately destroyed by laser cannons stationed around the ring perimeter. No warning was given. Everyone knew the rule: break the invisible ring barrier, and you were toast.

Few people lived in the first ring. It was a fantastic jeweled marvel of buildings soaring into the sky. The second ring held all the high technology that enabled the first ring to function and was just as heavily fortified and secure as the first ring. Successive rings were progressively lower in technology. Less expense and effort were spent on infrastructure upkeep and the welfare of faithful citizens. By far the worst ring was the outermost ring where all levels of mayhem, lawlessness, and despair existed. The outermost ring also contained most of the population.

"Dom, are we headed to where I think we are going?"

"You got it, Jack. We are headed to see Fast Eddie." People sought out Fast Eddie when they needed a lot of credit fast and were willing to take a big discount. He was the king of the black-market bartering system. Rumors were that, with enough credit or goods, it was even possible to purchase a black chip from Fast Eddie. A lot of people had heard about Fast Eddie, but hardly anyone knew where to find him. Jack and Dom knew his whereabouts because they had an inside deal with him. From time to time, they needed to find specific criminals, and for a price, Eddie would locate them.

To deal with criminals, it's best to know the criminal mind. While Fast Eddie was a criminal, he was only in the commodity business. He did not break any sacred leadership laws that required immediate execution. In the hierarchy of offenders, he was low level—a rich and successful low-level criminal.

There were only four laws—the Mortal Laws—that were enforced by the Authority. Those who broke the laws were subject to immediate execution or imprisonment: Citizens must display absolute obedience to the leadership. Citizens must attend their retirement ceremony when they reach forty-four years and four months of age. Citizens must never say anything negative about Authority leadership. Citizens must never be involved in any way in any religious group. For all other situations, Authority police were commissioned to "manage with judgement." The police had absolute discretion with regard to the use of force, and Dom and Jack had seen many of their fellow brother and sister police officers abuse their powers. Thankfully, Jack and Dom were never able to be so coldhearted or evil. It was another reason they made such a good team.

"Let's see if the rumors are right, Jack." Dom and Jack had frequently bought information from Fast Eddie, but never sought him out for this level of "trading." They approached a series of warehouse buildings that looked like something from a war zone. No lights at all in the area—no streetlights, no building lights. The only illumination was the full moon, and it cast waving shadows of the buildings that made the buildings almost seem alive. As they got close to their destination, Jack turned on the aero car's night vision cameras so they could home in on a particularly beaten-up warehouse with a red brick exterior. It was the same as all the other warehouses except for a rusted metal door that looked more like an aircraft hangar door that extended nearly all the way to the roof of the warehouse. They approached low and slow, and when they were about one-hundred feet away they stopped and hovered. Dom gave a signal with a directed spotlight: three short flashes, three long flashes, three short flashes. It was an old maritime "SOS" Morse code for "save our ship" or, as some said, "save our souls." Fast Eddie had a good sense of humor. And then they waited not making a move. Exactly seven minutes later, the huge aircraft doors opened, and Dom and Jack slowly flew the aero car into what Fast Eddie called the bat cave. Eddie was also a history buff and a fan of the old comic books.

As they entered the warehouse, Jack asked Dom, already knowing—or fearing—the answer, "Dom, what are we selling to Eddie that's worth black chips with lots of credit?"

"You're sitting in it, brother," Dom responded.

Jack whistled. "In for a penny, in for a pound. Looks like we're all in on this one, Dom."

"You got it partner. What else do we have? Only one way out of this mess—forward." Dom landed the aero car at the back of the warehouse next to an elevated dock that was used to unload the old street-bound, rubber-tired trucks. To keep order in society, the infinitely wise leaders kept the people in the Stone Age and left the high technology to the few who "managed" the masses. Beyond the elevated dock, the wall was all metal with a vault-like door to the side. The warehouse was a front for a fortress.

The massive door even had those old-fashioned wheels that bankers used to spin to open the door locking pins once the proper code was entered. The wheel began to spin with accompanied sounds of gears in motion. Fast Eddie loved history, and he loved drama even more. The door swung open to reveal a short, dark-skinned, dark haired, Middle Eastern man. Fast Eddie always stayed extremely fit and was always well dressed. He looked like the consummate olden day's mafia man—another throwback that Fast Eddie loved. He just loved the movie drama scenes. He approached the aero car and stopped about ten feet away with his hands on his hips.

That was Dom's and Jack's cue. They popped the aero car door. It gave a soft hiss like gas escaping a pressurized airtight lid when opened. The doors lifted up silently like the wings of a bird unfolding, just like the old DeLorean car from the movie *Back to the Future*. The vehicle was elevated a bit from ground level, so the bottom segments of the doors opened downward providing a few steps for ease of getting out of the vehicle. The aero car doors and steps all moved in one seamless motion. Dom threw out his left leg and placed his foot on the step. He grabbed the door handle that was above his head and levered himself out to the floor in one smooth move like a choreographed, synchronized ballet move. Jack knew the drill, so he did the same. Dom and Jack walked to the front of the vehicle and stopped just a few feet in front of Fast Eddie making sure to stand aside so he could get a full view of the beautiful, state-of-the- art aero car.

"Woo-weee!" Fast Eddie said. Then he whistled. "You two sure have a sweet ride. I would give anything to have a machine like that. A man could disappear into the void and never come back." That was the same remark that Fast Eddie had been telling Jack and Dom for the last ten years even when they'd had their older model aero car. This time, however, his voice had a bit more gut to it. Before it had just been fantasy play, but this time the situation was subtly different. Dom stared at Fast Eddie and took all of him in. His face was a bit more weathered, his hair a touch thinner, and Dom could make out a few white hairs around the fringes of Fast Eddie's hairline. Maybe Fast Eddie was closer to the magic forty-four number than Dom had thought he was. With all the money in the world, a person could not escape "retirement." Normally, Dom would respond, "In your dreams, Fast Eddie." This time, however, he paused a bit longer than normal and pivoted his head to Jack. Jack replied with a silent nod and then turned back to Fast Eddie.

Dom addressed the crook: "Well there, my good friend, today may be your lucky day. Jack and I are in need of heavy credits— black market credits. And we want to discuss with you what we can get for the aero car."

Fast Eddie froze like a statue at Dom's request. Jack worried that he might have a heart attack. He just stood there and stared at the aero car. The detectives knew his mind was going a thousand miles an hour as he projected what it would be like to own one of the most advanced pieces of equipment on the planet. Fast Eddie was a great poker player and knew how to keep his cool. That's how he had been so successful at making credits in the black-market bartering game. But this completely threw him off guard. And, of course, Dom and Jack were close with Eddie—almost friends … almost.

"Wow, Dom! You guys must be in hot water to be thinking of parting with that machine. That would be signing a death warrant for you two once the Authority leadership finds out you stole the aero car!"

"We know that, Eddie. We don't plan to ever surface again once this deal is done. Jack and I are disappearing into the shadows of society. We just need enough credits on a couple of black chips to do it."

"Well, well, my two friends!" Eddie retorted quickly. "You certainly have come to the right place, and, I might add, at the right time as I have recently also been pondering my own future. Just like you two, I have precious few years left, and I have been thinking about time—or the lack of time to be more accurate."

"Eddie, we need just two things from you," said Dom. "Then we'll show you how to disarm all locating devices, and we'll give you the rundown on all the newer features of the aero car."

"That sounds great, Dom!" Fast Eddie didn't bother to hide his enthusiasm. "I've been studying up a lot on the newer aero cars, and think I know all the newer features."

Jack responded, "Eddie, the literature doesn't cover half of the features this one has. Its virtually untraceable, unlocatable, maintenance free, and has a power source that lasts over a hundred years."

Eddie looked as if he was about to burst in tears of joy and give them a big hug. He began to sweat profusely, and Dom could swear a bit of drool formed in the right corner of the short mafia-type man's mouth. Regaining some sense of composure, Eddie gestured with a large sweep of his right hand. "Right this way, my brothers. Come into my office. We can have a drink and talk more about your needs. I am always here to help my friends out in their darkest hour." As they followed behind him, Fast Eddie stopped short of the vault door. Turning and looking at the aero car, he barked to his top security guard, "Finny, double the guards around the aero car. If anyone gets near it, shoot him!"

CHAPTER 7

Changing Sides

F ast Eddie's interior abode beyond the metal vault door did not match the décor of the dreary exterior building or the open interior area that was like an old warehouse. Dom and Jack felt as if they had walked into a Fortune-500 tycoon's house. The room they entered was circular, and they stepped down into a recessed open floor area. Recessed soft lights hone from the high ceiling. Plush leather couches and chairs; dark, rich wood flooring; and a large floating holographic globe hovering right in the middle of the room gave the place an air of extravagance. The entire perimeter wall of the circular room was covered floor to ceiling with display screens. At the moment, the visitors found themselves in a rain forest. Speakers everywhere played the soft noises of the jungle—wind whispering through the trees and the far-off calls of native birds and even some frog croaks.

Just as Dom and Jack sat down in the plush chairs, a steward floated in like a ninja providing them with drinks, and then he departed as silently and swiftly as he'd entered. Dom spoke with admiration. "I've been in here many times, Eddie, and I am always awestruck at the amazing beauty of this room. Simply incredible." And that was no remark to boost Fast Eddie's ego. Dom truly meant it. An amazing place.

"Thanks, Dom," Eddie replied. "It took years to build it up to what it is today. Piece by piece. It's my sanctuary away from the strange world we live in."

They chit-chatted for about an hour about what was going on in the ring kingdom, and also touched on what Jack and Dom needed for credits, a car, and a place to hide out. "All that sounds very doable," Fast Eddie said. He was relaxed and in a very good mood after a few drinks and the thought of his new aero car.

Dom cleared his throat. "There is one more item we need, Eddie." There was always one more thing, and this got Eddie's gears back in motion. When negotiating, savvy people always saved the biggest "ask" for last. "We need access to some information."

"Hmm … what type of information do you two need, Dom?" Fast Eddie's tone changed from happy-go-lucky to cautiously concerned. He was especially cautious about dealing in information. Acquiring sensitive information from a paranoid regime could get a person killed.

"We need access to a library of books that detail symbology dating back through history."

Fast Eddie gulped. "Historical books? Why on earth would you want that?"

Jack jumped in. "Eddie, it's our only way out of the mess we're in. We need the information to find the two examiners who destroyed the body of the old dead lady we told you about."

Eddie's curiosity was quickly piqued. He was a history buff, and he knew a lot. He wanted to ask what Dom and Jack were looking for, but he stopped short. Sometimes—well most of the time—it was better not to know, especially when the subject at hand had to do with history. It meant automatic torture and death for those caught with distributing contraband information.

Fast Eddie looked over to Jack. "There isn't much left in the way of libraries in this part of the world anymore. Most of them had either been destroyed in the Great Conflict or were covered under by ice from the deep freeze. Let me think about that for a minute." Fast

Eddie turned to a small tablet device and began typing furiously. The holographic globe in the center of the room lit up. The image of Earth depicted the present ice-age world, showing areas covered in ice sheets. Dark blotches were areas devastated by nuclear warfare; each blotch had once been a thriving city. Dom and Jack watched as successive dots popped up. The globe would zoom in to the city. Eddie would mumble to himself as the image faded away and the globe zoomed back out again. This went on for some time until, at one location, the dot did not disappear.

"That's the one!" exclaimed Fast Eddie. "She's been known as one of the most beautiful book libraries in South America, and it's still intact. Not an electronic library that had all data wiped out by electromagnetic pulses from the nuclear war—but a real book library. "Ta da!" With a sweep of his hand, Eddie raised his finger up, and then, with a flourish, he depressed a key on his electronic pad. The holographic image zoomed in on a beautiful English-style mansion set in a charming neighborhood community. Fast Eddie touched another button, and a holographic lady appeared next to the building. She described the place in her soothing voice: "The Wilborada 1047 Bookstore is one of the most beautiful places one can visit in Bogotá, especially if you love books. It is located in a typical mansion in Bogotá that is surrounded by the high buildings of the Quinta Camacho neighborhood. This store is a unique place where you can enjoy a good coffee and a delicious empanada while you are surrounded by precious editions of the works of the best authors in the world. The name of the library-styled bookstore is derived from Santa Wilborada, the patron of booksellers and books. The building has four floors, each full of books."

The building exterior faded away, and the interior of the building came into view. Each floor was, indeed, full of books. Chairs were set out so visitors could sit and leisurely peruse a good read. *Ahh, the good old days.* The soothing lady faded away, and the holographic image changed to a view of the entire city of Bogotá with the bookstore a glowing green dot for identification in the zoomed-out view—the City of Bogotá in all of its glory circa the early twenty-first century. The year 2010 to be exact.

Dom was curious. "So, Eddie, why is this bookstore still around? It should have been destroyed by the nuclear war or destroyed by the Authority during the Cleansing."

The Cleansing had happened after the Great Conflict, unification under a single world leader, and the creation of the ten ring kingdoms. All hard-copy books and electronic data on the topics of religion, history, politics, and more were destroyed to cleanse the world and all her peoples of thoughts that provoked disunity and promoted conflict. It was a purge the likes of which had never been seen before. All bookstores, museums, and libraries were destroyed along with any structure that stored information. All citizens were directed to turn in their books, computers, and any device that stored data. All were destroyed. The world would start anew with a new history. The calendar was reset to year zero of the new age—the Enlightened Era (EE).

Fast Eddie typed furiously on his keyboard so he could show Dom the bookstore's history. The holographic image of the City of Bogotá flickered for a second and then started to change rapidly. Fast Eddie programmed the image to show slices in time. Eddie explained, "We are looking at images in ten-year increments." The Bogotá cityscape undulated with the construction of buildings, roads, and more buildings until the city changed from a large population of ten million people to a mega city with over thirty million people. As the images of all the demolition and rebuilding whizzed by, one of the few constants was the stately-looking Wilborada 1047 Bookstore. At one point, it looked as if the world had encroached onto all sides of the bookstore and yet it held its ground against all the massive construction activity. The image flickered again. Some of the buildings were destroyed. Curiously, all the green leaves disappeared and turned to brown. The images moved on. The brown disappeared, and all that was left were empty buildings and streets. No people, no plant life. Nothing. On and on the images flickered and moved forward in time until the date read year 2538 (420 EE)—the current image. Still nothing. The buildings looked crumbled and old, devoid of all life. Frozen in time, the structures were still standing, even though they'd been beaten down by centuries of weather. But there had been no deterioration or decay from plant life growth or animal destruction. By now, most cities in the world that were south of the freezing zone were either covered over by forests, completely destroyed, or had been re-habited and become part of the ten kingdoms. But Bogotá suffered from another fate. It had become a lost city.

"Bogotá is not the only city to suffer from this graveyard fate, my friends," Fast Eddie explained. "Over years of searching, I have found multiple cities—graveyard cities—frozen in time, just like Bogotá."

After thinking this over for a few seconds, Dom blurted out, "Neutron bombs!"

"That's right," retorted Eddie, impressed with Dom's knowledge. Eddie returned to his scholarly mode. "Otherwise known as enhanced radiation weapons—ERWs—low-yield thermonuclear weapons designed to maximize lethal neutron radiation in the immediate vicinity of the blast while minimizing the physical power of the blast itself. During the Great Conflict, they made the bombs especially 'dirty' using highly radioactive plutonium, not for blast effect, but to spread high doses of radioactive particles. It was never found out how many they dropped on Bogotá, but it was said that the radiation level is so high that it will kill anything and anyone in seconds for the next ten thousand years."

"That's just unbelievable!" exclaimed Jack.

"You got that right, Jack," Eddie replied. "The war motto was, if we can't have it, then no one can. Ever."

Dom mulled over what he was hearing, "So, Eddie, that's the only intact library in the world? In a place of super high radiation that would kill us in a second?"

Eddie scratched his head. "Well, I've searched for years, out of curiosity, for areas that survived the nuclear war. That is the only place that I've found that isn't buried under a hundred feet of ice and may possibly house some books that have survived through the years. The good news is that the place is so hot with radiation, it's not monitored by any satellites, and there are no security patrols anywhere near the city. You'll have easy access in and out."

"Thanks a lot." That was all Dom could muster for a reply.

After more conversation, the three men moved away from the holographic image to relax. Dom looked wiped out. "This is a non-starter. Uugh." He sat back down on the plush sofa and took a big gulp of Fast Eddie's fine whiskey. That helped a little to relieve the onset of a headache brought on by thinking about the radiation problem. Jack did the same, moving to a chair and resting his feet on an ottoman. The duo sat in silence for a few minutes, lost in thought as they gazed at the beautiful ghost city still glowing on the globe. Dom was about to say something when Jack jumped in. "Dom, do you remember the technical building fire about five years ago near the south edge of the city? We had to clear out a radius of ten miles due to a potential breach in an old nuclear fuel reactor. It was an old communication building that got its power from a self-contained fission reactor. There was a scare that somehow the reactor might have cracked open and was leaking radiation. We were coordinating with the Special Forces Unit, and they were gearing up for the worst. As I recall, I asked one of the guys who was suiting up how good the suit was. He told me they had just got new radiation suits that could handle radiation levels over one hundred thousand roentgens per hour!"

Dom added excitedly, "That's right, Jack! I do remember that incident. In the end, it was a false alarm. As I recall, they stored all their special containment gear in a special room. Was that in headquarters or the off-site facility?"

"From what I remember, the gear came from the main fire station located about four blocks away from headquarters."

"That makes sense. Looks like we'll have to pay a visit to our fire-fighter friends. If we do it quickly, we could be finished before the word gets out about the incident at the morgue. Let's hope for a break." Jack was about to speak when Dom added. "Yeh, yeh, Jack, I know what you are about to say. Hope is not a plan. We'll need to think this through with a couple of bail-out options in case we get into trouble."

Fast Eddie added additional input based on his amazing history knowledge. "If my memory serves me correctly, I think the worst nuclear disaster that wasn't related to war was the Chernobyl nuclear reactor incident. The worst-hit areas of the reactor building were estimated to be just over five roentgens per second, equivalent to more than twenty thousand roentgens per hour. A lethal dose is around five hundred roentgens over five hours. Those suits you described should easily handle the radiation levels in Bogotá." He paused and thought for few seconds. "Gents, a couple of those suits would be a great addition to the aero car! They would certainly bump up the offer price indeed!"

Jack and Dom looked at each other. Dom turned to Eddie. "But of course, Eddie, why not? As we said, in for a penny, in for a pound. If we're going to be fugitives, why not go all the way?" That put a huge smile on Fast Eddie's face. "Well then, my friends, let's have another toast to our partnership."

Jack was all in for another round, but Dom jumped in, putting a frown on Jack's face. "We'd love to, Eddie, but time is not on our side. Every minute is a minute closer to the exposure of our mishap at the morgue and our disappearance being made known to our superiors. If we're going to do this, we need to do it fast. And we'll need to use our aero car to avoid suspicion."

A frown came over Fast Eddie's face. It was a risk to let the aero car go. The chances of Dom and Jack getting caught or damaging the aero car if they had to escape were high.

Dom saw the wheels going around in Eddie's head and said, "Don't worry, Eddie. We'll be in and out in a flash and bring back extra high-level radiation suits to protect you in any situation that may arise in the future."

Eddie took in Dom's words with some thought and took a long swig of his drink. "Yes, yes, it's what must be done so you can get to your library. Okay, then, let's do this. Just bring back my aero car in pristine shape please." Eddie's voice cracked up a bit as if he was saying good-bye to a lover.

Dom tried to ease Eddie's concern, "We want full price, so don't worry. We'll take especially good care of her. Not a scratch!" Dom didn't think his assurances gave Eddie any comfort, and Jack was not exuding confidence in the plan—or lack of a plan—to get the suits and come out of the heist in one piece.

Dom and Jack departed the warehouse in the aero car in the middle of the day during peak traffic, opting for camouflage by keeping the aero car close to ground level and moving slowly along with the surface transportation vehicles. The multi-lane roads were crowded with passenger cars and large trucks. Staying in the middle lanes, they were invisible, lost in the mass of slow-moving traffic. Some might think it unusual to see an aero car amongst the ground cars, but most tried to mind their own business, figuring the officers were on patrol. One never questioned the law. Ever.

Jack was typing in the location on his clear pad device. "Okay, Dom, the fire station is just at the outskirts of ring four. From where we are now, that's about four hours away at this slow speed."

"Okay then, Jack. We have four hours to come up with a couple of options." Time seemed to pass quickly as Jack and Dom threw out all types of ideas and scenarios. They debated the pros, cons, and risks of each one. There were only two outcomes—success or death. Nothing in between. So, their plan A had to be a good one, and from there the fallback options had to follow "what if" diversionary scenarios. The last one, of course, was an all-out shooting match war, and they did not want to go there. The firemen at the station were good people. Would they kill their brothers and sisters who were not the aggressors? Surrender was not an option as the Authority leadership would torture Dom and Jack endlessly as a warning to others to toe the line and obey the rules. The duo decided to not think of the total failure option.

Dom and Jack had been in the police force for many years and had worked closely with quite a few of the firemen, many whom were still around. They talked about the ones they considered friends, the ones who "owed them" for something or another. Brothers and sisters in uniform watched each other's backs. There were those, of course, who would do anything to get ahead, and they were crossed off the list. Friend or not, the detectives couldn't take a chance with overachievers who saw Dom and Jack as an opportunity to make brownie points with the higher-ups.

"Okay, Jack," Dom finally surmised, "looks like we are down to two people we can trust to have our backs at the fire station." There was Phil, the senior medic. Jack had saved his life five years earlier when they had raided a warehouse full of contraband goods. In the raid, one of the officers was hurt, and Phil was called to provide treatment as he was the closest in the area. As Phil was treating the officer, a lone gunman came charging out trying to escape, and Phil was right in his way. The gunman was just about to shoot Phil when, out of nowhere, Jack tackled the gunman from the side like a charging rhinoceros. Phil had been white as a sheet, and to this day Phil called Jack on the anniversary of the day of the incident thanking him for giving him a new lease on life. It was time to call in the favor. But even Phil wouldn't go as far as to allow them to waltz in and take a few radiation suits. If Phil was caught—now or later—helping Dom and Jack, the punishment would be death not only for Phil, but also for his entire family. That was how it worked. Threat of total destruction kept the masses in line. So, Phil would help them get through the front door if they were lucky. Then they would need more help.

The idea was that no single person would help to get them all the way in and then back out again. If Dom and Jack were able to isolate their helpers to specific limited tasks, then no one could be entirely responsible for the break-in and theft, and therefore no one would be in danger. Or anyone suspected would be in less danger. It had to be a choreographed dance of multiple people, each doing his or her part in perfect timing and location. Okay, that was at least the dream.

The next helper they considered was Vivian. Vivian and Dom dated for a while, and they really connected well. But Dom's work hours were long, and he sometimes disappeared for months at a time while undercover. This did not make for a stable relationship, so they parted as friends. Vivian's support might not be as enthusiastic as the support of a person who owed his life to Jack, but she would be key because she was the head of the Special Forces Unit. One of the special subunits was the demolition, explosives, and radiation team. So, she would know where the suits were kept. The plan was forming. Dom and Jack knew how they'd get into the fire station, and they knew how to find the suits. Now they needed a plan to get the suits and then get out of there.

"Jack, do you remember how the suits were stored? I recall they could be rolled up pretty small and were not very heavy."

"Let me think about that, Dom. When we were talking to the Special Unit guy with the radiation gear, I did hear him mention that the suits needed to be lightweight and portable."

"Okay then, Jack, let's assume the suits are a duffle-bag size with no weight issues. So, each of us could easily carry two or three suits."

"Dom, even if we could carry them, the fire station alarm bells would be triggered by anyone who saw two cops walking down the hallway carrying three duffle bags each of gear. We wouldn't get ten feet without someone stopping us. Unless of course …" Jack's voice trailed off, and he seemed to be lost in his thoughts.

After a minute it was too much to bear. "Okay, Jack, spill it. What are you thinking?"

"Dom, this may be way out there, but what if we got into the fire station with help from our pal, Phil, and then made our way to the area where they kept the suits with help from your friend, Viv. And then, when we are close to the suit locker room, multiple emergencies broke out. A huge fire somewhere and maybe a radiation leak alert in another area. There would be chaos, and we would be right there to help out by bringing extra radiation suits to the emergency scene."

"Hmmmm ... yes. Well, Jack, I think you just earned your paycheck today. And you know Fast Eddie will be all over that to help us out with the 'emergencies.' Destruction and mayhem are his specialties. We don't have time, but we'll need some coordination to make it all work."

"Yeah, we'll need at least a few days at the very least to bring this all together. Every day we're missing in action brings about suspicion. We can't not check in with headquarters about what we're doing. Our esteemed Captain Morgan must be wondering where we are and how it went with the governor's favor."

"You're right, Jack. We need to check in. Seems like it's been forever, but it's been less than twenty-four hours since we started this whole favor-for-the-governor mess. It would be a miracle if no news came out of this whole debacle already. Jack, slide the aero car over in that alley, and we'll call the captain."

Jack smoothly navigated the crowded lanes over to the side street. It helps a lot when your car screams, "Police car! Move over or pay the price!"

"Okay then, Jack, let's get this over with." Dom keyed a few digits into the center console panel, and the familiar chime of the call going through sounded. In the middle of the console, a holographic image appeared between Dom and Jack—Captain Morgan's head in three dimensions. He was in his office sitting at his desk, and they saw his standard holographic background image of a white sand beach. "One can dream," he would always say. Oddly, he didn't seem put off or angry that they hadn't checked in sooner.

Dom decided to play it cool. "Hello there, Chief. How are things at the shop?"

The captain took a moment to respond. His eyes swiveled from Dom to Jack and then back to Dom. He rubbed his overgrown beard with his right hand. He often did that when he was thinking of the right reply. A few more seconds passed, and Dom could see Jack starting to break out in a sweat. *Play it cool my friend*, Dom's eyes told Jack.

"Well, gents, everything here is normal. No major crisis today. Not yet at least. The governor never got back to me on that 'favor' you two did for him, and I am not inclined to call and open a closed door. I don't want to know what happened or didn't happen. Just tell me that you two didn't mess it up too much."

Dom replied, perhaps a bit too quickly, "We did our usual, Chief. We didn't kill anyone that we didn't have to and didn't blow anything up."

That brought a chuckle from the chief. "Well, then, for now I'll say thanks until I hear otherwise. Say, what are you two doing anyway?"

Jack jumped in with a nonchalant, "Following up on some leads on the white whale."

"Are you guys still after that ghost? I'm telling you—he's a figment of your imagination! He doesn't exist. Just some random program glitch in someone's ID, and you think he's been eluding the law for what? How many years?"

It was Dom's turn to stumble in. "From my calculations, he's been around for literally hundreds of years."

"Guys! If you two weren't so dirt cheap, I'd have your heads for chasing ghosts! But, hey, I'm in a good mood, so I'll cut you some slack. Do whatever you want for the next few days. Just don't do anything that gets me in trouble. Okay?"

Dom and Jack replied in unison saluting. "Yes, sir!"

And just like that, the chief's big floating head disappeared, leaving Dom and Jack to their thoughts in the dark deserted street alley. "What do you think about that, Dom?"

"That's a million-credit question, Jack. I guess with the body gone and no one asking questions—yet at least—we're still safe. For how long, I'm not sure. We don't know who those goons tried to kill us work for. At least we know they don't work directly with our police department. Like us, they can't tell their superiors they failed to secure whatever information they were sent to find on that dead woman's body. There are two scenarios. One, the goons keep a low profile and find us, beat out of us any information we have, and then kill us. Two, the goons tell their superiors they lost the woman, but we may have the information, and then their employers and the goons hunt us down and carry out option one. Perhaps in option two the employer kills the goons and then hunts us down. Either way, we end up tortured and killed."

"Wow, Dom. Thanks for the pep talk, partner. I feel better already!"

"Just telling you the way it is, brother—the truth, the whole truth, and nothing but the truth, so help me God. I think that was the line they said in the olden days."

"We can't hide out long, Jack. Those people had powerful forces behind them to think they could kill us without any backlash. We need to move fast before it all crumbles down around us."

"You bet, Dom. Let's get this plan in action."

Dom and Jack spent another exhausting day planning, rethinking, and replanning multiple scenarios with Fast Eddie. Finally, the three men had it all coordinated, and they were in agreement. Eddie wanted to actually detonate a nuclear device to cause maximum distraction. Dom and Jack, still cops and human beings, made it clear that a single person dying or getting injured in their pursuit of a few radiation suits was just not acceptable. Eddie kept complaining that the distraction had to be real to deserve the kind of attention that they were looking for. They settled on one of the package nuclear plants at an older but still highly populated section of the city. The target fire station was also the closest one in the area. The idea was to place some low-level radioactive material near the plant sensors. It would trip the alarm, and all chaos would erupt in the densely populated area. All personnel at the fire station would be needed to secure the area and get residents out of the potential hot zone. Eddie had an inside man at the plant whom he could pay off to blow the minor radiation spike out of proportion to generate maximum panic in the area. He was disappointed at the lack of damage the plan would cause, but, hey, he wanted the aero car and the suits. The plan passed about a thousand "what ifs" they collectively threw at it. No plan was fool proof, and there was always something missed or an unexpected turn that required fast thinking and a lot of luck. Dom never thought a lot about God, religion, or any of that supernatural stuff, but if there was ever a time when they needed divine help, it was now.

Jack had been able to get in touch with Phil, who was thrilled to meet up with them. Dom connected with Viv. She was definitely not as enthusiastic about seeing Dom and Jack, but she reluctantly agreed to meet them when they arrived to hang out with Phil. Dom turned on the charm, but it didn't work well, so he stooped to bribery. Dom told her he wanted to give her a belated birthday gift. It was a very expensive bottle of perfume. That should do the trick to lighten her feet a bit and get them a tour of the emergency area.

CHAPTER 8

Fire Drill

D-day was upon Dom and Jack. In Jack's talk with Phil, he learned the least busy time with fewest firemen on duty was seven at night—dinner time. Viv and Phil were pulling night shift, so they would both be there at that time.

The evening before D-day, Dom and Jack called it an early night to get rest. They took extra precautions by never returning to their apartments. Instead, they stayed in a hotel. Fast Eddie had booked them rooms using the names of two of his men. It was a nice hotel, but not so nice that their presence would attract attention. Dom and Jack had dinner in the hotel restaurant and washed it down with a couple of beers to unwind their minds. The plan was to meet for breakfast in the morning at nine at the same restaurant.

The next morning came quickly for the duo. Dom got to the restaurant about fifteen minutes before nine to get some coffee and orange juice as well as a smoke. Jack came in a few minutes later in his normal, easy-as-it-goes walking pace. He took a seat across from Dom—not so fast he'd draw attention, but not too slowly either for the same reason. He was a natural at blending in with the crowd. Jack always said the best place to hide is in plain sight. Just don't stand out and no one will find you. Dom asked as he took a gulp of coffee, "How did you sleep, Jack?"

"Ahh, it was okay. You know, Dom, it's hard to turn the wheels off at night, especially the night before a mission."

"I hear you on that one, Jack. It wasn't the best sleep for me either. It will be over soon enough."

Jack's head bobbed up and down in reply at the same time his face turned into a crumpled frown. Jack waved his hands around in front of his face. "Man, when are you going to lose that disgusting habit?"

Dom gave him the "who me?" look. "What are you talking about? This is one of the finest cigarettes you can get for free!"

"Uggh! Smells like my toilet in the morning."

"Hmmmff. No class, Jack. No class. Some spy you'd make." That always gave Jack a smile. "Anyway," Dom went on, "let's partake of a big breakfast. We'll be needing all of our wits about us today."

"You got that right, Dom." Jack and Dom proceeded the buffet line. "Nothing like all you can eat, Dom." Jack's eyes lit up at the display of fruits, meats, egg dishes, and rolls. "Definitely could get used to this lifestyle."

Dom nodded in reply. "Yep, for sure, brother. For sure."

They drank coffee, orange juice, and grapefruit juice, and ate anything they wanted. Their last breakfast so to speak. "Jack, it's ten thirty now. Let's go to my room and run over the plan one more time and revisit the what-if scenarios."

"Sounds like a plan, Dom."

They spent the next several hours going over everything. Then they contacted Eddie to confirm all was in order on his end. To make sure "the distraction" happened at the right time when they were in the right place, Eddie had given them a tiny black box. The lid opened to reveal a single button. When the button was pressed, a signal would be sent straight to Eddie's mobile device: the *go* signal. Dom had asked him why they couldn't have done the same with their mobile device. Eddie pointedly reminded them that wasn't possible, and Dom could have kicked himself for not remembering. In most government facilities, mobile devices were blocked from the outside world to ensure security and prevent data from leaking out. This was mainly to prevent terrorists from signaling to detonate a planted bomb, coordinating attacks, or anything else the paranoid leadership could think of. The Authority was an expert at terrorism themselves, so they knew the deceitful hearts and plans of its proponents. Fast Eddie's black box was a one-of-a-kind invention by his crew that could bypass the jammers to get a signal out.

Eddie's mind was as brilliant as it was corrupt. He fancied himself like the legendary Robin Hood, taking from the rich and giving to the poor. Except in his case, he kept a percentage as a good-will service fee. It was funny that, when Dom had asked who the poor were to whom Eddie so graciously gave freely, he replied, "Look around! My subjects are everywhere."

Dom had needled him, "Oh, you mean your workers are your poor?"

Fast Eddie had put on a face of fake disdain. "Well, of course. We help the poor by giving them employment and lifting them up from rags to riches."

"Dom. Dom!" Jack nudged him out of his memories about Fast Eddie.

"Right, Jack. Sorry about that mental lapse. I was thinking of Eddie and his Robin Hood talks."

Jack murmured, "Oh, yah. I remember those talks. I've got to say that Eddie is brilliant but insane."

"Jack, the station is about twenty minutes maximum from here with traffic. Let's get some rest and leave here at six fifteen this evening. That'll put us inside the main fire station not later than six thirty-five. We'll have about thirty-five minutes to chat with Phil, find Viv, and walk to a point near the radiation gear storage room. More than enough time." They headed off to their rooms and settled in to sleep.

The alarm on Dom's handy mobile device blared its ugly tune. "Ugghhh!" Dom slapped it off his bedside table and looked at it with his bleary eyes. Five forty-five. Just enough time to take a shower, grab a cup of coffee, and meet Jack in the lobby. It was go-time, and Dom needed to pump up the energy volume. But not too much. They were supposed to be having a casual meeting with old friends.

Trained people can quickly recognize quirks in people's demeanor. Comes with the job. Phil and Viv were in the fire and rescue business and had dealt with many incidents caused by nefarious activities. They had been well educated both in class and on the job about reading people. It's what had kept them alive all those years.

Dom finished showering and hit the lobby at six to get a coffee in the restaurant. Jack was already there sipping a cup of brew at one of the back tables. Dom grabbed a cup and joined him. Jack looked up from his cup, "How are you feeling, Dom? Get any rest?"

"I got a solid hour of sleep time. Thanks for asking. I was so beat; it was hard to shake the cobwebs out of the brain. Cold shower helped a lot. How about you?"

"About the same. Felt good to hit the bed for a quick nap. Coffee helps a lot."

They sat there for a few minutes of silence lost in their own thoughts going over what they had planned. Six fifteen rolled around. "Okay, Jack. Let's do it."

Dom called Fast Eddie and let him know they were headed out. Their communicators would work until they were one hundred feet from the fire station. That was the perimeter of the jamming system. Dom and Jack would check in with Eddie one more time just before they hit the jamming perimeter so he would know when to expect the signal.

Fifteen minutes later they were at the jamming barrier, and five minutes after that, they were parked and at the front door of the fire station. Six thirty-five. Right on schedule.

The fire station, although located in the outskirts of the fourth ring, was a fairly new facility; that is, it had been built in the last one-hundred years. All new technology and new construction were concentrated on the inner rings one and two.

It was time. Dom and Jack stood in front of the main door. Dom took a deep breath, "Here we go, Jack." After entering the fire station, Dom and Jack walked directly to the security desk with purposeful strides to page Phil. As they approached, they saw that Phil was already at the desk chatting with the security guard. Phil was tall—about six foot three—and skinny as a rail. As a paramedic, he didn't have to do the heavy lifting the firemen had to be ready for. Upon seeing them, Phil quickly came around the desk telling the security guard, "These are my two best pals, Jack and Dom! The dynamic duo of detectives! I sleep easy at night knowing these two are out there bashing the bad guys!"

Dom liked Phil. He actually meant what he said, and his friend's words gave Dom a sense of worth. Jack jumped in. "Phil! Great to see you, my old friend! You are looking as trim and fit as always."

Phil gave Jack a warm hug and Dom a nice warm handshake. "So glad you two could come on down for a visit!" Phil continued, "Let's go in the back to the cantina and grab a coffee and a donut." With a wry smile Phil added, "Sorry, guys, no alcohol allowed on premise."

"But of course." Jack jumped in with a big smile and a fiendish look of disappointment. "But of course."

In the break room, they chatted for a while; it looked as if it was going to be a slow night. Phil appeared to be in no hurry, so Dom maneuvered the discussion to Viv. "Oh, yes, that's right." Phil remembered. "You and Viv were an item for quite some time. She's looking even better now, Dom. I heard she's seeing someone from a fire station in ring three. A brute of a guy, and he has a place in ring three."

Dom shrugged his shoulders. "She was always out of my league. Happy for her. I told Viv I would be here, and I'd stop by to see her. Mind if Jack and I take a walk to her area? Is she still stationed in in the back-office area?"

Phil thought for a second. "Yep, she's in the back and still managing the Special Forces teams. Go on, and before you leave, stop back over to see me. I'll be in the medical ward area."

Jack gave Phil a warm slap on the back. "Will do, Phil." And off the dynamic duo went in search of Viv.

All that chitchat with Phil had put them about ten minutes behind schedule, so they picked up the pace a bit as they walked to Viv's area, but not so fast they would draw attention. Fast Eddie knew the timing was unpredictable, and Dom and Jack had given him a window of plus or minus a half an hour. Eddie had assured them that, once they pushed the button, the fire station alert alarm would sound within a minute. Eddie didn't fool around when mayhem and destruction were involved.

A few minutes later, Jack and Dom were in Viv's office. Phil had been right—Viv looked amazing. She must have lost thirty pounds and had definitely been working out hard every day. Her eyes beamed as she gave them a wry smile. Dom knew it was in response to the expressions on his and Jack's faces. Their faces said it all: Viv you are at the top of your game! After Dom picked his jaw off the ground, he stammered a lame, "Hey there, Viv! Great to see you after all this time. You are looking amazing!" Jack just stood there and nodded with appreciation at her hard work.

"Why thank you, old friend," Viv replied. The old "friend" stung Dom a bit, but what could he say about love once alive and now lost. "You're looking good yourself, Dom." Obviously, a weak attempt at a return compliment from Viv.

Dom was looking okay, but had let himself go over the last few years. He'd become a bit mushier around the waistline—just the opposite of Viv's trimming up. "Thanks, Viv. Unfortunately, these last few years have not been as kind to me as they have been to you."

After an awkward silence, Jack jumped in. "Well, it's nice to have all of us together again. It's been quite a while since we all used to go out and do some damage around town. I know a few bars made a lot of credits on us back in the day. Say, is Wild Frank still around?" That broke the ice, and they all had a good laugh. Frank had been truly wild. Get a couple of drinks in him, and he'd be jumping on tables looking to swing from chandeliers.

Viv chimed in. "Yah, Frankie is still here in the station. Still working the fire brigade. But wild no more. He found a nice lady who doesn't let him off the wagon. He even trained for our Special Forces Unit team."

A slight opening—and Dom dived at the chance. "Really. Special Unit, huh! That's great news and a real step up for Frank. I remember there were several units including that really neat one you head up, Viv. You called them the radiation team. I was here one time during a potential incident. I was with a fella in the unit's room as he was gearing up. He was going to show me some of the real special gear, but he never got the chance. Would you mind if we took a peek?"

Viv took it all in. Not really thinking too hard, she replied. "Why not? I haven't been there recently myself, and as the Special Forces Unit commander, I am supposed to inspect all units. Let's take a quick walk. It's right down the hallway." Dom turned to Jack and lifted his eyebrows to signal *Game on!*

They stepped out of her office and started down the hall. It was shockingly bright with white walls that reminded Dom and Jack of the hallway at the hospital. A bit of sweat popped out on their foreheads as they hoped this wasn't going to turn out like the hospital episode. They had barely got out of that incident alive. Dom surreptitiously depressed Eddie's special button as they got close to the Special Force's Unit area. Within seconds, a loud siren erupted, doors flew open, and people came pouring out into the hall. "What's going on?!" Dom shouted. The alarm was so loud it was hard to hear his own voice.

Viv yelled back. "Priority one alert! The type of alarm indicates the incident type. This alarm is for a major building fire. Our fire crews will handle it. It's not a Special Unit incident."

"Glad to hear that!" Jack shouted back. Phase one in action. Deplete the fire station of as many staff as possible. Phase two should be kicking in a minute later. Like clockwork, another type of siren sounded. This alarm was a series of short blasts from a blaring horn. Viv's face went white as a sheet.

"What now?" Dom yelled.

"Oh, no!" Viv yelled. "Radiation alert!" Just then a few men came running around the corner. One of them yelled, "Viv! We have a live one, and I heard it's bad!"

"Only you three?" Viv yelled back.

The sergeant in charge looked a bit sheepish. "Sorry, Viv. Just us three. The first alarm fire is so bad they asked for our unit's help, so they went. We're all that's left."

Wasting no time, Dom jumped in. "Tell you what, Jack and I will help you get extra gear out to the radiation site so your team can meet up at the scene without having to come back here again after they put the fire out."

Viv's sheet-white face regained a bit of color. "Dom, you're a lifesaver. Go with Sergeant Foster. He'll load you two up."

Jack and Dom responded in unison, "Will do!" And off they went with the sergeant.

Viv yelled as she headed the other way, "Foster, I'll be in the command center tracking you all and giving you updates!"

Arriving at the locker room door, Foster quickly typed in a code on the keypad as a facial recognition scanner swept his face. The door was much wider than a normal door to enable the rescue to team to move through two to three side by side. It opened immediately after the recognition scan because seconds count when there is a radiation breach alarm. Dom and Jack followed the sergeant to the back of the room where there was a whole line of duffel bags arranged on three tables. Foster barked quickly, "The bags are lined up on the three tables by size. Each bag contains everything necessary. The left table is for under five feet eight inches, the middle for under six feet, and the right for over six feet."

Before Foster could say another word, Dom interjected, "Got it, chief. Thanks. Go on ahead. Jack and I will load up our aero car with as much gear as we can carry."

Foster and the other two were suiting up, and within a minute, they were headed out of the room. Foster yelled, "Viv will send you the location. Thanks, guys!" And off they went leaving Dom and Jack alone in the room.

Dom excitedly said, "Let's go!" And he turned to the table. The bags each weighed about twenty pounds, easily handled by them except they were a little bulky. Dom and Jack were able to take four each in a range of sizes. The duo needed mediums, and Fast Eddie needed a small. They decided to take two small, four medium, and two large. They were about to leave when Jack saw a stack of duffle bags in the corner of the room that looked just like the radiation bags. Quickly, he ran to them and "restocked" the tables. "Good thinking, Jack! That may just buy us a few more days."

In a few minutes, the dynamic duo were loading the aero car, and a minute later, they were gone. When they were moving at full speed, and only after they had crossed into ring five, Dom called Eddie. He picked up immediately. "Tell me." His voice hoarse with anticipation.

Dom replied, "Made it to ring five, all secured." Dom punched the end transmission button. That was it. Dom and Jack were to rally back at Eddie's warehouse.

Their aero car locater was off so no one could track them. As Dom and Jack monitored the emergency transmission lines, they heard Foster's gruff voice. "Viv, we just got here to the location you gave us for the radiation alert. Looks like a faulty sensor. No leak. We're heading back to the station."

"That's great news!" Viv replied. "Fifteen minutes to the scene. That's a bit slow, Sergeant. We'll have to review and run some drills to bring the time down."

"Roger that," Foster replied. Then silence. Dom and Jack were waiting for it. Perhaps it wouldn't come in the confusion. Then the transmission crackled to life again. It was Foster. "Say there, Viv. It was great of your police friends to help, but they're not at the scene yet. Maybe they got lost. Would you let them know it's a false alarm?"

"Will do, Sergeant."

A second later, Dom's wrist device rang to life. He picked up the incoming call. "Dom here."

"Hey, Dom, it's Viv. Where are you two?"

"Sorry, Viv. We got a bit mixed up and punched in the wrong coordinates. Just heard your exchange with Foster. Thank goodness it wasn't a real event. We'll swing on by and drop off the gear."

"Thanks for the help, you two. It was great seeing you, Dom. Take care of yourself. You too, Jack. Keep him out of trouble."

Jack replied, "I'll do my best, but you know Dom. Clouds of trouble follow him wherever he goes." They all laughed.

Viv jumped back in. "Stop on by to see us again, you guys. Stay safe."

"Will do, Viv." Dom replied. He turned to Jack. "Let's see how long our luck holds up, my friend."

CHAPTER 9

The Medical Examiners

After placing the deceased woman in the cremation burn box, the two medical examiners quickly left the hospital autopsy room and immediately departed the area, knowing that others would be right behind them to examine the body—or lack of body as was the case. They felt bad about leaving the two detectives behind to bear the brunt of any blowback that might result from the examiners' burning of the body.

Needing to hide out in a place that gave them privacy, they made their way to a Chinese restaurant, Mimi's Café, deep in the fifth ring. The fifth ring Chinatown was a huge sprawling series of old buildings that ranged anywhere from two-story crumbling buildings to ten- to twenty-story buildings all packed in about fifty city blocks. The size of Manhattan, it was more like a China city than a Chinatown. Millions of people crowded the streets and sidewalks twenty-four hours a day. There was only one rule here—safety was an individual responsibility. Mimi's Café was over a hundred years old, and in places, it looked much older with traditional red tiled flooring, square tables, and bench seating along the walls. The main dining room was long and narrow. The back booth next to the kitchen was a good spot to sit for viewing the entire restaurant while keeping a low profile.

Sitting in the back booth, having changed clothes, the medical examiners blended in with the local crowd. The man wore jeans, a black long-sleeved shirt, and a baseball cap that hid his short, dark-brown hair. He was of average build, about five feet ten inches tall, had a fair Western European skin color, and looked as if he was in his early thirties. A few wrinkles around his eyes and his forehead indicated a rough life. Like many who lived in the fifth ring, his time on the planet had probably been no basket of joy. Across from him sat the other examiner, a young woman in her mid-twenties, slim. She wore jeans with a dark-gray shirt with a high open collar. She too wore a baseball cap to hide her face, and it bulged with her full head of black hair. A ponytail hung down just past her shoulders. Their caps prevented anyone standing next to them, including the waiter, from easily seeing directly into their faces. On their table sat a large bowl of rice, a steaming plate of stir-fried vegetables, a plate of beef broccoli, and a pot of tea. They were alone, and they ate in silence for a few minutes, seemly enjoying the quiet period.

The man spoke first. "We made it out of there just in time. I heard the 'others' come in just after we did. That was a close call."

The young woman picked up her hot tea and took a sip. "What of the two officers?"

"I don't know," he replied. "We haven't heard any word about them since we left. You know how they work. No witnesses."

The woman nodded slowly, a bit of sorrow coming over her face. "John, they were two innocent men caught up in something they had no way of understanding. Let's say a quick prayer for them."

John nodded, and they briefly closed their eyes. Religion was banned, and any outward show of anything tied to religion, such as praying, making the sign of the cross, or speaking about religion resulted in an automatic death sentence. The Authorities provided a hefty reward for anyone who turned in suspected religious people. And prying cameras were everywhere, although many of the cameras in the fifth ring frequently had "maintenance issues."

The woman spoke again. "Should we find out what happened to them? Maybe we can help." John put up his hand and adjusted his cap—a nervous habit. "You know there is nothing we can do for them, Sara. When we left, they were in God's hands."

"Yes, of course. You're right, John. There was something about one of the two officers—something familiar that I can't quite put my finger on. Could we have met before?"

"Perhaps," John replied. "One never knows."

When they had finished the meal, the waiter came back to pick up the dishes and serve the standard Chinese complimentary desert, a bowl of cold almond-flavored custard cubes. After the waiter left, Sara spoke again. "We have to get back to the Cave. It's been a few days now since we left. With what we saw at the morgue and then with the 'others' coming so soon afterwards, we can't use any communicators to call ahead."

"Agreed," John replied softly. "There is so much technology that we don't know about out there. The Authorities may have broken our codes already. The last time that happened, we lost hundreds of people in the ensuing raids." Sadness came over Sara's eyes. "I'm sorry to bring that up, Sara. I know how hard it was for you."

"Everyone lost someone in those raids, John," Sara replied. Both looked down at their desert and finished eating in silence.

John paid the bill with his wrist ID chip, and they left the restaurant. They walked several blocks down the street, trying to make sure no one was following them, but the streets were so crowded with people, it was hard to tell. The only way was to go forward slowly and then suddenly cut across a street or take a turn and then see if anyone in the crowd changed their speed and direction to match theirs. After doing this for about half an hour, they felt safe. John flipped his device open and called an aero taxi. What showed up was a real beater. They wouldn't be able to lose anyone with that hunk of junk, but it did blend in well with the rest of the old aero cars flying around.

"Where to?" the cabbie asked.

"Take us to the Tanker Hotel in the Waste Industrial Zone," John replied.

"That'll cost you twenty credits and an extra five credits for night differential." The cabbie decided not to mention that the extra five credits was actually for hazard pay. The Waste Industrial Zone, commonly referred to as the WIZ, was a mix of waste product recycling factories, landfill dumps, and shanty towns filled with people trying to make money off the landfills. No matter how far society progressed in technology, there was still a mass of outlying people that scraped by for a living. Needless to say, the area was not safe at night, and the Tanker Hotel was notorious for its seedy customers.

Knowing it was better to not ask any questions, the cabbie punched in the location, and the aero taxi sped on its way with the onboard computer doing all the driving. It was a wonder that a real person was needed to drive the cab. In the third and fourth ring, most were automated. It was only in the fifth ring that it was normal for aero taxies to be manned by cabbies. There were several theories about why the system operated that way. One theory was that automated systems were at risk of potential hijacking by computer hackers. At least with a person on board, the chance of theft was reduced. Another theory, and the most likely one, and the one that no one talked about, was that a taxi mafia was paying off Authority officials.

It took about a half an hour to reach the hotel. John paid the bill with his ID chip, and the cabbie quickly departed. John and Sara entered the hotel, stopping for a few minutes in the lobby. The Tanker Hotel had seen better days. The lobby, although small, felt somewhat grand with winding staircases on each side of the check-in desk that spiraled up to a mezzanine level. The carpet in the lobby area was a faded and worn red as was the carpet on the spiral staircases. The trim on the staircase railings had been painted gold, but the surface was cracked from use and old age. A few worn-out chairs and coffee tables littered the sunken open area in front of the check-in desk.

Seeing no one around except one lonely worker at the check-in area, John and Sara moved to the back right corner of the first floor where a narrow corridor led to the back exit. They left the hotel and stood in a dimly lit parking area. A few old beat-up cars and a couple of beat-up small trucks dotted the lot. Moving to a black aero car, John dug out a key fob from his pocket and pressed the door button. The aero car rumbled to life as the engine started, and the doors opened.

The first thing John and Sara did when they slipped inside the aero car was to remove the ID chips from their wrists and place them in a shielded container. ID chips were supposed to be implanted under the skin and were equipped with sensors that prevented their removal from the body. Disabling the sensor without compromising or disabling the chip was very expense and risky. And those caught tampering with their chips were immediately sentenced to death. But the chips that John and Sara were using were removable chips, which were rare.

Once their chips were locked in a magnetized case that isolated the chip from transmission to the outside world, Sara breathed a sigh of relief. "Let's get out of here, John."

"Yes, ma'am!" With a smile, John levered the throttle, and off they went.

They meandered around the city for about half an hour to make sure no one was following them while also monitoring transmissions from the local police forces thanks to a handy "black box" that intercepted and decoded police, fire, and hospital transmissions. It didn't work for the more secure government-coded transmissions, but what they heard was enough to keep them safe. Most of the time.

Not seeing any tails, John slowed the aero car as they approached a medium-rise apartment building in a part of town called Little Mexico. It was a bustling area, about a half a million people, the size of a small city. People and transport vehicles were moving at all hours, which made it easy for anyone to disappear in the crowds. The apartment building was relatively new, about fifty years old, and constructed of concrete with smallish windows and tiny balconies. Standing ten stories tall with no exterior cladding or paint, it was typical mid- to low-class housing. One good feature was the underground parking structure. Just as in Chinatown, everyone minded their own business in Little Mexico. No one wanted to get involved with anyone else's affairs unless they could make a credit off someone else's misfortune. Spying on a suspected neighbor paid off sometimes. More often than not, it got the people who were spying killed before they had a chance to turn in their suspects.

After parking in the lower level of the garage, they moved quickly to the elevator. John punched a ten-digit security code into the elevator keypad, and immediately they were rocketed up to the tenth floor. The elevator door opened into a square lobby area that had the look and feel of an office main lobby rather than a narrow residential apartment hallway with doors leading to multiple rooms. The area was not more than ten feet by ten feet and was empty of all furniture. The off-white painted walls made it completely sterile looking. It was just a white square box with a single solid metal door with a keypad and biometric scanner. There were only two anomalies in the room. There were hundreds of little dots of light on the ceiling that looked like stars and bathed the room in soft light. And shiny black spheres mounted in each corner of the ceiling warned people in the room that they were being watched. Sara moved to the keypad and punched in a code. A laser scanner scanned them both, and then a second later, the mechanism in the large metal door clicked, and the door slid sideways into the wall. Sara and John moved quickly, and the door closed immediately behind them.

They walked into a large room with high ceilings. Unlike the claustrophobic lobby, this open area felt warm and inviting. The tiled floor was well built but not extravagant, and the room was filled with a few couches, coffee tables, and a large dining table that comfortably seated fifteen people. One whole side of the room consisted of a large, open kitchen. It almost felt like a nice lobby of a hotel with an attached open kitchen. The entire tenth floor was one huge apartment.

A man and a woman were sitting on one of the couches deep in conversation. They both looked up at the same time as John and Sara walked in the room. The man was of average height, about five feet ten inches, trim in physique, and had dark-brown skin. He had short hair, and his brown eyes sparkled with intensity. The woman was of Asian descent. She had black hair and brown eyes and was quite slim. They both appeared to be in their late twenties. The woman jumped up to her feet immediately "John! Sara! Thank God you're okay!" The man was right behind her, and they all embraced.

Sara replied, "Yes. Thank you, Lord, for protecting us. We made it out of the morgue just in time before the 'others' arrived. Matt, Christie, we were able to view the woman's body and confirm she was one of us. She had the sacred mark on her wrist."

Matt spoke. "Were you able to transfer the data from her chip?"

John jumped in. "Yes, I passed my wristband over her wrist, and it picked up the embedded chip. The data was transferred, but we don't know how much." John took off his wristband and handed it over to Matt, who was eagerly awaiting it. As soon as it was in his hands, Matt walked quickly across the room and set the wristband on the table. The table surface lit up; it was a bright screen. A small green light on the wristband lit up as well and began to blink. Matt called out, "Downloading now. It should take just a few seconds. Then it will take about an hour to decrypt the files. From the size of the download, it looks like a large program and a lot of documents. Not much to do but wait now. How about you two tell us what happened at the morgue."

For the next hour, John and Sara walked Matt and Christie through their adventure at the hospital morgue, including meeting up with the two police officers.

Christie asked Sara, "Do you know what happened to the two officers?"

Sara's face turned sad. She frowned and started to speak, but she choked up and couldn't talk. John took over. "We listened in the police communications for several hours after we left, and there were no reports of officers down or other officer emergencies in the area." In ring four, it was unusual to have officer fatalities. In ring five, police officers were injured or killed daily. "But of course, that doesn't mean anything," John continued clinically. "They may have escaped, bribed their way to freedom, or, heaven forbid, they could have been taken away to somewhere in ring five and neutralized. There are so many murders in ring five every day; they would just be another statistic."

After getting herself under control, Sara was finally able to speak again. "There was something about one of the police officers. I mentioned it to John. His face seemed so familiar, and there was something distinctive about him. I think it was his eyes that really caught my attention. There is only one other person I know who has that same green eye color."

"It's you," John said. "I noticed the same thing. His eyes were not nearly as brilliantly green as yours, but they were still unusual. What are the chances of that?"

Matt chimed in. "There are no chances with our Maker. Let's pray for the two officers." For the next several minutes, they prayed for safety of the two officers who had been caught up in their web of intrigue.

All four sat down at the table and watched the tabletop screen stream through a series of numbers as the software unraveled the complex coded files. Sara asked the group, "All I know of our Maker, the Lord of all creation, are the stories told to me by my caregivers when I was younger. It was all so secretive that nothing was ever written down. They learned from their caregivers, and so on and so on. The information passed down through the generations by word of mouth only. They were more stories than anything else." The others nodded in response. Sara continued, "I was told never to talk about our Lord to anyone except those with the sacred mark."

They all instinctively extended out their wrists. They each bore a tiny mark just where their palms met their wrists. Two arcs coming together to make an oval with a small triangle at the end. It was the same symbol that had been on the dead woman at the morgue.

Sara continued, "The mark on the older deceased woman at the morgue was much larger than ours." She made a size comparison with her thumb and her finger. "It must have been about an inch long."

"Whew! Wow—that is huge!" Christie blurted out. "There is no way you could ever hide something like that. She must have been in seclusion for most of her life. Anyone on the street would notice a mark that big, and we all know what the penalty is for having anything at all to do with a religion. That's instant death."

Musing on Christie's words, John chimed in, "From what we know of the woman, she was very well connected. We know this because the ring-four governor himself wanted to clean up the scene where the woman died, and he didn't want any official records. That means that he knew of her advanced age. Did he also know about her mark? She was very well dressed and had no signs on her body that she had died by foul play. In fact, from what we heard on the secure police transmissions, her body was recovered at the governor's office."

Matt weighed in the conversation, "Wow, intrigue about her case goes right to the top!"

It was Christie's turn to think out loud. "You're right about that, Matt."

Sara asked, "What do we know about the governor?"

Christie continued, "The highest levels of the ring-one leadership appoint the governor to his position, and we understand that the governor makes regular visits to ring one. Some even say that the ring governors meet with the leaders of the ten ring kingdoms for future planning. And there are whispers that they even meet with the One." Christie broke out in a cold sweat as she spoke, and there was an uncomfortable silence as everyone took in what she had said.

Fear engulfed the group just from thinking of him. No one dared to speak of him in public. One wrong word about the absolute leader brought instant death to the offender and everyone close to him or her. There was no mercy or forgiveness. So absolute was his rule that all were taught from childhood to obey without question.

After a minute, Matt spoke softly, "Do you think the governor could be one of us?" That thought warmed the hearts of the group and cast away evil thoughts of the governor.

"It would be an incredible blessing to have an inside man like that," Sara whispered back.

Just then, a burst of short rings sounded from the tabletop. The table surface lit up with a series of lines moving like a cascade of water, and a holographic image rose out of the table. It was the dead woman from the morgue! Sara said, "She must have recorded this before she passed away. She was wearing that same necklace at the morgue. She has the same hair style and looks just as I saw her except, in the morgue, her skin was that awful pale color from lack of blood circulation."

John nodded in agreement. "You're right, Sara. She must have recorded this message that same night." The four of them gathered around the table, mesmerized by the woman's face. Her hair was full and black, and she was wearing a nice shade of makeup—not too much, but just enough to look natural. They could see creases around her eyes and mouth. She was a very attractive older woman. The group had never seen anyone over the age of forty-four years and four months and could not guess her age.

The woman's floating head and shoulders turned to view each of them around the table. Matt whistled as her head turned to each of them. "Very sophisticated technology. Artificial intelligence built into the recorded message."

The woman spoke "Greetings, friends. I pray this message has fallen into the right hands. Before I continue, please show me your wrists." No one moved. Could this be a trap by the Authority? Were the events of the entire night a big ruse to expose the hidden religions?

The woman waited patiently, and she seemed to understand their dilemma.

It was John who spoke up first. "Sara and I saw this woman at the morgue and took the file transfer from her body. If this is a trap, this woman paid the ultimate price for our capture. I think she is legitimate." John turned to each of them, and each nodded slowly. All at once, they extended their right hands, exposing the small, barely visible marks. The holographic woman examined each of their wrists; she seemed able to identify the marks from that distance even though they were small.

She continued "Two arcs coming together with a triangle at one end. That is the sign of our most secret society. Thank you for sharing that with me. If you are watching my holographic image, then I am dead and with our God. Do not trouble yourselves, for I am in a much better place. My life ended in this mortal world, and my soul has been lifted to heaven. I look upon your young faces and see myself some years ago—full of hope and unable to understand what my elders had taught me when I was young. I just knew that I was different from everyone else. I knew I wasn't special because of any particular gift; I was special because I had a peace in my heart and a yearning to learn more about the one true God who had given me such peace and love. My mentor had great knowledge of our God, and he passed that knowledge on to me. Ours is such a difficult time. Whom can we trust? Many of us have been caught and tortured mercilessly for what we know, and we have been made to give up our fellow brothers and sisters. There are so very few of us left who have detailed knowledge of what was stripped from our society hundreds of years ago. All digital and hard-copy books— anything that had to do with any religion—were destroyed. The price for whispering a religious word is a fate worse than death. I come to you today, my friends, my brothers and sisters, to tell you of our God. To tell you the whole truth of Him and to provide you with an assignment—one that I was tasked to fulfill but am no longer able to do. I lay it upon your shoulders as it is God's will."

For the rest of the day the woman discussed the Bible's New Testament and spoke of Jesus and the apostles. She speed talked through Jesus's four years, and finally stopped short of the last supper. They took a few breaks and one short meal. The hours seemed to fly by. John, Sara, Matt, and Christie were so wrapped up in her message that they didn't realize so much time had passed until the woman stopped talking.

"You four need to think about what I have said," continued the woman. "Rest and pray on the words I have spoken, and we will continue in the morning. I will present a series of lectures over the next week. By the way, my name is Mary." She smiled warmly, and her head and shoulders slowly faded away.

The four friends sat in silence for a few minutes trying to take in the mass of information Mary had given them. Christie was the first to stand. She stretched out her arms. "Wow! I had not even the faintest idea of how much power, love, and grace our Lord has! Why would anyone want to keep this information secret! The words of Jesus are the cure for all humanity's problems. We should be shouting his words at the top of our lungs to anyone and everyone!"

"Amen to that!" John jumped in. "It makes no sense why anyone would keep such a loving and caring God a secret!" Following Christie's lead, the other three stood up and walked around to stretch their bodies out from the long session.

"I don't know about you," Matt said, "but I've had to take a pee for the last hour. Just didn't want to miss any of Mary's words." He turned quickly and walked off to the restroom.

"I need some water," Sara mumbled, and she headed toward the kitchen area. They were all lost in their own thoughts after listening to Mary's lecture. It would take a lot of time for the sheer volume of information to sink in.

Matt returned from the restroom, proceeded directly to the table, and started typing on a pop-up display on the table. "Guys, I am transferring the New Testament to your devices. It will be encrypted, and only your thumbprint will decrypt the file."

All replied in unison, "Thanks, Matt!"

After drinking her water, Sara returned to the table. "It's been a long day, everyone. Let's get a good rest. No alarms tomorrow. Wake up when you feel you've had enough rest, and we will reconvene for Mary's next session." All nodded, and with that the group shared hugs and departed to their rooms. Anticipation wafted in the air for what Mary had in store for them tomorrow. Each knew they needed rest but wanted to stay up and hear more.

CHAPTER 10

Complications
(The Authority Three)

R epeated chimes rang out as the elevator door kept attempting to close. The body of the Spaniard was blocking the way. Blondie and the Giant were at the elevator looking down at their unconscious teammate. Blondie was huffing and puffing, and the Giant was sweating profusely. He had taken off his jacket and wrapped it around his left hand.

Blondie and the Giant had been waiting below for over ten minutes for the elevator to come back down for them. Sensing something was wrong, they finally ran fifteen floors up the emergency stairway. It was exhausting, and the air in the stairway, with no air-conditioning, was stifling and hot. With a disgusted look on his face, the Giant bent down and dragged his partner out of the elevator so that the door would close. He slapped the Spaniard once on the face, and the Spaniard started to move. His jaw and nose were broken. "Aggggg, what happened?"

"You got clobbered, you fool!" bellowed the Giant. "We'll never find them now!"

The big man stepped forward and was about to hit Jackson again when Blondie raised his hand. "That's enough, Hector! We're in enough hot water as it is. It'll take all three of us to sort this out."

Hector replied, "Okay, okay. What's the next move, Saul?"

"Let me think about this for a minute. We can't call in and say we lost the woman's body and didn't examine her for any marks or data devices. We would suffer the penalty for failure." He looked directly at Jackson and Hector. "You two have seen what the price is for failure on a mission." Both men looked down at their shoes. Both had very uncomfortable looks on their faces. Yes, they had seen videos, and on occasion, they'd been live witnesses. The Authority leadership took great pains to force members of the Authority to witness the long and agonizing torture of their comrades. Slow death and pain served to remind all about the price of failure.

Saul continued, "Let's go somewhere where we can think through our options. We'll wait a few more hours, and then we'll call in and say that all is fine. We took care of the body, we acquired the information, and we're following up on a lead before returning to the office. That should buy us some time. With all that's going on now, let's hope our mission is not critical."

Jackson mumbled, "Yeh, yeh. I'm sure that old hag was just a low-priority nuisance." That reply warranted slap on his head. "Ouch!"

Saul said, "That was for messing up and then saying something dumb. How in the world would you know if that old lady was high priority or not? Just the fact that there were two officers in the morgue when we got there means she was of some importance! What am I to do with you two? Come on. Let's get out of here!"

After leaving the building, the trio got into a new aero car. It wasn't police issue with all the high-tech gear like the one that Dom and Jack had, but it was nice enough that an inner ringer would admire it. Anyone living in the first, second, or third ring was referred to as an inner ringer, one of the upper class.

Jet black in color with tinted glass and sleek side molding, their aero car looked like a sedan version of the Batmobile. The back of the aero car even sported flared winglets. It had the look of a "special government" official vehicle, and all citizens knew to stay far away from them.

After traveling at normal speed for about thirty minutes, they made their way to an Italian restaurant. A nice place with the look and feel of an old Italian trattoria, it was known for good food at reasonable prices. What was more attractive was the fact that it was out of the way in an area that few Authority officials ever visited. It was located on the outskirts of the fourth ring close to the industrial sector and near to the border of the fifth ring. Saul had grown up in the area; it was his hometown. No one would mess with them there.

As they walked into the restaurant, the owner came up to them. "Saul, it's been a while! How are you doing?"

Hanging in there, Pete. Hanging in there."

With a smile, Pete shot back "Saul, you still hanging around those two clowns—Hector the Giant and the brown man Jackson?" This produced the desired effect as Hector's and Jackson's faces turned sour. "Whoa, gents, just kidding. First round of beers for you three are on the house." Their faces immediately responded with smiles.

Hector replied. "Always great to see you too, Pete! My thirst buds are your best friend."

"Well, come on over. I got your table waiting." Pete led them to the back of the restaurant, through the kitchen, and into a private room.

Saul spoke as the trio sat down. "Thanks, Pete. We'll start with the usual and then go from there." The usual was a round of beers for the three of them with some bruschetta, pitted olives, and Parmigiano-Reggiano cheese—a typical Italian *aperitivo*, the beginning to a good meal.

"Right away, my friends!" And with that Pete disappeared. He returned in a few minutes with their food and drinks. As Saul insisted, for trust reasons, only Pete could serve them lest anyone else eavesdrop on their conversations. Before they spoke, Jackson whipped out his device and scanned the area. "No bugs, Boss. The area is clean of any listening or video equipment."

"Glad to hear that we can still trust Pete," Saul mused. "He keeps a tight ship here and makes sure his clientele are well served." The payment for such good service to the three was that Saul made sure the Authorities looked the other way when seedy characters visited Pete's establishment. Pete also paid a smaller amount in tax than did most restaurants.

After each of the trio had consumed about half a beer and some food, they all began to unwind a bit. Feeling better because of the slight buzz from the alcohol, they began to figure out what to do next. They looked at the projected timeline from the time Saul got around to calling in their status. If they received no immediate blowback, they probably had a week or so of cover until they would have to return to headquarters and submit an official report—a week to find the two detectives who had escaped them and the two imposter autopsy examiners, ring out of them all the information they knew, and hope that would be enough to satisfy whoever needed to be satisfied at the Authority.

The main course was *pasta vongole*, Saul's favorite because Pete had the freshest clams around town, and slow-cooked beef stew, a house special. As they made their way into their third round of beers, the trio laid out the next steps they would have to take. Saul tapped his clear pad device, bringing up a holographic image of the hospital. "We'll have to circle back to the hospital to get all the information we can from the video camera feeds. And we can sweep the floor area for bio traces they might have left behind. We'll then search the Authority database as well as real-time information to find out who they are and where they are. From there it should be easy to do a grab and snatch."

Jackson reasoned, "I'd say we're looking at two to three days tops."

Saul replied, "Probably right about that. The detectives are, no doubt, in some form of hiding knowing we'll be after them. And those two autopsy examiners are probably lurking in the shadows of society.

Hector jumped in as he munched on a piece of bread. "As long as I get the chance for some payback. I can foretell the future. Pain for our friends. Lots of pain." And with that they raised their glasses in a toast.

Saul spoke in a quiet but firm tone. "No mistakes, my friends. This time our lives are on the line. We have to get this one done."

Dinner was topped off with Pete's signature tiramisu. The chocolate coating was so flaky that a fine mist puffed from the plates when Pete set the dish on the table, making Hector cough. "As always, a perfect tiramisu, Pete," Saul exclaimed as Pete made a formal bow and retreated to leave them alone to savor the desert with a round of restaurant-roasted Italian espresso. Pete made everything from scratch.

About half an hour later, Saul reluctantly looked at his device. No bigger than an old-style mini-iPad, it was made of a clear, glass-like material. A black edge framed the four sides. It was about a quarter inch thick, it weighed less than two ounces, and it was almost indestructible. The clear pad device was available for almost all citizens because it was cheap and easy to use. The devices were customized with software that drove functions as well as access to information. The devices of secret Authority enforcement men like Saul and his team were set up with specific security that took in the user's entire biometrics before opening any of the programs. The sophistication of the security encryption was seamless for the user. Saul just picked up the device and spoke: "Authority main headquarters Steven Banks." The device lit up, and within a few seconds, a face appeared on the device slightly raised from the screen. It was not a full holographic image, but the image of Steven did appear to have some depth against the background. He was at home at his dining room table looking a bit tired from a long day. But he didn't look at all surprised by the late call. His staff called him at all hours.

"Hello there, Saul. I trust all went well at the morgue."

"Nothing ever goes exactly as planned, sir, but we got what we went there for, and we'll spend a few days following up on some leads before heading back to headquarters to file a full report."

"Okay, Saul. I haven't heard anything from my side, so it looks like you have some time to do whatever you need to do. Just keep your communicators on in case this blows up and I need the report sooner rather than later."

"Will do, sir, and have a good evening." With that, the device went dark. Hector and Jackson breathed a big sigh of relief; they had been holding their breath during the entire conversation.

Saul breathed out too. "We dodged a blaster round for now. Let's lie low for a day just to make sure that call wasn't a ploy to lull us into the open. I'll check a few sources tomorrow, and if all seems normal, I'll ping you two the code word *go*. We'll then meet up at the café around the corner."

"And if we don't receive your go message?" Jackson enquired.

"Well then, my friends, that means that, when I checked my sources, I discovered we're in hot water and I'm either dead already or running for my life. So, if you don't get my message, if I were you, I 'd try to escape as well."

Hector jumped in. "Where would we go, Saul?"

"You two have a day to think about your own escape route. Sweet dreams." And with that troubling thought, the three dispersed.

CHAPTER 11

Deeper Truths (The Medical Examiners)

I t was nearly ten in the morning when John woke up. The sun was peeking its way through half-closed shades in his room. About fifteen minutes later, he was padding around the kitchen area making a cup of coffee. Everyone else was still asleep. They had stayed up so late listening intensely to Mary's history lesson that, by the time everyone went to sleep, it was after five in the morning. He looked at his device and read the time: ten thirty. He'd had about four and a half hours of sleep. Not enough, but his mind was racing with thoughts of Jesus: *Jesus, so that is the name of our God. Through hundreds of years people have passed down the Bible's history from one generation to the next by word of mouth. The Bible has been reduced to shadows and ideas of our Lord. No one even dares say his name for fear of torture and death. Over time, little by little, verbal erosion has taken its toll. But now no more. We have information; we have the truth. What will happen now?* Lost in his thoughts, John spent the next hour in prayer, thanking Jesus for the opportunity to reunite with Him.

The others crept out of their rooms a few hours after John had got up. By early afternoon, they were once again settled around the table. It was John who spoke. "Let's say a prayer before we begin."

They clasped hands. "Jesus, we thank you for this opportunity to get to know you again and to hear the full and real history of your life here on Earth so many thousands of years ago. Lord, we are thankful to know your name. We are thankful to hear of your mighty powers. We are thankful to hear of your love, your grace, and your compassion for us. We pray that our hearts remain open. We are so excited and blessed to hear more of your time here on Earth. Amen."

As they opened their eyes after the prayer, Mary's head was once again in the center of the table. "Thank you for that prayer, John," she said. "Praying to our Lord Jesus is the most powerful communication we have. Continue to pray and speak with him constantly throughout your days, for he is forever by your side."

Mary continued with her lectures, starting with the Last Supper and moving on to the Crucifixion of our Lord. She stopped at the point where Jesus's mortal body finally gave out. A deep sadness overwhelmed the group. So much pain and suffering! Their questions were the same as those of the twelve apostles because they did not know the rest of the story: *What will become of us now that Jesus has died?* There was confusion among them. Matt said softly, "How can we pray to Jesus? He died like any other mortal man and is no longer with us!" John, Sara, and Christie were so overwhelmed with grief that they could not talk. Their throats choked up.

Mary said, "Let's break for an hour. You all need to get something to eat, and then we will continue." Mary had intentionally stopped at that point to let the magnitude of Jesus's sacrifice it sink in to their hearts. To fully grasp the meaning of sacrifice and of faith, people had to feel the grief and pain before they could experience light and restoration.

The foursome snacked on a variety of sandwiches. It was Christie who broke the silence as they ate. "After all that Jesus did—his miracles, healing of the sick, and preaching of love and forgiveness— is that the way his life ended? What does that say about us? And look at what we are now! After nearly destroying our world through massive shifts in the weather to all-out war, we live in a totalitarian one-world government where life for all but a few privileged inner ringers is short and hard." Christie kept on talking for a few more minutes before her energy seemed to drain. She stopped talking and went back to munching on her sandwich. The others just nodded at her words. What was there to say?

Matt finally replied solemnly "We are the ancestors of those who persecuted our savior Jesus; we reap what we have sowed."

It was Sara's turn to chime in. "Jesus spoke only of forgiveness and a path to heaven through him. Even as he was crucified on the cross, he reasoned with Father God that those who tortured him did not know what they were doing. He saved the wretched thief who was being crucified next to him. There is always hope for us."

John rounded out the conversation. "Jesus sacrificed his life for us. Our Lord died and went to heaven. He sits there waiting for us and judging us. If he is really God, did he die on the cross? This is all so confusing." They all nodded; John had said what others were thinking. *If Jesus was God, how can he have died? What does that mean? And how can a god die at the hands of mortal men?* A bit of confusion and discomfort spread through the group. Just as the apostles were scared and full of doubt, the group of four were also filled with that same fear and doubt. Now that they had crossed the line and knew more about this Jesus, they were marked for death by the Authority. *Have we made a mistake? Will we be killed for knowing Jesus without knowing if Jesus is really God?* thought John.

About half an hour later, they slowly made it back to the table where they watched Mary's translucent head get a bit brighter as it reformed into a solid figure. Her closed eyes opened, and her expression was warm with a hint of sadness. They all felt similar emotions to what they saw on her face. But, unlike Mary, their faces also had underlying masks of fear and dread. What next?

Mary continued where she had left off. "The apostle John was there at the feet of Jesus when he died. Also there were Jesus's mother Mary and Mary Magdalene. Also there was a rich man by the name of Joseph of Arimathea, who was a respected member of the Jewish council. Joseph had not consented to the council's decision to arrest and crucify Jesus because he, himself, was a secret follower of our Lord. Joseph asked Pilate, the governor, if he could have the body of Jesus so he could perform a proper burial. Pilate granted his request, and Joseph, with the help of other followers of Jesus, took his body, washed him, and bound his body in linen cloth with ritual spices. They had to undertake the ritual washing and cleaning of Jesus quickly because the Sabbath was drawing near, and no Jewish person was allowed to work on the sabbath. They placed Jesus in a man-made cave cut out of the face of a hill.

"The Jewish leaders came to Pilate with their concern that the followers of Jesus would steal Jesus's body so that they could proclaim that he had risen from the dead in three days as Jesus had said he would. Then even death wouldn't stop them from proclaiming that Jesus was the Messiah. Pilate agreed and sent soldiers to guard the entrance of Jesus's tomb all day and night. The tomb itself was sealed by a huge rolling stone.

"On that Sunday, the third day after Jesus was crucified, Mary Magdalene went to the tomb to anoint the body of Jesus with spices. When she arrived at the tomb, there was a great earthquake, and the stone rolled away from the tomb, opening it in front of her. She went into the tomb, and the body of Jesus was gone! Only his linens were left on the tomb floor. The guards were greatly distressed and concerned. They had never left the tomb entrance. How could his body have disappeared?"

The floating head of Mary now quoted from the Bible, John 20:11–18:

> Now Mary stood outside the tomb crying. As she
> wept, she bent over to look into the tomb 12 and
> saw two angels in white, seated where Jesus' body
> had been, one at the head and the other at the foot.

They asked her, "Woman, why are you crying?"

"They have taken my Lord away," she said, "and I don't know where they have put him." 14 At this, she turned around and saw Jesus standing there, but she did not realize that it was Jesus.

He asked her, "Woman, why are you crying? Who is it you are looking for?"

Thinking he was the gardener, she said, "Sir, if you have carried him away, tell me where you have put him, and I will get him."

Jesus said to her, "Mary."

She turned toward him and cried out in Aramaic, "Rabboni!" (which means "Teacher").

Jesus said, "Do not hold on to me, for I have not yet ascended to the Father. Go instead to my brothers and tell them, 'I am ascending to my Father and your Father, to my God and your God.'"

Mary Magdalene went to the disciples with the news: "I have seen the Lord!" And she told them that he had said these things to her.

Then Mary quoted John 20:19–20:

On the evening of that first day of the week, when the disciples were together, with the doors locked for fear of the Jewish leaders, Jesus came and stood among them and said, "Peace be with you!" 20 After he said this, he showed them his hands and side. The disciples were overjoyed when they saw the Lord.

Mary's image in the middle of the table expanded so they could see her full body from head to toe. She spread her arms out to her sides and lifted them up to heaven. With passion, she shouted, "Jesus is alive! He has risen from the dead!"

John, Sara, Matt, and Christie just sat there unable to completely comprehend the magnitude of Mary's words. The holographic Mary shouted again, "Jesus is alive! He has risen from the dead!"

With that, the most amazing thing happened. The soft hiss of the air conditioner in the background ceased, and the room became still and silent. Forms around the room slowly appeared. Wearing beautiful, white, flowing linen and white feathered wings attached to their shoulders, twelve men and two women encircled the four sitting around the table. With great smiles and glee, they, too, shouted as they raised their arms up and opened them wide: "Jesus is alive! He has risen from the dead!"

Confusion reigned amongst the four at the table. Even holographic Mary did not know what was going on. Christie furiously tapped on the clear top table and exclaimed. "Those other voices and images are not coming from the table's databanks!"

John, Sara, Matt, and Christie at once dropped to the floor on their knees. John prayed. "Jesus, forgive my sins, wash me new. I believe you are the Son of God, the Messiah. Thank you, Jesus, for your sacrifice." They were all crying with joy.

Even holographic Mary was speechless. After a few more prayers and shouts of gratitude, Mary continued her teaching until dinner time. When they took a break, there was a bounce to everyone's steps. The air was so much lighter now; there was no more heaviness caused by sorrow and pain. Like the dawn of a new day, everything was new and bright. They all chipped in to make dinner. John and Sara did the prep work and handed it over to Matt and Christie to cook while John and Sara cut up salad vegetables.

When they were sitting around the table, just as Mary had explained the other day, John held a large piece of bread in his hands and gave thanks. Then he broke the bread and passed it on. After everyone had a piece of bread, John quoted Matthew 26:26–28:

> While they were eating, Jesus took bread, and when he had given thanks, he broke it and gave it to his disciples, saying, "Take and eat; this is my body."

> Then he took a cup, and when he had given thanks, he gave it to them, saying, "Drink from it, all of you. This is my blood of the[b] covenant, which is poured out for many for the forgiveness of sins.

The rest of the meal was filled with laugher and joy—sheer joy knowing that Jesus had risen from the dead. Not even death itself could stop Jesus because he was the Messiah, the Savior!

After dinner, Mary continued for just a little while, allowing time for the four get a good night's rest. For the next five days, Mary taught the four new disciples more about Jesus and the apostles as she told them about the rest of the New Testament.

On day six, Mary introduced to the group the final book of the Bible—the words of the apostle John, written when he was sentenced to live on the Greek island of Patmos: the book of Revelation.

CHAPTER 12

Fragments of the Apocalypse of John (The Medical Examiners)

Mary started the session: "Friends, the final book of the Bible, called Revelation, was written by the apostle John. It is about the end times of the world. The book is also known as the Apocalypse of John. This will be the time when humanity will be judged by God and will feel the wrath of heaven and hell brought down because of our evil ways. We destroyed Earth with our greed. We refused to adhere to the commandments of the Bible. We lost ourselves in the physical world of pleasures and material gain. We let our brothers and sisters suffer and die because of our greed and lack of caring. For our sins, God let loose the evil one, the angel who turned away from heaven and was outcast. The dark angel will come and manifest himself on Earth to rule the planet and make all suffer. He will rule with an iron hand and devastate the world with his evil power. He will decimate all until the second coming of our Lord Jesus. God will do this not just to punish humanity but to give everyone one final chance to repent and accept Jesus as savior—to shock and give us one final opportunity, one final plea, to accept Jesus, have our sins washed away by the love of Jesus, or suffer eternal darkness.

"The book of Revelation—the Apocalypse of John—warns us and tells us what will happen in these end times. It will not happen all at once. The end will come through a series of horrific events."

Mary proceeded to quote Revelation 5:1–5:

> Then I saw in the right hand of him who sat on the throne a scroll with writing on both sides and sealed with seven seals. And I saw a mighty angel proclaiming in a loud voice, "Who is worthy to break the seals and open the scroll?" But no one in heaven or on earth or under the earth could open the scroll or even look inside it. I wept and wept because no one was found who was worthy to open the scroll or look inside. Then one of the elders said to me, "Do not weep! See, the Lion of the tribe of Judah, the Root of David, has triumphed. He is able to open the scroll and its seven seals.

"The Lion of the tribe of Judah is none other than Jesus," explained Mary, and then she quoted Revelation 6:1–4:

> I watched as the Lamb opened the first of the seven seals. Then I heard one of the four living creatures say in a voice like thunder, "Come!" I looked, and there before me was a white horse! Its rider held a bow, and he was given a crown, and he rode out as a conqueror bent on conquest.

> When the Lamb opened the second seal, I heard the second living creature say, "Come!" Then another horse came out, a fiery red one. Its rider was given power to take peace from the earth and to make people kill each other. To him was given a large sword.

"These are the first two seals," she said, "and they mean that world war will be unleashed." She quoted Revelation 6:5–6:

> When the Lamb opened the third seal, I heard the third living creature say, "Come!" I looked, and there before me was a black horse! Its rider was holding a pair of scales in his hand. Then I heard what sounded like a voice among the four living creatures, saying, "Two pounds of wheat for a day's wages, and six pounds of barley for a day's wages, and do not damage the oil and the wine!"

"The third seal refers to a great famine," Mary said. And she quoted Revelation 6:7–8:

> When the Lamb opened the fourth seal, I heard the voice of the fourth living creature say, "Come!" I looked, and there before me was a pale horse! Its rider was named Death, and Hades was following close behind him. They were given power over a fourth of the earth to kill by sword, famine and plague, and by the wild beasts of the earth.

"The fourth seal describes death and destruction caused by the wars and man's destruction of the earth," Mary told them. She quoted Revelation 6:9–11:

> When he opened the fifth seal, I saw under the altar the souls of those who had been slain because of the word of God and the testimony they had maintained. They called out in a loud voice, "How long, Sovereign Lord, holy and true, until you judge the inhabitants of the earth and avenge our blood?" Then each of them was given a white robe, and

they were told to wait a little longer, until the full number of their fellow servants, their brothers and sisters, were killed just as they had been.

She explained: "The fifth seal describes the persecution of Christians." And she quoted Revelation 6:12–17:

> I watched as he opened the sixth seal. There was a great earthquake. The sun turned black like sackcloth made of goat hair, the whole moon turned blood red, and the stars in the sky fell to earth, as figs drop from a fig tree when shaken by a strong wind. The heavens receded like a scroll being rolled up, and every mountain and island was removed from its place.
>
> Then the kings of the earth, the princes, the generals, the rich, the mighty, and everyone else, both slave and free, hid in caves and among the rocks of the mountains. They called to the mountains and the rocks, "Fall on us and hide us from the face of him who sits on the throne and from the wrath of the Lamb! For the great day of their wrath has come, and who can withstand it?"

"The sixth seal describes more death and destruction," she said. And then she quoted Revelation 8:1:

> When he opened the seventh seal, there was silence in heaven for about half an hour.

"The seventh seal describes time," she said. "Now, we don't know exactly how much time. It's clearly written 'about a half an hour,' but from our years of research our thoughts are that perhaps we don't fully understand or comprehend the same meaning of time as does our Lord. So much of what we hear and what we see is taken in the context of what we can understand as mere humans.

"That is all we have of the book of Revelation; the rest is lost. So, we know about a time of unprecedented changes to Earth's climate, war, decimation of the world's population, and the persecution of Christians. Beyond that, we just have at pieces of the book. A small fragment speaks of seven trumpets, and another speaks of seven bowls. If these are anything like the seven seals, then they would be frightening events! We have a larger fragment from chapter thirteen that describes the rise of an Antichrist, the devil himself, the evil one, returning to earth." Here she quoted Revelation 13:1–5:

> The dragon stood on the shore of the sea. And I saw a beast coming out of the sea. It had ten horns and seven heads, with ten crowns on its horns, and on each head a blasphemous name. The beast I saw resembled a leopard but had feet like those of a bear and a mouth like that of a lion. The dragon gave the beast his power and his throne and great authority. One of the heads of the beast seemed to have had a fatal wound, but the fatal wound had been healed. The whole world was filled with wonder and followed the beast. People worshiped the dragon because he had given authority to the beast, and they also worshiped the beast and asked, "Who is like the beast? Who can wage war against it?" The beast was given a mouth to utter proud words and blasphemies and to exercise its authority for forty-two months.

"The fragments of Revelation that we have describe the Antichrist and some signs we can use to recognize him. The Antichrist will have a fatal wound that is healed. He will have authority for forty-two

months. We have another snippet from the book of the Apocalypse."
She quoted Revelation 13:18:

> This calls for wisdom. Let the person who has
> insight calculate the number of the beast, for it is
> the number of a man. That number is 666.

"And we have just a few other fragments that tell of the second
coming of Jesus and his defeat of the evil one. Throughout all of
history since the time John wrote Revelation, people have been
trying to figure out what the book means and when the foretold
calamities will occur, signaling the beginning of the end of the
world, the appearance of the Antichrist, and finally the second
coming of our Lord Jesus. So many times in history people have
looked at their current situation and declared the end of times was at
hand, the evil one was living, and Jesus was to return soon. We too
are searching our history—at least what knowledge of our history
that is left to us. We search to see if the end times are at hand. We
have some information that goes back over four hundred twenty
years. In the old year two-thousand one hundred when the world's
weather systems went haywire, the beginning of the new ice age
started, and then the Great conflict. It was not a war born only
out of scarce resources and land; it was also a war of religions—
Christians, Muslims, Jews, Hindus, and adherents of other religions
all fighting each other, blaming each other for the state of the world.
The radicals from every nation seized control and led the drumbeats
of war. To almost everyone, this seemed like the beginning of the
end times. The sequence of events seemed to match perfectly with
the description of the first six seals from the book of the Apocalypse:
calamity, war, starvation, and massive waves of death throughout
the world.

"The few sections of Revelation that we have left describe the
rise of the Antichrist and fit so well with what happened after the
nuclear war—the promise of peace by the newly crowned one-world

leader in the year two thousand one hundred and eighteen, our so-called Father of the World, Shoa Khad. He changed everything to a one-world government and a one-world currency. He even reset the calendar to year zero, the start of the Enlightened Era (EE). In his early years, after the start of the Enlightened Era, there was an attempted assassination. It was a horrific suicide bombing, and his whole protective detail was killed. There was no way he could have survived. It was said he too even died for a few minutes and then somehow miraculously recovered. The whole world was in awe of his miracle return to full health. Some shouted that Shoa Khad was a profit sent from heaven; others even called him Messiah! As the newly ordained one-world leader, Shoa abolished all religion as evil proclaiming that there is no heaven or hell; there is only the physical world. He burned all religious books and wiped all religious records. In fact, he wiped out all history before two thousand one hundred and eighteen so he could start a new world with himself as the sole ruler. His campaign washed over the world as he conquered and slaughtered all those that defied him. He brought the world's population down to six hundred sixty-six million and declared that, from then on, that would be the world's population to ensure the remaining resources would last. He instituted the retirement age of forty-four years and four months.

"Shoa's reign of terror and control only gained more radical approval as time went on. Everyone came to think of him almost as godlike because he didn't appear to age. That was another sign to many that he was a god. The scriptures say the evil one would rule for forty-two months, but his reign never ended. It started in the new EE year zero, the start of the Enlightened Era, and is still strong today, four hundred twenty years later. No one has seen our world leader, Shoa Khad, but there are rumors that he still lives! Every year he gives a speech to all people. It was thought that they were prerecorded messages. Our inside contact says he lives! And he looks exactly the same as he did in the new year zero, four hundred twenty years ago!

"We have an informant who is a part of the Inner ring government in the highest levels of the Authority. He reported that, over the last few years, tension has been growing in the top Authority leadership. Our supreme leader himself has become more paranoid. Shoa Khad, if he is still alive, started to meet with his inner staff much more regularly, and he questions their loyalty. Any sign of hesitation from his staff results in torture and death. The purges have become more frequent, making people in all the ten ring kingdoms nervous. Shoa has been heard talking to himself, saying that the time is drawing near. Near for what no one knows.

"We have an idea forming regarding his erratic behavior, but we need the complete book of Revelation to understand what is supposed to happen in the end times and when the events will occur. This is the theory we have developed: What if, in the writing of the book of Revelation, the disciple John could not comprehend the full magnitude of what the angel was telling him. What if he wrote the timeline wrong? Or what if someone mistranslated John's writing? What if the first part of the Antichrist's reign of terror was not forty-two months but four hundred twenty years? We just started our four hundred twentieth year in the new Enlighted Era a couple of months ago. What will happen after this year? Are we on the verge of starting the next wave of calamities foretold in the book of the Apocalypse of John? We must know more. The authority has been getting unusually harsh with their penalties and less tolerant of any religious activities in the recent years."

It was getting late in the day, and Mary ended her Apocalypse lesson. The four "students" all stood up and began to walk around to stretch their bodies. It had been a long, tense session. "What do you make of all the end-of-the-world Bible writings?" John asked out loud.

Sara blew out a long breath. "It's quite a story filled with imagery of strange creatures and unimaginable amounts of death and destruction. It's hard to take it all in."

"And yet," said Matt, continuing Sara's thought, "the massive events—the world's climate change, a world war on a scale never seen before, and it's terrible aftermath—did result in the death of most of the world's population."

Christie chimed in, "And then the world was miraculously saved by a man coming from nowhere to unite the world, making himself the ruler of all mankind, erasing all religion, and beginning the persecution of all Christians that continues today. It all matches the seals from the book of the Revelation except, of course, the timing. And what if it's true? Now, four hundred twenty years later, we are soon to face disaster and death even more horrible than what happened so long ago. Seven trumpets and seven bowls—that's fourteen worldwide calamities yet to come!"

Silence filled the room, and they settled back down, John and Sara on the sofa, Matt and Christie planting themselves in a couple of recliner chairs, all lost in their own thoughts of what may come. "Well, team," John said as he levered himself up from his chair, "it's been a long session, and it's late. Let's all move on to the kitchen and cook some dinner. I don't feel much like venturing out into the city tonight to look for a meal. We have leftovers from last night and the previous night that we can combine into something."

"Sounds like a good plan, John," Christie replied also getting up from her chair and heading to the kitchen. Matt and Sara followed with enthusiasm. Dinner sounded good. And washing it down with a glass of wine to soothe their tension sounded even better.

By nine o'clock the next morning, the four were back at the table with Mary's floating upper body alive and mobile ready for the continuing lessons. Before starting, Mary asked the group if they had any questions. Sara asked, "Mary, it's all so much to take in, this Apocalypse of John—war, destruction, death, and famine. Then the rise of the Antichrist, the devil himself, walking the earth! And maybe he is even still here today! Then you tell us the devastation is not over yet, and in fact, it may come upon us very soon in our own lifetime! What are we to think about all that? It's nearly too much to comprehend that it can all be true." The three others nodded in agreement.

Mary also nodded as she replied, "I know it's a mountain of information. It's all written in the Bible, written thousands of years before the calamities that befell us, foretelling exactly what would happen, and it did happen. Now, the only thing left to find out is when the rest of the calamities will happen and what the coming devastations will be. We are missing crucial information."

"But what good is knowing the rest of the story, Mary?" John spoke up. "So, the world will face another series of devastation and death. What good is knowing what will happen or when it will happen? We will all die from it anyway."

Mary looked at John and thoughtfully replied, "That's a great question, John. Remember what we learned from the first four books of the New Testament." Mary's head swiveled slowly to make eye contact with each of the four students. "Jesus said no one can enter the kingdom of heaven except through him. If the end times are upon us, it is up to us to preach the Good News of Jesus to as many as we can so they have a chance to accept Jesus before it's too late and they have to spend an eternity without our Lord in heaven. You must be bold and go out and tell others of what's coming. They will hear you and then see the Bible coming to life, and they will have a chance to accept Jesus before it's too late. It's not an easy road, and we must first know what will occur. We must know the contents of the rest of the book of the Apocalypse."

CHAPTER 13

The Journey (The Detectives)

Both Jack and Dom had a sense of déjà vu as they headed toward the old, abandoned warehouse district in the seedier area of ring five to Fast Eddie's hideout, the aero car flying close to the ground at low speed so they would not draw any attention. Just a couple of cops on a slow, boring night patrol in the area. As they approached the familiar beaten-up warehouse with a red brick exterior, the duo held short of the big doors, and Dom flashed the aero car's lights with the sequenced signal and waited. On cue, the big doors parted, and Dom silently glided the aero car into the warehouse. He eased the throttle and stopped at the back end of the warehouse. Several days ago, when they had first come to the warehouse unannounced, the area had been silent and empty; this time around, there was a greeting party waiting for Dom and Jack. Eddie was all smiles to see "his" aero car in top shape with no scratches.

As Dom and Jack stepped out of the aero car, Eddie ran up to them. "Great job, guys! It went like clockwork! And from the looks of my ... oops ... *our* aero car, there were no incidents or issues during your getaway."

"We were lucky, Eddie," Dom replied. "Very lucky."

"You know, in this business, there is not much luck, Dom. It's all about good planning and execution. And maybe a little bit of luck as you say."

Jack added to the joy. "We even got more radiation suits than we planned for." He opened the back trunk, which was stuffed to the limit with eight bagged suits.

This encouraged another big smile from Eddie. "Well played, gents. Let's go inside, have a drink, and celebrate."

Jack grinned. "Sounds like a great idea, Eddie!" Jack's mouth almost appearing to dribble from thoughts of a nice strong drink after their ordeal.

Jack, Dom, and Eddie enjoyed a few drinks and a great dinner served in a private dining room next to Eddie's circular cave. It was a feast—a three-course meal with steaks as the main course. Eddie made sure his guests knew that the steaks were not from genetically produced factory cows—otherwise known as warehouse meat—but from the finest stocks from ring six. Most meats came from enormous warehouses in the food factory section of ring five. Various animal meats were "grown" in the lab like bacteria in petri dishes, only on an industrial scale. Full-size animals were manufactured from genetic strains that yielded the fastest and biggest quantities in the shortest time.

Ring six, the outermost farmlands, contained fields where all forms of plants were grown. There were also pasture lands that supported free-roaming animals. From these lands, the innermost ring citizens ate the best of the best leaving everyone else to make do with factory foods. The outer ring six also helped to supply the needed genetic variety for plant and animal life to ensure that no single bacteria, virus, fungus, or pest would wipe out a crop to extinction levels.

"Amazing beef, Eddie!" Dom exclaimed with a hint of sadness as he took the last bite on his plate.

Eddie replied with a bow of his head, "We spare nothing for our friends. Enjoy, as this is also our last supper together, for tomorrow we will part our ways."

Dom replied, "You are right, Eddie. Jack and I need to get on with our journey. We'll pack up and head out under the cover of darkness tomorrow night." In reality, with all the surveillance technology in the rings, it didn't matter if it was day or night, but the cloak of darkness always seemed a comfort to those traveling under a cover of secrecy.

The next day started early for Dom and Jack with a light breakfast and a couple of cups of strong coffee. The morning was all about packing a used civilian aero car that Eddie had given to them as a part of the exchange. It was average in speed but had a lot of room for their gear with extra space to spare. In the afternoon, Eddie made his "artists" available who worked over Dom and Jack's appearance for extra stealth. Both Jack and Dom went from clean-shaven faces, military-style haircuts, and fair skin to a grunge look with long hair, pierced ears, full beards, and dark-brown skin.

"What do you think, Dom?" Jack, smiled.

"Jack, I think we've hit rock bottom now. We look like a pair of delinquent drifters with no jobs, no money, and no sense of morality. I guess it's a perfect disguise."

"Well, I don't think anyone is going want to bother with us now," Jack replied rubbing his full beard with his hand. "Not even the police will want to mess with us."

"That's for sure, Jack. Especially with these on our arms." He indicated his right bicep, which was decorated with a large tattoo of a skull and crossed bones—the mark of the fifth-ring mob aptly known as the Crossbones. The Crossbones were the seediest of seedy characters. For some reason, the police never bothered with the Crossbone mafia, allowing them to terrorize and control much of the fifth-ring businesses, extorting "security fees" from business owners. They also sold drugs and were into all types of nefarious activities. Nothing seemed to matter to the Authority as long as the people of the outer rings produced their quota of products, paid their taxes, and left the inner ring citizens to themselves. The Authority almost seemed to enjoy the cruelty and hardship of the outer rings as if that dark energy was a form of fuel for them.

The plan seemed simple. With the disguises, fake identification chips (black chips), and fake traveling permits, Dom and Jack would take their aero car through the ring-five and ring-four checkpoints to ring three where they would buy tickets on the Transit Tube (known as the TT).

The TT was a high-speed hyper loop transit rail in a magnetic levitating tube that was the only transportation from one ring kingdom to another, and transport happened at speeds that exceeded seven hundred miles an hour. Because it was a completely enclosed system, the Authority was able to completely control the populous. The worldwide nuclear war had laid waste to most of the countries, and high levels of radiation existed outside of the protected ring kingdoms. Because of the radiation, the ice age, and other natural disasters that had befallen Earth, most of the planet was an uninhabitable wasteland. After hundreds of years, no one knew what was left outside of the protective domes—paradise or devastation. There were always those who tried to escape and see for themselves what the world had left to offer, especially the runners who did not want to "retire" at the young age of forty-four. No one ever escaped, however, and no one lived to tell the story of their attempted escape. Rumors of those who had made it out stayed rumors as the runners had never reported back what they might have found.

The duo's final destination was the Wilborada 1047 bookstore in Bogotá, Columbia, where they hoped to unlock the secret of the old woman's tattoo. Once Dom and Jack got the information, they would use it to track the two medical examiners.

The nearest ring city to Bogotá was the South American Ring Kingdom in Brazil. To get there, Dom and Jack would travel using the TT from their home (the Middle East Kingdom) to the Central Africa Ring Kingdom in Nigeria. From there they would transfer to the TT going to the South America Ring Kingdom. One transfer station wouldn't be too risky. The hard part would be getting from Brazil to Columbia traveling out in the open wastelands. Escaping the South America dome would be the hardest part. Luckily Eddie had contacts in all ten ring kingdoms. That's how he did so well for himself in black-market trading. All Eddie had given Dom and Jack was a contact name in the South America Ring Kingdom. He said that if anyone could find a way to breach the dome, it would be Crypto Casanova. For a price anything can be obtained; this was Crypto's philosophy. Eddie did warn them to watch themselves around Crypto. He believed only in money. If someone was offering a bounty on Dom and Jack, Crypto would turn them in unless they offered to pay more. He might even be tempted to take their money and then turn them in for two payoffs! Either way, the advice was watch out!

It was early evening when Dom and Jack said their good-byes to Fast Eddie and his crew. Eddie told them to keep him apprised of their progress and to ask if they needed any help. Fast Eddie meant it too. Not that he was an honorable man; Eddie loved adventures. If he could live vicariously through Dom and Jack to get the thrill of the action he would gladly pay for the opportunity. Dom and Jack's adventure made for good story telling and, it would be an even better story if Eddie himself was a part of it. There was also a bit of curiosity from Eddie about what they would find out and where it would all lead. *Life is far too short,* Eddie thought. *Is there more to this world than meets the eye? Is there something greater that we cannot see?* Questions with no answers.

"Jack, fire up the Batmobile!"

"Sure thing, Dom. Let's get this show on the road." The Batmobile was Eddie's name for the car he had given to them and was based on some old document he'd uncovered about a bat-like man who had a bat car, a bat cave, and other mysterious bat equipment. Times surely had been strange back in the past.

It took a few hours to get to the Transit Tube in ring three. Almost half the time was wasted in the two ring gates between rings five and four and between rings four and three. True to Eddie's word, his documents provided them with easy passage; it was the long lines at the border gates that soaked up time. Dom and Jack decided to check into a hotel and rest up before they went to the Transit Tube station. They needed to have all of their wits about them at all times. Mistakes happened when people were tired, like forgetting and using their real names or making some other small mistake. That would be all it would take to tip off the Authority personnel and end their best laid plans.

The hotels in ring three, even the cheapest ones, were worlds apart from hotels in ring five. The "motel" they stayed in near the station had three restaurants and a full-sized gym that overlooked a swimming pool and Jacuzzi on an open deck on the roof deck ten stories above ground level.

"Whoa, Dom! I could get used to this ring-three life. Yesseree, living good is the way to go."

"You said it, Jack. We've been scraping a living with the underbelly of society spending most of our lives in ring five for so long that I forgot how the mids lived." Mids was slang for the ring-three people—those who lived in the middle ring. They were not as privileged as those who lived in the inner rings one and two, but they were not like the lower middle-class people who lived in ring four or those at the bottom of society who lived in ring five. They were upper middle class, or just mids for short.

The duo stretched out on the pool deck for a while taking in the sights and then enjoyed a nice Italian dinner and called it an early night to save their energy for what was to come. The next morning, Dom and Jack took their aero car to the TT. In the parking lot area, they met up with one of Eddie's associates who took the aero car in exchange for a lump of credits transferred to Dom's black chip. Eddie had given Dom and Jack special black chips to which he could add credits at any time. Eddie had enormous resources.

The TT journey from the Middle East Ring Kingdom to the South America Ring Kingdom, a distance of just over seven thousand miles, took about eleven hours including a one-hour stopover in the Central Africa Ring Kingdom in Nigeria. Thankfully, the same TT train was going to Brazil, so Dom and Jack did not have to transfer trains; they were able to keep their private cabin for the entire trip. Better to be unseen than to be seen by prying eyes. It was even more important to avoid video surveillance, which was everywhere, along with DNA trackers that sampled surfaces that people commonly touched. To fool the DNA trackers, Dom and Jack wore special transparent gloves that did not build up heat and sweat but prevented skin particles from escaping. They were part of Eddie's hide-in-plain-sight kit, and the detectives were thankful that he'd thought of everything. They even wore special lenses in their eyes to thwart the Authority's surveillance and identification systems.

Fast Eddie was vested in their adventure, and to ensure his continued help, Dom and Jack had to provide to Eddie with access to their travels. The lens implants in their eyes passively transmitted video feeds, and ear implants transmitted everything they heard. Eddie had access to everything they did twenty-four hours a day. Through the implants, Eddie could also talk to them. Dom mused that they would need Eddie's dark intellect to navigate the South America Ring Kingdom's notorious fifth ring. The Middle East Kingdom's fifth ring was a dangerous place, but nothing compared to the South America Kingdom's fifth ring.

Disembarking from the transit station at South America Kingdom's third ring, the two detectives stepped out into the street and were immediately hit with hot and humid air. Their senses were inundated with the sounds of land-based street vehicles, aero cars, and thousands of people walking like swarms of ants on enlarged sidewalks. The buildings were old in style with no flair and seemed to stretch on and on for miles, the 120-story-high buildings blocking out the light coming from the top of the ring dome. Rectangular buildings with reflective mirrored glass gave the illusion that their route was through a hall of mirrors—a very old hall of mirrors as the reflective surfaces were streaked with mold and other stains. Obviously, no one ever cleaned the glass. The air carried the slight stink of exhaust as old model land cars and aero cars still used conventional carbon-based fuel oil. Technology enabled vehicles to get a hundred miles to a gallon or more, but oil fuel was still dirty power, and the vehicles exhausted carbon dioxide and other noxious fumes.

"Whoa, Dom! If this is ring three, I wonder what ring five will be like. Back in the Middle East, our ring five is better than this place."

"I definitely agree with that, Jack. This place is a dump. I can hardly wait until we get to ring five and find Eddie's friend Casanova."

Just then, a beep sounded in their ears, and a familiar voice spoke, sounding as if he was right next to them. It was Eddie. "Wow, guys! Ring three Brazil is just like I remembered. It's a dump. Be careful there. Authority surveillance systems are everywhere. Mind what you say in open public areas, and get to ring five as soon as you can."

Thankfully only Jack and Dom could hear Eddie. The trick was to reply to him while making people think they were talking to each other. So, looking at Jack, Dom replied "Great advice. Let's grab a cabbie and get out of here." It took them three tries to hail an aero cabbie who agreed to take them to ring five. Looking like a couple of degenerates in their clothes and makeup, they couldn't blame the cabbies for not wanting to stop for them. The journey cost them a ton of credits. Apparently ring five was even more dangerous than they had imagined.

The rings were set up in a curious way. The ring barrier fields that separated one ring area from the next ring area extended to the top of the dome and, in addition to being force field barriers, were also giant screens on which were projected images of blue sky. This kept people from being able to see from one ring into another ring. Since each ring kingdom was enclosed in a dome, there was no time change from one ring kingdom to the next, and the dome field turned day into night on the same schedule. The ring kingdoms were mini worlds unto themselves, self-contained from outside destruction and disaster that humanity had called down upon themselves many hundreds of years ago.

As Dom and Jack passed through the checkpoint from ring four to ring five, the voice in their heads instructed them to go to the East Asian Mall located in Chinatown. When Dom told the cabbie where to take them, the cabbie said it would cost them another one hundred credits. "Blackmail!" shouted Eddie so loud it hurt the detectives' ears. Thankfully the cabbie didn't flinch. Only Jack and Dom could hear the voice in their heads.

"That's robbery!" blurted Jack in response to Eddie's voice. The cabbie turned to back to face them where they sat in the backseat. In an accented Chinese voice, he said "Five ring Chinatown bad place. Last time I took someone there, I held up and they take my credits at gunpoint. It's one hundred credits or I drop you off after checkpoint. You find own way. Good luck."

Jack conceded. "Okay, okay." And he proceeded to transfer to the Asian man one hundred additional credits. Jack stuck out his right wrist and the cabbie did the same. Jack then said, "Transfer one hundred credits." A light flashed, the reader on Jack's wrist lit up "-100 credits," and the cabbie's wrist ID lit up "+100 credits." Jack pulled back his wrist so the cabbie wouldn't see the flash of his balance. A few seconds later, Jack's wrist ID lit up with his credit balance—"9,900,000 credits" remaining. A sly smile appeared on Jack's face. He couldn't spend that many credits in two lifetimes! *So, this is what it feels to have no worries about money.* If it weren't that they were fugitives and in one of worst places on the planet, life would be good. He briefly lost himself in dreams of being in a beautiful hotel lounging poolside in one of the distant ring-three kingdoms, or even ring two with the right connections.

Dom nudged Jack on the shoulder. "Stay sharp, partner. We are cleared from the checkpoint and entering ring five."

The South America Kingdom ring five was the armpit of the planet. The buildings were low rise, made of concrete, and had few windows. Low and squat, about ten stories high, each building covered an entire block making the city look more like a chess board. All the buildings were exactly the same. A grid of narrow streets ran between them. Even the height of the dome ceiling was depressingly low. Normal domes were at least thirty thousand feet high—enough to give the feeling of open space with high artificial clouds. Here the ceiling was only about a thousand feet, and there were no images of clouds, just a dirty brown layer cover that clearly showed the limits of the dome above. It all felt a bit claustrophobic. As they flew, the aero taxi skimmed at the height of the building rooftops down the street corridors. It was illegal to fly over structures; this was to prevent vehicle crashes landing on the buildings. They could see the air itself—smog from a filtration system that couldn't keep up with the city's belching fumes. The low-dome ceiling also did not help, providing a lower volume of space that required a higher amount of air recirculation. "It looks like this ring could fit a billion people," Jack said.

The cabbie replied in his broken English. "It could, but only fifty million people in five ring. Most buildings you see hundreds of years old. No upkeep. Buildings abandoned in place and new building built. New building, old building fill up every square foot of area. Who knows? Maybe a huge unreported illegal peoples are living here? No one go into abandoned buildings. Bad places." In the distance, they saw several plumes of black smoke rising from multiple areas. The cabbie continued, "Here always buildings on fire from bad circuits, homeless people, bad people. Here is Wild West."

Dom asked the cabbie, "Where are all the law officers?"

The cabbie smirked. "Police? What police? Police in ring good parts not bad part. Police protect big manufacture plants. People on own. You have protection?"

Jack replied, "We have."

"Well, you show it. You need power."

Eddie's voice in their heads replied, "Good advice." Jack and Dom reached into their duffle bags. They had brought one duffle bag each full of gear and very few clothes as they planned on buying standard items as they needed them. Taking out their guns, they slipped them into holsters on their waist bands and untucked their shirts to provide concealment.

They neared a series of blocks guarded by a wide gateway at a large intersection. The gateway was framed by two enormous terracotta soldiers that stood twice as high as the buildings in front of them. Between the two soldiers, a faded red and cracked painted sign read "Chinatown." The aero taxi cabbie threaded through the gate and then he noticeably speeded up while mumbling. "Here Chinatown. I no stop. Faster you go, the less likely the gangs chase you down. They look easy targets. Me make it hard, they lose interest."

"Not to mention," Dom mumbled quietly, "this cabbie's aero car is so beat up who would want to rob it anyway?" Jack and the cabbie overheard Dom, and they chuckled, easing the tension a bit.

The cabbie replied with a smile. "Say what you want. My beater cab—it camouflage."

Dom thought he was going to throw up as the cabbie swerved at high speeds zig zagging around the blocks while saying that it would be better to keep on a chaotic path so no one had a chance to see them for very long. *Ugh, it's torture*, Dom thought. Finally, the cabbie slowed down the aero cab as they approached a very old gray brick building that was about five stories high. The windows on the upper level were all boarded up. On the ground level, there was a small double steel door, and above it was an illuminated sign that looked like it could be a couple hundred years old. The sign was flashing with a few letters missing: "Welcome East Asian Mall." The area around the mall was dark and depressing. Homeless people were rummaging through a few overflowing trash cans. At the corner there were about ten seedy-looking characters who were staring at their aero taxi. A chill ran down Dom's spine as he observed them. They were looking at them the way a pack of wolves might look at some lost sheep. Dom swore he could see them begin to salivate in anticipation of a kill.

Jack sensed the same and blurted out, "You have got to be kidding me! This is a kill zone here."

Dom said, "Only one way to play this—get the big guns out of our duffle bags to show them what they're up against."

"Right with you, Dom. Let's show them some fire power." They dug into their duffel bags, each bringing out a high-powered auto rifle that could shoot up to a thousand rounds per minute with explosive launchers under the main barrel. Moving quickly, they strapped on the power magazine backpacks that held fifty thousand rounds and five hundred explosive charges. The duo also donned their tactical head gear with display that enabled a 360-degrees view for enemy locating and auto targeting. The weapons were unique. The rounds were target seeking rather than the old-style straight-shot rounds. Each target was lit up with a laser dot, so targets knew they were on the hit list. These babies made anyone a one-man army. If the enemy got too close, the auto detonate feature could wipe out an entire block. The cabbie stared at them. "Wow! You prepared! No way anyone touched you now. You should tell me you big firepower. Save you a few credits. Please stay until I gone."

Jack replied, "No worries." And they stepped out of the aero taxi.

The corner gang started to walk toward them just as the cabbie departed, leaving them alone in the street. "Jack, let's light them up."

"Roger that, Dom." They swung their riffles up and shouted a command to their head gear: "Auto lock all targets." With that, a small halo of red dots on the heads-up display on their head gear illuminated, and a small red dot appeared on the chest of each member of the corner gang. The approaching gangsters immediately stopped in their tracks, seemly confused for a second. Then they realized what the dots were. Seeing Dom and Jack's auto rifles, they quickly lost interest in pursuit and backed off into their corner, not looking at the duo anymore. The newcomers' gear screamed of high-quality Authority weapons, and no one in their right mind messed with senior-level Authority personnel.

As Dom and Jack walked to the front entrance of the East Asian Mall, the street people continued to mind their own business, trying not to look at the two wild-haired, bearded newcomers with the impressive hardware. Dom motioned by extending his arm forward and then pointing his thumb to the right. "Jack, I'll open the door and walk in quickly. I'll move to the right. You come in straight after and go left."

"Gotcha, Dom."

At the door, Dom hesitated and then took a deep breath. This was either going to be easy or a cluster. The door gave way easily and opened outward. The lighting inside was bright as would expected if it were truly a mall. Dom moved quickly to the right. Jack followed a second later and crouched to the left. Taking in the scene, they swiveled their heads left and right and up and down. The inside of the building opened to a massive warehouse-type setup. The ceiling was at least three stories high on the first level, and the wide-open space was filled with small kiosks selling all manner of goods and foods. It looked like a Chinese bazaar. Seeing no active threat, Dom and Jack quickly stowed their rifles and headgear in their duffle bags. They still had their guns tucked away under their shirts just in case.

A bit of relief overcame them. "Whew, for a second there I wasn't sure what to expect, Jack. Thank the gods that this really is an Asian mall."

"You got that right, Dom. Let's move into the interior and put some distance between us and those characters outside. They may get curious and follow us."

As they moved inward, it was easy to disappear in the maze-like setup of booths and stalls that offered all manner of items. "Dom, where did Eddie say we needed to go?"

Dom whispered back. "He didn't. We need to establish contact with that voice in our heads."

Just then, right on cue, a voice sounded in their ears. "Man, what a sprawling mess of kiosks! This place hasn't changed since the last time I was here about ten years ago. This is so exciting. Just wanted to thank you guys for this adventure."

Jack replied, "Hey, Eddie. We're glad you're entertained. Wish you were here with us, my friend."

"Now, now, Jack. You know I'd be with you if I could. Nonetheless, seeing and hearing through you two is the next best thing. Anyway, keep going straight, or as straight as you can. Get to the middle of the ground floor of the mall area. There should be a kiosk selling all kinds of fruit juices. The name of the stand is The Fruit Juice."

"But of course," Dom replied to the voice in their heads. "What else would it be called?" Laugher rang in Jack's and Dom's head.

"You know, Dom," Jack muttered, "this twenty-four-seven voice in our heads could get tiring pretty quickly." Dom replied with a smile and a nod.

Eddie continued. "Okay, when you get to the stand, ask them for a large Crypto juice. They will just stare at you without saying a word. Don't respond. Just wait until they speak again. That is the routine. The man will ask. 'Small, medium, or large?' You respond, 'The Crypto is always large.' He will then guide you to the back of the mall through a few back corridors where Crypto works. You'll have to tip the man pretty well. I expect he will ask you for fifty credits or so. That was the going rate ten years ago."

Meandering around the place and trying not to look as if they were specifically headed straight for the juice stand, Jack and Dom took their time stopping at various booths. Jack even bought a T-shirt that had the layout of the Brazil rings on it with names of famous places. That got a groan from the voice in their heads. "Man, guys, can you move a little slower! An eighty-year-old would have been at the juice stand already. And what's with the T-shirt?"

"Hey laugh it up," Jack replied. "But when we get lost, who will have the map on his back? It'll be none other than Jack the map man." That got a big laugh from Dom and Eddie.

"I'm not sure if I'd bet my life on a T-shirt map to get us out of a jam." Dom mused out loud. People began to stare at the duo. "Jack, people are looking at us a bit funny. It may sound weird to others who hear our three-way conversation when they can only hear only the two of us."

"Right on, Dom. Let's be a bit cautious about that."

After meandering for a few more minutes, they arrived at the juice stand, and Jack ordered the Crypto drink following Eddie's instructions. Just as Eddie had said, the man guided them to the back of the warehouse and then through a few winding, dimly lit corridors. A great place for a mugging. Dom and Jack kept their hands low at their sides near their blasters just in case. Finally, they stopped at a steel door that had no seams in it. It was flush with the wall. It was an impressive, hardened-looking door for such a ratty old place. This area had definitely been upgraded for security. Up in the left corner on both sides of the door were two tiny round black spheres—video and audio obviously. Before the man knocked on the door, he lifted his right wrist. It was payoff time. As Eddie had advised, Dom used his wrist chip to transfer fifty credits to their guide. The juice man looked at his wrist with a smirk and then held it up again. Dom guessed there had been a bit of inflation in the last ten years. He tapped in another fifty credits. That did the trick. Juice man cracked a slight smile and then proceeded to knock on the door in a specific pattern. Then he turned and departed leaving the duo alone at the closed door. They waited about a minute. Finally, a voice sounded from one of the black spheres. "Who sent you here to me?"

Dom replied, "We are friends with Fast Eddie."

The disembodied voice laughed "I didn't know Fast Eddie had any friends."

The voice in their heads erupted in curses. Dom translated, "Fast Eddie shares the same sentiments."

"Oh," the voice replied. "Fast Eddie is doing his video and audio feed thing through you two is he? Well, come on in and we can talk, and I can catch up with Eddie." And with that, the steel door parted in the center with a silent swoosh. The interior was completely dark, and Dom and Jack walked into the void.

CHAPTER 14

The Search
(The Authority Three)

aking up at eight in the morning after another restless night, Saul wondered how he had got so far into this mess. A routine snatch and grab had gone horribly wrong. And the grab and snatch had been a corpse!

Getting up was a bit hard after the late-night dinner at Pete's Italian restaurant. It was the combination of all the great food and that last night cap that hadn't been necessary but sure felt right in the moment. Saul's head was pounding, and his stomach wasn't in much better shape as it tried to digest all the pasta and drink. The cheap hotel they were staying at in ring four didn't help either. Noisy neighbors and outside noise from the street cars and aero vehicles had been constant all night long.

Getting old, Saul. I bet the other two lads aren't in much better shape. After washing up and donning a new set of clothes, Saul was back on the street walking to the local café a couple of blocks away where they had agreed to meet for breakfast. It was half past nine. Both Hector and Jackson were already at the café in their normal booth at the back of the restaurant. Spying Saul walking in the restaurant, Hector blurted out, "Saul, we thought you'd had a stroke or something!"

Jackson gave up a big grin as well. "Yeah, you two just wait a few more years and see what a night of eating and drinking will do to you." Smiles all around. Sitting down, Saul wiped his hand over his hair. "Guys, I am definitely feeling a bit rough today. Need a coffee bad." Right on cue the waitress came over to pour a hot cup of brew for Saul.

Hector and Jackson lifted their cups for her to refill. "I'm glad not to be the only one needing a coffee fix."

"You said it, Boss." Jackson replied. "Nothing like a caffeine jolt in the morning."

During breakfast, Saul laid out the plan. Hector and Jackson would go back to the hospital and review all the video and audio logs from all monitors. Saul would go to the central security building where video and audio were kept from street surveillance monitors as well as the upper dome ring monitoring systems. There was aerial surveillance at the roof of the dome of every ring that captured all activities below. They would meet back at the café at five pm to compare information.

From the café, it took about an hour with all the morning traffic to get to the hospital. "What do you think, Jackson? Are we going to get some images of our two detectives?"

"We should, Hector," Jackson replied with confidence. "Those two detectives didn't look like they'd done any preplanning. Just a routine body grab and delivery to the autopsy room that went bad. Now, the two medical examiners the detectives mentioned is another story. They may have erased the videos. At least of themselves."

As Hector and Jackson entered the hospital through the front entrance, Jackson tapped on his hand-held device, and a map of the hospital and directions to the security office popped up on his display. The hospital interior was brightly lit with the same whitewashed walls they had encountered the other night. The ambiance was more subdued, and the air had an antiseptic smell that made his senses come alive, elevating his natural instincts to be alert. As they approached the back office areas the monitoring systems read their

ID chips, and the unmanned security gates lit up green. The security "gates" were two bands of yellow light on either side of the corridor that provided a visual cue that they were approaching a checkpoint. As Authority officials, Hector and Jackson had access to most public building secure areas. If they didn't have access, solid doors recessed in the wall would immediately close off the corridor before they were a few feet from the gate, and the entire area would lock down immediately. Security guards would be on them within seconds.

After passing several of the yellow checkpoint gates, they finally arrived at the security office door. There was no identification—just a plain closed door with a round hole in the wall next to it. Jackson proceeded to stick his right wrist into the hole allowing a full scan of his ID chip along with a genetic sample for added verification. "Ouch! I hate those genetic readers. Why do they have to poke you with a needle? Can't they upgrade to the more sophisticated systems?"

Hector gave Jackson the look. "That's pretty wimpy, Jackson. Man up."

They entered the security office from the sterile white corridor. The lighting changed immediately. The darkened small square room was about fifteen feet by fifteen feet. A table stood in the center surrounded by four wheeled chairs, and a series of screens filled the far wall. A man sat on one of the chairs. Wheeling his chair around, he faced Jackson and Hector. Not getting up, he took a few seconds to take in the skinny Spanish-looking man and the Giant. Both Jackson and Hector wore their official black mob-type suits. Clearing his throat, the security guard gave them a formal welcome. "Gentlemen of the Authority, to what do I owe the pleasure of your unannounced visit?"

Actually, the Authority never announced a visit. Hector boomed, "Cut the niceties. We are here to review some of your monitoring logs from last night."

"Right away!" The security guard knew not to ask any questions. Swiveling back on his chair, he faced the table and waved his hand over its surface. The tabletop screen illuminated, and the security man furiously started to type on the screens. "Which sections of the hospital do you want to see and what time frames?"

Jackson and Hector now sat in the chairs on either side of the security guard and were hunched over the table screen. Hector directed, "Show us two nights ago just before nine in the underground medical autopsy chamber."

"We have two autopsy rooms in the basement. Which one do you want to see?"

"Pull up both as well as the corridors leading to them."

A few strokes and taps on the table screen caused the screens on the far wall to change and show two autopsy chambers and all the corridors leading to them. The time stamp on the feeds showed nine p.m. Not a soul in sight. Hector continued, "Now move forward in five-minute increments." The right screen flickered, and then four figures appeared and entered the room—one large man with an occupied body bag hoisted over his shoulder followed by three other men. Hector said, "Stop there. Now go to real-time speed." One room faded away, and the screen showing the four figures enlarged on the wall. The large man walked to the center of the room and proceeded to plop the body bag on the table. A wall phone intercom rang, the man took the call, and then he departed with a smaller Spanish-looking man leaving the room with the two detectives. The security guard obviously picked up that the Giant and the Spanish man on the video were the two sitting on either side of him, and he had the good sense not to say anything.

Hector continued, "Okay. Now speed up to five-minute increments." After the security guard typed in commands, the images on screens began to speed up. The images of the two detectives flickered as they moved around the room. Then the room was empty again. The two detectives were gone along with the body. The image kept on moving in five-minute increments.

Jackson jumped in. "Get back the image that shows the last moment the two men were in the room and then play at normal speed." The image on the screen quickly rewound and showed the two detectives with the body bag on the table. Then the room just went blank.

Hector yelled, "What happened?" He turned to the security guard and placed his right hand on the skinny man's shoulder.

The man broke out into a sweat and furiously typed into the table board. "Not sure what happened, sir. Looks like they were in there one moment and then there was a glitch in the software program that saves the video and audio. The time stamp jumped forward. We lost an hour of video feed."

"What about backup?" Hector continued to squeeze the man's shoulder. The guard typed even more furiously now, and his face went ashen white. "Looks like all backups were also wiped out."

Hector was about to pummel the guard when Jackson jumped in from the side. "Take us back and get a good shot of the two detectives." With an obvious bit of a relief, the security guard provided clear face shots of Dom and Jack.

Jackson pulled out his device, and the security guard transferred the images onto it. "Hector, I'll run a trace. At least we'll get the details about our two detective friends."

Hector cursed, directing a couple of foul words at the security guard. "Let's get out of here before I do something to this security guard that he will regret."

Meanwhile, Saul was nearing the ring four central security building. Every ring had its own surveillance system. All data then all fed to the main security center in ring two. The front entrance of the security building opened into a massive reception area with high ceilings. It was just one large room with no waiting chairs, and all the walls were white. It reminded Saul of the hospital. Saul mumbled to himself, *What is it with all this antiseptic white in all the Authority buildings? Makes everything look sterile and void of life.* At the center of the hall-like area was a circular desk where two receptionists sat facing the front entrance. Low semi-clear glass-like monitors in front of them looked like hand-held devices but were much larger. Behind the circular desk on the far was a series of silver doors. None of them had any markings.

As Saul walked up to the desk, one of the receptionists, also dressed in all white, looked through her clear screen and chimed with a pleasant voice, "What may we do for you Mr. Saul?" Saul looked a bit surprised she knew his name. *The security system is fairly good! It probably read my ID chip even before I entered the building.*

"I need to get into the surveillance system to review a case I'm working on."

The young woman at the desk swiped at the clear screen and tapped a few buttons. A few seconds later, one of the silver doors in the back of the area opened, and a tall thin man, also dressed in a white uniform, approached. "Mr. Saul, right this way. I'll take you to our command center." The two went through the steel doorway and disappeared down a long corridor. This building was just like the other secured government buildings. They passed through a series of security gates that turned from yellow to green as they approached and quickly turned back to yellow after they passed through. At the end of the corridor, a glass door opened, and they passed through another gate, but this one led into a small vestibule. The glass door closed quickly behind them, and a few feet ahead, another glass door opened. They walked through a series of beams that recorded, measured, and analyzed every feature of them to the genetic level. "Impressive security," Saul observed.

The man in white replied, "We have to be extra sensitive because information for all ring-four activities are accessed here in our command and control room. We can also activate drones from here as necessary."

A chill ran down Saul's' neck. The drones were killer machines that could be as small as a fly. They could take out a single person or a machine the size of a small aero car. They even had enough firepower to wipe out an entire city block.

Entering the command center was like entering a small movie amphitheater. The room had a high ceiling, and a massive set of screens covered the front wall. They appeared to be showing hundreds of scenes throughout the city, overlaid on a background of a detailed map of ring four. There were about five rows of desks, each with seating for five people. Each person sat in front of the same type of semi-clear glass screens that Jackson had seen at reception, and each one of them was typing and swiping their hands on the screen as corresponding video images popped up on the large map on the front wall. One of them called out to the man who had escorted Saul from the receptionist desk. "Gal, I just got a location on the Thomas gang. They are in the industrial section at the border with ring five, grid 33.3152, 44.3661, ground level."

Gal replied, "Pull it up." The desk jockey closed in on the woman sitting at the desk. She swiped her screen, and a live video appeared on the theatre-screen-sized map on the wall. It was, at first, an aerial view of a few city blocks that quickly zoomed in on the coordinates at street level. Four men and one woman were walking down the street. From the angle of the view, they could see only the tops of their heads as they walked. A red dot was zeroed in on each of them. The woman's screen showed five faces. "Data system confirms all five." Gal got closer to her monitor. "Okay, great job. Get ready to launch two-five-five. Those fools think they can kill someone from the Authority and walk the streets with impunity. We will set an example of them."

"Target locked," the desk jockey stated with no emotion at all.

Gal, on the other hand, seemed as if he was about to hyperventilate. "Launch!" he yelled. She depressed a toggle on her clear pad. The room went silent as everyone stopped what they were doing to look up at the massive screen. Gal continued to give orders: "Zoom out to block level." The video image that was tight on the five zoomed out to show the entire block. There was still a red dot on each of their heads. Suddenly, a flash of white erupted on the screen, and the room reverberated with the sound of the blast. Saul had to cover his ears it was so loud. The others in the room seemed immune to the loud noise. A few seconds later, the explosion area started to clear. Half the block had been obliterated. They heard the screaming of what looked to be hundreds of people. Bodies were strewn everywhere, and most of the glass from the building frontage well beyond the blast area had been destroyed. The desk jockey spoke in a monotone voice. "Targets eliminated. Collateral damage estimated at two hundred killed." The image on the screen disappeared. The staff got back to work as the map on the wall and the other images of ring four popped up again. Back to business as usual.

Gal turned to Saul. "That will send a message: don't mess with the Authority."

Saul had heard about the ruthlessness of some Authority personnel, but this guy took it to a new level. Curiosity got to Saul. "Gal, do you need to get authorization for an action that does such massive damage?"

Gal responded with a slight grin. "I am the security section leader for ring four, and I get to do whatever I want as long as it doesn't disrupt the flow of goods and materials to the inner rings. I could wipe out a million people if I wanted to." Saul was about to laugh as if that was a joke, but he stopped short when he realized that Gal was dead serious. He was a stone-cold mass murderer. Apparently that's how the Authority liked their leaders. Thoughts rolled around in Saul's head. *Is this what we are? Robots led by killers with no remorse or morals?*

"Hello, Saul? Did you hear me?" Gal snapped Saul out his thoughts.

"Sure, Gal. Pardon the mental lapse. I was just so enthralled with the devastation scene."

"Yah, me too, Saul. Me too." Gal smiled big as if on an adrenaline high. "So, what were you needing to look at today?"

"Of course. Thanks, Gal. Really appreciate your help. I'm looking for all video and audio footage in the area around the City West Hospital a couple of nights ago from eight to midnight. We're looking for any movement at the rear service entry area."

Gal replied, "Of course."

Before Gal could motion to his staff, Saul added in a soft whisper, "One thing, Gal. Our mission comes from the highest Authority. There must be the minimum number of people involved with this search request."

"Yes, I see, Saul. Understood." Gal's interest was piqued even more with the new level of intrigue. He clapped his hands loudly to get everyone's attention and then directed his team, "Clear the room. This is a level-one operation." All operators immediately stopped what they were doing and headed for the exits. Gal waved to the desk jockey who had worked the screens during the previous action. "Drusilla, I need you to stay and work the problem."

The desk jockey responded, "Ay, sir!" And she sat back down. Gal gave her instructions, and she began to type furiously on her screen. The large map on the rear wall zoomed in to the portion of the city where the hospital was located. Multiple video feeds popped up showing the rear of the hospital with time stamps on them. A large aerial video looking straight down at the hospital took up the center screen, and to the left and the right were other angles of the alleys and streets behind the hospital. Amazingly, all the videos looked as if they had been recorded in the daytime, the area images were so sharp.

Saul spoke with admiration, "Amazing video, Gal. Even at night the whole area is in sharp detail."

"Yep, it's the latest technology, Saul. Day or night, our cameras are so sensitive they pick up everything using combinations of heat sensors, enhanced light gathering lenses, radar waves, and other systems that fuse all the data into clear video streams."

They intently watched the monitors as the scene fast-forwarded. "There!" Saul remarked as an aero car came to a stop outside the hospital in an alleyway. They slowed the video feed to real time and watched two men exit the car carrying a body bag. Saul anxious now said, "Okay, let's fast-forward now." When they speeded up, no action occurred. "There!" Saul exclaimed again. They watched two people exit the rear of the building in the same alley area, quickly run into the main street, hail an aero cab, and depart. They were much smaller in size than the two people who had come out of the aero car previously carrying a body bag, and they were wearing medical gowns.

Saul directed, "Get as much as you can on them." Drusilla furiously went to work, and the video screens pulsed with various views. After a few moments, a few static pictures appeared on the wall screen. They were close-ups of the two medical examiners. Their faces were hidden under the hoods they wore over their heads.

"Wow!" Gal let out. "These two are professionals. They knew where all our cameras were located, and they never tilted their heads up even a fraction. We can't get a read on their faces. Even more amazing is that we don't have any feed on the aero cab they left in because that cab had no markings and no transponders." They intently watched the screens as the feed followed the aero cab down the road until it went into a large underground structure and never came out. Vanished!

Gal nodded his head in appreciation. "Saul, looks like you're hunting professionals. Sorry we couldn't help you more. When you find another lead, let me know, and we'll track them for you. If you want, we can even exterminate them quietly or with a public showing." Gal's voice started to rise as he mentioned a possible extermination.

Saul replied, "Thanks for the offer, Gal. I'll be back—hopefully soon—with more details so we can track them. Appreciate all your help. Can you tell me anything about them?"

The desk jockey Drusilla tapped a few commands into her screen. "Looks like you're looking for a man and a woman by their outline features. The man is approximately five feet ten inches tall and of slim build. The woman is five feet seven inches tall. Also slim build. That's about it."

With that, Gal took Saul back out to the front reception area.

Arriving back at the café a little early, Saul ordered a coffee and a muffin. Munching on his muffin, he didn't notice Jackson and Hector coming over to the table. "Hey, boss, you're early," Jackson muttered as he sat down and Hector slid into the booth next to him.

Somewhat startled from his thoughts, Saul looked up at the two. "Hello, gents. I hope you had better luck than I had. I got nothing from the meeting at the security building except a cold sweat rolling down my back after watching that security team."

Hector spoke up. "We got zeros on the medical examiners, but we did get good facials on the two detectives. Searching the system, we got their names—Simon Halos and Jack O'Leary." Hector swiped his hand over his device, and the information ported over to Saul's device. "They're detectives from the ring four twelfth precinct. Their records look good. From the cases they were on, looks like they specialize in the dirty and off-book jobs."

"Just the type of people you would want for a quiet cleanup job," Saul replied as he perused their file.

Jackson added, "We called their supervisor who cryptically told us that the two are on assignment for the next few days and are undercover, no communication."

Saul sat back and thought for a few moments before he replied, "Well, then, you two head down to the security building in the morning. Ask for Gal, and let him know you're working with me. Get a trace on Simon and Jack. I want a complete record of all the places they've been in the last few days. Get an active patch on their aero car so we can track them live and remotely on our devices. I want us to be able to find them ourselves. I don't trust our security friends yet to keep this low profile. I've got a contact at the twelfth precinct station and will do a little bit of snooping around. Let's have a quick dinner and call it an early night. I'm beat."

Jackson and Hector nodded. Hector said, "It was a long night last night, and it's been a long day today too." After dinner they made their way back to the cheap motel for a good bit of rest.

CHAPTER 15

The Quest
(The Medical Examiners)

I
t was John who spoke up next, addressing holographic Mary. "So, we need to find the rest of the Apocalypse of John before we can understand what is yet to come—when these yet-to-be-known next series of horrific events will occur. And we need to be able to decipher what is going on with the Authority leadership."

"Precisely," replied the voice from the center of the table. Mary's floating head and shoulders swiveled slowly to address each of the four as she spoke. "We just recently came upon more information about the remaining book libraries in the world. There was such devastation from the war and the changes in weather that there are only a handful of places left that may remain. It was hard to get the information, and many have died over the years seeking that knowledge. But, thanks to God, we have a firm lead on where we may obtain an intact bible."

In front of Mary, another holographic image started to form. It was a three-dimensional map of a large city in a mountainous area. It was obviously a very old image, dating back before the wars as there were trees, street cars, and people everywhere. The image began to zoom in to a small section of the city with smaller buildings in a neighborhood area. The image continued to zoom in as it focused on a beautiful English-style mansion. Mary continued. "This is the Wilborada 1047 bookstore located in Bogotá, Columbia. That's in South America Ring Kingdom, north of Brazil."

"Ooooh," came the reply from the group. Not good news. The South America Kingdom was notorious for being one of the roughest ring kingdoms.

Mary continued, "Our intel says that the bookstore is still intact and may still contain its library of books." Another image took the place of the beautiful neighborhood landscape. This time it was of a neighborhood devoid of all life—not a single tree or plant. The buildings were old and crumbled. But the structure in the center view was unmistakable. It was the old stately-looking building of the Wilborada 1047 bookstore. It was weathered and looking worse for the years, but still intact. "Our sources say this image is less than fifty years old."

"Amazing," Christie remarked. "After hundreds of years, the building and the surrounding area look very well preserved. You would think it would be all crumbled and destroyed by now."

"That's what we were thinking too," Mary's floating head continued. "In our research, it looks like Bogotá was hit with a series of dirty bombs late in the Great Conflict. Low-impact, high-radiation bombs killed everything but left the structures intact. Somehow, that helped to preserve the area. No life was left to grow and take over the area. Now the problem is that we don't know how much radiation is left in the area. From the image, it appears that the area is still highly radioactive. There's no plant life at all in the area."

Matt said, "Well, that is a dilemma. It's great news that this may be the only remaining library in the world that may contain books, including the Bible. But if we go there, we'll be dead from the radiation. Mary, are you asking us to go on a one-way mission to retrieve and send the contents of the Bible to your group?"

There was silence in the room. No one had thought of it before, but what Matt suggested could be a real possibility. They had learned about Jesus and his sacrifice to save the souls of all humanity. Were they now being asked to also sacrifice themselves? To die in horrible pain from radiation sickness so that others may have a chance to enter the Kingdom of God? The silence was uncomfortable as each of the four contemplated Matt's words, and Mary's floating head slowly turned to each of them and looked them in the eyes. She seemed to assess their worthiness and resolve for such a task. Each of the four stared directly back at Mary's gaze, not looking down or up. Seeing resolve in their eyes, Mary appeared to be satisfied. Mary's eyes shone. Her face showing the same mask of determination as theirs, and her head nodded in appreciation of the determined faces that stared back at her.

Mary continued with an understanding sympathetic voice, "We have been working on this for some time now—how to get to the Wilborada 1047 without needlessly sacrificing lives. It may be still so radioactive that people might not even make it to the library without succumbing to the radiation. Every life is precious in the eyes of Jesus, and we will not needlessly send people to their deaths. In our planning, however, we have found a possible solution. It will require daring and cunning. The mission will require dealing with underworld characters to get the required equipment and passage. And in the end, it may very well be a one-way mission. We will need to prepare what we can and leave it up to Jesus to guide the way. For this mission, the stakes are high. The souls of millions are in the balance. The price to pay may be the ultimate sacrifice one can give to our Lord. This is voluntary, and each one of you must decide."

There was silence in the room for several minutes as each contemplated Mary's words. John spoke up first. "I have known something about our Lord for many years, and now it is as if a great fog has lifted, and I can see clearly. What was the passage you told us? 'Though I was blind, now I see.' I will go on this mission even if it requires my life."

Nodding her head in agreement, Sara spoke. "I too have survived too many years in the dark. It is time to live."

Christie spoke with tears in her eyes. "My tears are tears of joy that I may have such an opportunity. To be called by our Lord for a mission to help others is something my soul has been yearning for all my life. Finally, my destiny has appeared in my life."

Lastly, Matt spoke, also having a very difficult time keeping his emotions in check. "It's hard to believe that the Lord would entrust us to such a mission. I have lived such a small life, living day to day with no real purpose. Until now. What is it that was once said by an old-world revolutionary—William Wallace I think? 'Every man dies. Not every man really lives.' I fear for my life and for the lives of my dear brothers and sisters here. But I will not let my fear detract me from this great task."

They all held hands as Mary said a prayer: "Lord, be this your will for your four disciples to go on this mission to retrieve what is now lost. May they be successful and bring back your Word to us and to the rest of the world before it is too late. Lord, give John, Sara, Matt, and Christie strength to hold fast to your love, your peace, and your grace as they do your will. Amen." All four continued to pray in silence for a few more minutes, and then Mary spoke, "Break for lunch, and we will continue later with our plan of action."

There was a feeling of energy in the air as they chatted over sandwiches. Questions abounded: How would they do it? Where should they even start? Who were the people that Mary had talked about? How many underground Christians were there in their ring kingdom? How many Christians were there in the other ring kingdoms?"

The other internal questions remained unsaid as they ate their sandwiches: I talked big before with Mary and the others, but when it comes down to it, will I have the strength to sacrifice my life, to endure pain and suffering as Jesus did? Or will I scatter like the apostles did when Jesus was arrested?

John broke the silence. "I pray that I have the strength when the time comes."

All nodded in agreement and with a sense of relief that everyone felt the same way. Faith is difficult, and increased faith is only born out of the trials that we face in life.

When they gathered back at the table after lunch, Mary's head and shoulder reappeared. "Our Christian underground spans all ten ring kingdoms as well as many of the ten posts. Some are in high places of authority; others are at the working level. We even have Christian brothers and sisters who are in touch with the criminal elements in society. Jesus called on us to proclaim his Good News to everyone, and that goes especially to the ones who are disenfranchised from society. We will need our full combined unity to pull this one off. You will first take the Transit Tube to Brazil in the South America Ring Kingdom. From there you will have to work with our fellow Christians to be transport to the Venezuelan Post. There you will procure the necessary transport and radiation suits to travel to Bogotá, Columbia."

Sara scratched her head and asked Mary, "I've heard only very little about theses post cities. We are not supposed to talk about them, so I don't know much about them." Matt, Christie, and John also nodded in agreement.

Mary explained, "Each of the ring kingdoms is paired with a satellite city called a post. The posts are much smaller than the ring kingdoms, and their main function is to help to manage potential threats. No one knows what these threats may be, who they are, or how many there are. Asking those types of questions normally makes the questioner disappear very quickly. The posts are self-sustaining and therefore rarely need direct contact with the ring kingdoms. All communications are set up from the posts directly to the inner rings of the kingdoms. Rumors are that the posts have about a million people with only two rings: an inner elite ring, and an outer ring where everyone else lives and works, which makes sense due to the small population. There are also rumors that the posts are very heavily armed. Who they are fighting is a mystery as the whole world outside the ring kingdoms is supposed to be desolate and unlivable because of the Great Conflict and the ice age. There remain a lot of questions with no answers, and since there is no direct interaction with the posts, there is no one to talk about it."

"How firm are 'our' contacts in the South America Ring Kingdom and at the Venezuelan Post?" John asked.

"That's a good question, John." Mary's head swiveling to look at him. "Although we have active contacts in all ten ring kingdoms, they are not regular, and sometimes we go months between contact sessions. This is especially true for the rougher kingdoms such as South America. But, thanks to God, our last contract with them was just a month ago, and our group there is still strong. We can rely on them, and they are awaiting a response from us. We will contact them and let them know of your coming to them. For security purposes, we will not reveal your mission. It's best that, when you meet with them, you give them only the information needed to help you to your next stop. That's it. No more. They will not ask for more information. Less is better in our shadow world."

John pressed for more, "And the Venezuelan Post?"

This time Mary's face crinkled as she composed her words. "I will not sugar coat the difficulty of this mission. As you know, the posts are independent facilities with no public Transit Tube access or direct communications. They are remote islands unto themselves, and rarely does anyone get in or out. For that reason, it has been over fifty years since we had any communications with our underground Christian brothers and sisters there. We had only a small group, but they were strong and growing in numbers."

"Fifty years!" Christie almost yelled out. Everyone felt the same. "Mary, fifty years is more than a lifetime in the current world we live in! Who knows what happened to the group in that time!"

"I know it's hard," Mary told the shaken group. Just a few minutes before, the four had worn masks of determination. Now everyone's face showed uncertainty and doubt as the reality of the difficulty of the mission set in with the real possibility of failure, torture, and death. Mary's floating head slowing turned to each of them. "Faith is something that we are not born with. It is something we work on every day of our lives. Look at the twelve apostles and the struggles with their faith in Jesus even after they'd been with him for over four and a half years. Have faith that Jesus will see you through the mission. I will not lie. Some of you may be called home to our Lord during the mission. We will all die someday. Look upon me. You see me, but this is a holographic artificial intelligence model of my former self. I am with our Lord now in heaven. Have faith, friends. That this is the task that has been given to you. It is okay to be scared. It is okay to have doubts. Do not let that make you falter. Take everything one day at a time, and our Lord will see each of you through this."

Sara spoke for the group. "Yes, of course, Mary. We apologize for our hesitancy. We are all committed to our Lord and this mission he has given to us. Although we are afraid, we will go." The three others nodded in agreement, their faces turning from dread to determination once more. Sara continued, "I pray that Jesus gives me strength when the time comes to do what must be done, no matter the consequence to my life."

John spoke for the group. They all nodded in agreement and whispered the name of Jesus as John said, "I pray that Jesus gives us strength when the time comes to do what must be done, no matter the consequence to our lives. This is our calling. This is our quest."

They continued for the rest of the day as Mary told them more about the South American Ring Kingdom and the Venezuelan Post and what contacts they had there with the Christian underground.

Over dinner, the four sat at the dining table picking at their food. None had too much of an appetite thinking of what was yet to come in their lives. Up to that day, they had lived somewhat regular lives. They had experienced some dangerous moments as part of the Christian underground, but nothing compared to what this task promised. Up to now, the most dangerous mission any of the four had experienced was retrieving the data from Mary's corpse. They had never done anything else that would be considered life threatening. John and Sara were actual medical examiners; that was why they had been picked for the task of retrieving the information from Mary's corpse. Matt was an industrial engineer for a manufacturing plant that produced machinery parts for aero cars and other types of transport vehicles. Christie was an IT specialist who worked on the computer system hardware and software at the same manufacturing plant where Matt worked. They had all lived together for many years. Matt and Christie had been friends since they'd attended their first secret meeting of the underground Christian group a long time ago. The Christian groups were small, comprised of ten or fewer. They didn't want to be picked up as suspicious activity. And the groups rarely interacted with each other so the Authority could not tie them all together. If one group was captured and tortured, they could not give up the rest. No one knew how many groups there were, but there were rumors that it was a lot more than most people thought—potentially millions of people in the ten ring kingdoms.

Pushing his food around his plate, Matt was the first one to speak his thoughts. "I'm just an engineer with a normal job and normal life. I never professed to be a superhuman capable of doing daring deeds. I've never sought after an adventurous life. I live day to day doing my job. Yes, we go to our Christian underground meetings, and that is a huge risk, but nothing that requires a presence of mind and body like this mission that Mary is talking about—sneak undercover to the most notorious ring kingdom, meet with people we have never met, maybe even having to bargain with thieves and hoodlums, somehow get to an actual post that no one knows anything about, and connect with people whose last feeble contact was over fifty years ago. Then somehow from there traverse open wasteland to a radioactive zone that supports no life, find an intact Bible—if there is one—and get the information back to others in the underground Christian leadership team. And, for now, our only contact is a woman who is already deceased. If all goes well and they decipher the next calamities to come, our real work will begin because we will have to warn the rest of the world to repent and accept Jesus as their Savior before it's too late, saving millions of souls. Is that who I am?"

Finished with his soliloquy, Matt buried his head in his hands with a dejected look on his face.

Sara spoke. "We all feel the same way, Matt. We are all so small and insignificant. Our lives to date have been normal and unspectacular. Can we do this task that Mary asks? By ourselves or the four of us together? Of course not. None of us is trained as a spy. None of us has any military stealth training. We would be caught within moments of starting out and then tortured and killed. Only with Jesus can we accomplish this mission."

Matt lifted his head out of his hands, and he looked a bit better. John put in his thoughts. "It will take all of us together to accomplish this task. One step at a time. We will press on until there are no more steps to make."

"Well, then, I'd better bring my new running shoes," Christie said with a smile. That got everyone laughing, breaking up the heaviness of the conversation, and the mood turned much lighter.

"Well, team," John said, getting out of his chair, "let's clean up the dishes. It's time for some sleep. Tomorrow we finish planning with Mary, and then we need to pack up for the mission. I think we'll need to give our little team a name. How about The Quest?"

Christie replied, "Short, simple, and powerful. I like it."

Matt replied, "Sounds great to me."

Sara said, "Me too."

John finished, "The Quest it is then! Jesus be with us on our Quest!"

It was another restless night for the four. John and Matt got up first at seven. Sara and Christie were about one hour behind. Coming up to the dining room table, Sara took in a deep breath. "I love the smell of fresh-brewed coffee in the morning! Thank God for the little things in life."

"You said it, Sara," Christie added as they approached the two guys sitting at the table.

Matt pointed toward the kitchen. "There's a full pot in the kitchen. Today it's Italian roast with some Arabic beans mixed in. Freshly ground. Our chef of the morning, John, made some scrambled eggs, bacon, and sliced fruit." John acknowledged Matt with a bow of his head.

Both Sara and Christie clapped their hands in good cheer. Sara said, "You two are our angels this morning." And she reached for the coffee pot.

After breakfast, they moved to the table where Mary's floating head and shoulders hovered. "I pray you four had good rest last night." Weak head nods came in response. "Well, I must say it was a lot to give to you yesterday. Don't worry. After a restless night, it's usually easier to sleep the next night, if nothing else from sheer exhaustion." That got a few smiles and a laugh. Mary continued, "Today we will go over the detailed plans to get you to the South America Ring Kingdom and to our contact there. Your contact will direct you to the next contact who will get you to the Venezuelan Post. Then, from there, further contacts will get you to the prize—the Wilborada 1047 bookstore. I am sorry if the information and directions are compartmentalized. It is for the safety of everyone that you and each cell know only as little as possible about the mission." Concern once again came over the fearless four. Mary continued, "Worry not, friends, for you have found Jesus, and in him you have eternal life in heaven. What we do here on Earth, at this time, in this moment, is just a prelude to eternity. Let's do our best to enable the Good News of Jesus to spread to as many as possible and ready as many as possible for the times to come."

Through the rest of the day, Mary went over the plan again and again. She allowed the four to take notes, understanding that they had to commit everything to memory. Nothing could remain written down. All four must commit the plan to memory. If one or more of them didn't make it, the remaining members of the team must be able to fulfill the mission on their own. It was a sobering thought, but everyone acknowledged that it may very well come to be that not all of them would see the Quest through to the end.

The plan was simple. They would buy passage to the South America Ring Kingdom using fake ID chips (black chips) that had been delivered to their door early in the morning. Somehow Mary was in touch with other Christian underground elements far beyond the knowledge of the four. The black chips could be used by anyone, and all intrusive features, including tracking and recording, had been disabled. These chips were the holy grail of freedom within a system that tracked and recorded everything about its citizens.

Once in Brazil, they were to grab an aero taxi to ring five. There they would tell the aero cabbie to go to Chinatown to the East Asian Mall. It was a huge pavilion surrounded by shops and restaurants. In the square they were to go to the Seven-Seven-Seven Lucky Duck Restaurant. They were to ask the server for back table number twelve. They were given several phrases to say to get to their contact. Of course, it sounded simple. Mary stressed the need to take their time in transit, meander around, and look for tails. Above all, they must look and act normal. Very easy words, but the application seemed much more difficult.

The aero cabbie was set to pick them up the next morning at eight o'clock. They were to bring only one backpack each; they would purchase necessities as needed. There was sheer anticipation in the air that evening because the next morning their lives would change forever. No notices would be given to their employers. Matt, John, Christie, and Sara would just disappear. After a few days, they would become missing persons. They would probably be labeled as fugitives by the Authority at some point, and their identities would be put on a wanted list. After tomorrow, there was no turning back.

CHAPTER 16

Escaping the South America Ring Kingdom (The Detectives)

Dom and Jack were at the end of the corridor at the back recesses of the East Asian Mall. To get to their contact, Crypto Casanova, they had to go through the open steel door. Beyond the door was darkness. They heard not a sound from the interior. Jack looked at Dom, who just shrugged his shoulders. The duo had come this far; there was no turning back at this point. "Come on, Jack. Let's get this over with," Dom said. "Looks like our new friend, Crypto, has the same flair for drama as Fast Eddie."

That got a laugh from the video dot on the outside wall. Dom's and Jack's heads rumbled with Fast Eddie's laughter as well. That helped at least to ease their tension about walking into the dark void. After they crossed the threshold, the steel doors closed silently and rapidly behind them leaving Dom and Jack completely in the dark. It remained a dark void for a few seconds—enough time for their pupils to dilate larger so they could take advantage of any light. Then, without notice or sound, the entire hallway lit up with light of blinding intensity made even more intense by the white walls of the corridor.

"Aggh! My eyes!" Jack yelled. "Dom, what is going on?"

Dom tried to shield his eyes as well from the sudden blast of light. As they squinted their eyes and looked forward they saw shapes emerge—several large men and one slim but very fit man, all in classy all-black shirts and slacks. They were all wearing dark glasses, and their intent became clear. That was a great way to ensure safety. With Dom and Jack blinded by the sudden onslaught of bright lights, there was no way for them to ambush anyone. The men stepped forward, picked up the duo's duffle bags, and searched them for weapons as the two detectives stumbled around, still trying to get their bearings. This Crypto character understood security well. Crypto's guards, satisfied that they had all the weapons, returned to stand behind the slim man. The well-dressed man approached. "Pardon the need for that, gentlemen, but you must allow me to make sure of my safety. There are a lot of unsavory characters in this world, and especially in our ring five. It rarely gets tougher than these areas."

Rubbing his eyes, Dom looked toward the slim man. "That's a good security measure, Crypto. We do appreciate your measures for your protection as well as ours. I'd say that Jack and I are in good hands with you."

Crypto made a show of making a slight bow. "Thanks. And, yes, you are correct. I am Crypto. May I get your names again?"

"I'm Dom, and this character next to me is Jack."

Crypto waited. Dom wasn't going to offer any more information. After a few seconds of silence, Crypto spoke up. "Well then, let's get on with your adventure. Come with us, and we'll go to my command center to talk about your needs." He abruptly turned around and headed down the hall. The duo followed, and the guards brought up the rear. It was a long and narrow hallway with no doors. At the end—some two hundred feet or more—there was a T intersection. It appeared there was only one way in or out, using the long narrow corridor. Without any rooms to break into, anyone caught in the long corridor would be easy pickings. No hiding places. Turning the corner to the left of the T intersection, they encountered another large steel door. Looking back to the other end of the T cross, they saw a dead end with no door.

Crypto punched a code into a keypad, and the steel door immediately opened to a room that was about thirty feet square, a decent size for a command center. The far wall was filled with video screens showing aerial views of the South America rings three through six. A series of work desks and monitors faced the video wall. In the center of the room was a large rectangular table with a clear screen surface. A few people sat on chairs. They were holding clear pad devices that connected to the table screen, which was also a holographic projector that allowed images to hover over the table. They seemed to be looking at maps of some small ring city. But that ringed city looked nothing like a typical six-ring kingdom system. There were only two rings—a very small inner ring and a massive outer ring.

Crypto motioned Dom and Jack to the table, which was not necessary because their curiosity about the holographic image of the strange ring city drew them to it anyway.

As the detectives came up to the table, Crypto, asked the lady who was manipulating the three-dimensional image, "What is the date of the image, Kayla?"

"Mr. C, we're looking at an image that is approximately ten years old. We found this in our research from the big download event."

Dom and Jack were confused. Jack asked, "The big download event?"

Crypto gave a small laugh. "That's what we call the data heist we made five years ago from a data center in the second ring. We found an inside man who was willing to help for a large payday, and we were able to siphon a massive amount of information out of the ring-two main data center. We 'found' so much data that I've had Kayla and two others sifting through and organizing it for the past five years, and we are only twenty percent through it all. As an information broker, this has been my most profitable venture to date by far. Selling information can be quite lucrative. Take you two, for example. Your benefactor in your head, Fast Eddie, paid handsomely for this information."

Dom said, "Crypto, I'm still confused. Jack and I need to get to the Wilborada 1047 bookstore in Bogotá, Columbia. From aerials that Fast Eddie showed us, we know that the bookstore is located in an old abandoned town in the suburbs. It's not in some strange-looking ring city."

The hovering image of the two-ringed city looked like something out of Dante's "Inferno." Both detectives had seen various paintings inspired by the poem. There was a small gleaming inner ring surrounded by massive fortified walls. The large second ring contained a sprawling mass of old buildings, fortified wall encampments, and factories that appeared to belch out black smoke from huge stacks. Spread in a haphazard layout were massive industrial buildings and plots of farming land. The entire area reminded Dom of an old Jason Pollack painting: sheer chaos. The voice of Eddie in Jack's and Dom's heads exclaimed, "What a strange place! I thought the fifth ring of the South America Ring Kingdom was the bottom of the pit, but this place takes it to the next level." The voice of Eddie also came out of Dom's hand device so Crypto and others could hear him.

Crypto said, "Hey, great to have you on this mission, my friend. Still living vicariously through others, I see. I was wondering if you were with these two on their one-way mission."

The voice from Dom's device laughed. "You bet, Crypto. How do you think I've lived so long and yet had the opportunity to go on such great adventures! And this one is by far the best of all. It has everything—danger, intrigue, journeys to far-off forbidden lands, and clandestine meetings with seedy characters!"

"Hey, there! Wait a minute, Eddie. Just who are you calling seedy characters?"

"Wooohhaaaa!" Erupted in the room from everyone.

Eddie replied, "The only thing I miss is sitting down for a few drinks with you, my friend."

"Yes, indeed, Eddie. I hear you on that one. Yes indeed." Crypto turned back to gaze at the three-dimension image of the vast, sprawling ring from hades. "Gentlemen, you are looking at your next destination along the way to your bookstore. What you have hovering in front of you is the Venezuelan Post. It is the nearest post to Columbia and the only place where you will be able to find a terrain vehicle to get you to your final destination."

Jack spoke up. "Crypto, why can't we take an aero vehicle from here or from the Venezuelan Post to Bogotá? That would make it so much easier and faster than trying to traverse all the way using a land vehicle."

"Good question, Jack. There are several reasons. First, from here to Bogotá is over four thousand seven hundred miles—too far for you two to travel in an aero vehicle large enough to make the trip without getting caught by the Authority's sensors. Although they are limited outside the ring kingdoms, the Authority maintains some monitoring stations as well as patrols. Using a land vehicle from here to Bogotá isn't feasible due to the distance and terrain as well. From the Venezuelan Post to Bogotá is nine hundred miles at most. That's a short enough range for a smaller sized aero vehicle, but all around the Venezuelan Post there are Authority sensors watching the airspace. The only way to get there safely is to use a land vehicle."

Dom asked in curiosity, "Tell me, Crypto, why are there authority sensors outside of the ring kingdoms and the posts? Are they concerned about runners trying to escape to avoid retirement at age forty-four?"

"That's what we thought at first too, Dom. However, the regularity and number of patrols and sensors in close proximity to the ring kingdoms as well as the size of the post military compounds suggest other concerns. Take a look at the Venezuelan Post, for example." Crypto pointed to the holographic image of the post. "At the edge of the outer ring, see how tall and thick the walls are? There are also huge military-type encampments, vehicles, and storage facilities near the perimeter wall at regular intervals. On the walls themselves there are lookout towers every several hundred feet fitted with weapons."

Dom had a realization. "They are concerned about invading forces from the outside!"

"Exactly, Dom! Regardless of what we have been taught—that there was no life left on Earth after the Great Conflict except within our ring kingdoms and posts—there is obviously something or someone out there. And a lot of them."

Jack retorted nervously, "So, if by sheer luck and good fortune, we make it from here to the Venezuelan Post, will we be able to hook up with another 'character,' acquire a land vehicle, and somehow make it through the Authority's security net and escape the post? That's the easy part. Then we'll have to contend with mutant creatures from hades for nine hundred miles to Bogotá?"

"Whoooa!" The voice of Fast Eddie crackled from Dom's hand-held device. "Looks like I bought myself the adventure of a lifetime! Dom and Jack, thanks for this. Consider anything you need along your journey on me!"

Dom jumped in. "Thanks, Eddie. So glad to hear your enthusiasm for our trip. I wish you were here in person to share the fun with us."

Smiles and laughter erupted around the room. Crypto, all smiles, turned to face the duo. "Well then, gents, it looks like we'll be able to kit you out right for your journey compliments of the host in your head!" Crypto rubbed his hands together savoring the payday and the challenge. "Yes, yes. I'll work with my team to get a plan together for you. It will take another day or so to get the pieces and people in place. Our place here is a one-stop shop. Not only do we work here, but the crew and I also live here. We have full living quarters with kitchens as well as a central kitchen and a dining area for those who want to cook and eat together. We also keep several free apartments for our guests. Jason here will see you two to your rooms. Feel free to shower, rest, unwind, and explore our little community."

Crypto handed small wrist bands to Dom and Jack. "Wear these at all times. They're both communicators and tracking devices. We all wear one. It is highly encrypted and allows internal communication within our area only. Just say a person's name and you will be patched into them. If you don't know the name, say what they do or what they look like. Our recognition algorithms will find the person you're looking for. In case of emergency, the band also allows us to track and organize everyone. We've been raided a few times by the Authority, and the trackers were life savers because they enabled us to quickly organize and escape."

Dom replied with genuine appreciation, "Amazing, Crypto. The more we learn about you and your team the more impressed I am. You all take security to the next level."

Crypto gave a slight bow of his head. "Thank you, Dom. We are a small group and consider everyone here family. Make no mistake, the South America Ring Kingdom is a dangerous place, and our business is equally dangerous. No matter how careful we are, we lose people every year. That is a fact of life here in the South America fifth ring."

With that grim note, the security muscle man, Jason, turned to Dom and Jack and started walking across the room to a back door. Stopping short of the door, he turned to the duo. "Your wrist bands also serve to access all authorized doors in our facility. Wave the wrist band near the keypad, and the door will open. If it doesn't, then you don't have access. Yours are coded to your rooms, the kitchen and dining area, open community break rooms, as well as this command center. In case of an emergency, your wrist bands will illuminate and an arrow will point you in the direction you need to go for an emergency exit. Follow your band, and specific doors will open for your escape."

Dom was in awe. "Crypto thinks of everything."

Jason replied as the door silently opened and they walked down a dimly lit corridor. "All of these measures have been developed over the years from hard lessons learned."

Dom and Jack were assigned adjoining quarters that were fairly large. Each had a separate bedroom, bathroom, and a small living area with a dining table and a small kitchen. Anyone could live there for an extended time very comfortably. Their duffle bags were in their rooms on their beds. Dom opened his to see if everything was there. All weapons and gear were accounted for. They had passed Crypto's security check, no doubt aided by their close relationship with Fast Eddie.

A voice came over Dom's wrist band. It was Jack. "Hey, Dom, some pretty nice digs here. Crypto sure knows how to treat his guests."

"That would be paying guests, gents." The voice of Eddie sounded in their heads.

Jack responded, "But of course, Eddie. Thanks for your support, Eddie. Now, gents, if you would excuse me, I think I'll shower and take a nap for a few hours."

Sounds like a great idea, Jack," Dom responded. "Let's set our alarms to meet up in about three hours. Call me when you're ready, and we'll head out together to find the community kitchen area."

"Sounds good to me, Dom." With that it was time for a shower and some rest.

"What is that?" Dom moaned realizing he had been more tired than he thought. An alarm was sounding. The hours of rest had passed in a blink. After showering and getting ready, Dom heard Jack's voice on his wrist band. "Hey, Dom. Will be at your door in ten minutes."

"Okay, Jack. Take your time. I'm getting too old for this adventure stuff."

"Well, look on the bright side, Dom. This is our last one no matter what. Do or die time, my friend."

Dom replied, "I'd kill for a cup of coffee right now, Jack."

Jack chuckled. "See you in ten, Dom."

Ten minutes later, as they were walking down the hall, Dom asked, "Jack, how are we supposed to find the main kitchen area?"

"Good question. Let's see how smart this wrist band is." Holding up the band just a bit closer to his mouth, Jack commanded, "Show us the way to the main kitchen." Nothing. Then, a second later, Jack's band lit up with an arrow pointed straight ahead. They followed it to a T intersection, and the band pointed to the right. When they had walked about fifty feet along the corridor, the arrow disappeared, and a green circle materialized as they approached a door to their right. Dom passed his wrist band near the door keypad, and the door opened to a large room bathed in soft lighting. There were several people there eating at tables. The kitchen area was very impressive. Two figures who appeared to be androids were busy working away at the stove area. As they approached, one of the androids, whose gold steel skin gleamed, looked their way. "Greetings, Mr. Dom and Mr. Jack. What would you like to eat? We serve anything and everything from breakfast, lunch, or a full three-course dinner."

Dom replied immediately with enthusiasm, "I'll take a couple of scrambled eggs, bacon, sausage, and toasted bread with butter please. And a big cup of hot black coffee."

"Right away, Mr. Dom. And you, sir, Mr. Jack? What would you like to have?"

"I like the way Dom thinks. Give me the same."

The Android's mechanical face made a weird-looking smile, and the machine turned to prepare their food. "Have a seat anywhere, and we will bring your food when it is ready."

It was a big room, and the tables were comfortably spread out so that conversations remained private. No one really bothered to look at Dom and Jack. The two were paying clients, and the staff respected their privacy.

"I've got to say, Jack, this is a comfortable place. Wouldn't mind staying here a while before our adventure continues. Safety combined with comfort is hard to beat."

"You said it, Dom. I feel the same way. Like you said, we aren't spring chickens anymore."

A silver metaled android came over a minute later to deliver two steaming hot cups of coffee. As they sipped their coffees in bliss, Dom's wrist vibrated, and then a voice crackled to life. It was Crypto. "I hope you and Jack had some good rest. You're going to need it."

"Thanks for the cheery conversation, Crypto. Jack and I are in the dining area about to eat."

"Great! Take your time. Afterwards, head on over to the command center where we were looking at the post earlier. We've got your next moves about solidified. Just a few more tweaks and we'll have your itinerary completed."

"Okay, Crypto. Thanks. We'll see you in a bit. Jack, let's take our time and eat. I think this is the last chance we'll have for a good meal."

An hour later, Dom and Jack were in the command center. The table in the center of the room where they had examined the holographic image of the Venezuelan Post was gone, and in its place was a three-dimensional map of the South America Ring Kingdom. Crypto waved his hands to zoom in and around the image. "Dom and Jack, take a look here." Zooming into ring two, Crypto moved the image to an underground transport tube that started in the South America ring two and headed north.

Jack said, "That's definitely not the Transit Tube we came in on from the Middle East Ring Kingdom. For one thing, all the Transit Tubes I know of start and end in ring three not ring two."

Dom chimed in, "And look how small that system is. It looks like a quarter the size of a normal Transit Tube."

Crypto nodded his head. "Very observant, you two. This is how the Authority has access to the posts. In every ring kingdom, there is a small Transit Tube that connects ring two to the nearest post. We speculate that they are much smaller for several reasons. One, not much traffic ever goes in or out of a post. Two, the small size reduces the ability of an invading force to use the tube to invade the ring kingdom." A chill ran up Dom's spine—and Jack's too—just thinking of what could be able to survive outside of the protected dome kingdoms.

"So, Crypto," began Dom, turning to face him, "you've found a way for us to get into ring two and then catch a ride on the TT to the Venezuelan Post?"

That got a laugh out of Crypto. "No. No, my friends." You know as well as I do that no one is allowed from the outer rings to the two inner rings. And, certainly, there is no such thing as a ticket to a post. Only the most senior Authority officials are allowed to use the ring-two TTs to the posts."

Dom asked, "Okay, Crypto, I give up. How in the world are we to get to the Venezuelan Post? Walk?"

"That is one option." Crypto rubbed his chin and smiled. "But we have a much more elegant and efficient way to get you passage." Crypto then continued to zoom into the entrance area of two TTs in the small ring. "You see here that the TT has an inner tube and an outer tube. The outer tube contains all the power, ventilation, and other utilities needed to run the inner TT. In the outer tube, there is a guideway that houses a maintenance cart that travels alongside the tube the entire way to allow workers to maintain and service the tube. We just happen to know the two people who work on the service tube cart, and they are due to go out tonight to fix a problem circuit in the tube that is located about ten miles from the Venezuelan Post."

Dom asked, "Crypto, why wouldn't a service crew from the Venezuelan Post go out and fix the problem if it's so close to the post?"

Crypto turned to look directly at Dom. "For security purposes, the Authority limits the qualified service crews to two crews of two people—one crew of two from the South America Ring Kingdom and one crew of two from the Venezuelan Post. Unfortunately, this morning there was an accident, and the two crew members of the Venezuelan Post were killed. It will take them a month to find replacements."

"Well," Dom replied, looking straight at Crypto's cold dark eyes, "their misfortune is our lucky break."

"Can't ask for more perfect timing," Jack murmured to himself.

Crypto moved along. "We'll sneak you two into ring two through a tunnel we dug at the border between rings two and three. Our two service men will meet you at the tunnel exit. They have a full kit in their service vehicle that will enable you two to disguise yourselves as maintenance men. Once in your disguise, you four will make your way to the outer tube service cart, and off you'll go. Easy, huh?"

"Sure. But somehow I don't think it will be that easy," Dom replied.

Crypto continued, "Of course there are some risks. The temperature in the outer tube is over a hundred degrees. And did I mention there is no air? The outer tube is a vacuum. You will have to wear environmental suits and carry oxygen packs to access the service cart."

Jack rubbed his forehead in dismay. "Wonderful, Crypto. I knew it couldn't be that easy. Any other good news? How reliable is this service cart?"

Crypto hesitated before responding. "The service cart and the tube utilities are over four hundred years old. They say a service call has an eighty percent chance of success."

Jack was exasperated. "You mean twenty percent of the time a crew will go out and not come back?"

Crypto just nodded his head. "That's the game, gentlemen. This current crew has been working for over a year without a fatal incident. I sure hope luck is on your side."

The voice in Dom and Jack's heads and on Dom's hand device came to life. Fast Eddie again. "My, my, gents, this is truly exciting! I can hardly wait!"

"Yes, we feel the same enthusiasm you do, Eddie," Dom replied with very little enthusiasm in his voice.

CHAPTER 17

Following the Trail
(The Authority Three)

I t was nine in the morning when Hector and Jackson arrived at
the security building to execute the plan Saul had given them
the night before. Out of the information they had gathered
over the last few days, the only lead they had left was a clean image
of the two detectives who had been at the morgue—Simon (Dom)
Halos and Jack O' Leary. Hector and Jackson were to meet up with
the Authority lead security manager, Gal, to see if he could run a
trace on where Dom and Jack had gone the night they escaped from
the hospital. Meanwhile, Saul was going to snoop around the police
precinct where Dom and Jack worked to see what information he
could dig up on the whereabouts of the two detectives.

Gal met Hector and Jackson at the main entrance security desk
as he had met Saul the other day. Gal was intrigued by the thought
of chasing down two Authority detectives. "Gents, what did these
two detectives do that warrants our trying to find them? Are they
missing in action from one of their assignments or did they go absent
without leave? What are you going to do when you find them? If
they are AWOL and you need to terminate them, let me know. We
can do it remotely with one of our cyber drones." Just the thought

of a kill operation raised the tone of Gal's voice. It looked as if he was going to go into a spasm, he got so excited.

Jackson and Hector looked at each other briefly, and Jackson replied. "For now, this is just a routine enquiry. We just want to make sure they are okay. As you know, the other day, our boss, Saul, was looking for two medical examiners. Our two detectives were at the hospital with them, and then afterwards they didn't check in. We just want to make sure they are okay."

Gal looked a bit dejected when Jackson mentioned the two medical examiners because he had not been able to help in identifying or tracing them. Recovering from the thought, he replied, "But of course. We want to make sure our brothers in arms are all right. These are strange times, and we are seeing more and more unrest among the people. It's not unusual anymore to hear of Authority police disappearing. This morning four Authority police officers were taken out by a band of thieves in our industrial district. The unusual thing is that, normally, we get the call to hunt down the killers and wipe them out as well as their families, friends, and even beyond to serve as a lesson to others who might contemplate messing with the Authority. But no call came from the inner ring. It's as if the Authority leadership is preoccupied with other matters. This will make our job of maintaining security a lot harder. I'm glad to see you two are concerned about our fellow officers. If we find them and they are in trouble, we'd be more than happy to help launch a rescue mission."

Hector and Jackson took his offer into consideration. No doubt Gal seemed more than willing to kill anyone and everyone involved. Such was the man they had to deal with to help get them information. Hector jumped in this time. "Gal, we really appreciate your support. We'd be mighty glad to enlist your support for a rescue mission if it's needed."

Gal's glum demeanor perked up again at the prospect. "Of course. Of course. We are here to help in any way we can. Let's go to the control room and start looking for your friends at once." He hurried off, and Jackson and Hector had to nearly run to keep up with Gal.

Upon entering the security command center, both Hector and Jackson were taken aback by the sheer size of the room. The high ceiling accommodated massive sets of screens on which hundreds of scenes throughout the city were laid over a detailed map of ring four. "Amazing, Gal," Jackson noted. "You have a state-of-the-art facility here—the best I've ever seen."

Hector said, "I totally agree with you, Jackson." He did a three-sixty turn to take it all in.

Gall beamed and replied, "Thanks, gents. We pride ourselves in our ability to keep track of everything that goes on in our ring. Well, mostly of course. If one does not want to be seen, it is easy to hide in our massive ring system."

Jackson whispered to Gal, "Gal, as our boss mentioned the other day, this is a highly sensitive operation. Minimal eyes only."

"Oh, yes, of course. I remember. Thanks for reminding me, Jackson." With that, Gal cleared the room except for Drusilla, the same desk jockey who had helped when Saul had visited. Gal said with appreciation, "Dru is our best technician. She can find anyone anytime anywhere. She is a master of our security technology systems and also is extremely loyal."

Moving to the row of desks in front of the video wall, Gal called to Dru who was sitting at one of the desks. "Our friends here are looking for video feeds of that same hospital we looked at yesterday."

Dru enquired, "Same time and area of the hospital?"

"The same," Gal replied. "Those two authority officers we viewed—we need to see where they went after they left the hospital."

Dru clicked and swiped furiously at her clear screen monitor. After about a minute, the large map on the wall enlarged, showing an aerial view of the rear of the hospital. "Go three-D," commanded Gal.

"Yes, sir." After Dru executed a few more swipes and strokes on the monitor, the image popped out of the wall and hovered in front of them. It then twisted and turned until they had a three-dimensional image of the alley at the back of the hospital. They watched as two shapes—Dom and Jack—ran out of the back of the hospital loading dock and got into a sleek-looking authority aero car that had been hidden in the dark alley.

"Follow the aero car." Gal sounded excited and his voice grew high anticipating the chase. Dru clicked more, and as the aero car took off, they followed the detectives' journey with various camera views as the aero car rounded the corner and shot down the street.

"Adding the tracer," the desk jockey noted. The aero care lit up with a glowing red dot.

Gal spoke as if narrating a movie scene: "The red dot represents a transponder that all Authority aero cars are equipped with. It allows for tracking in all weather, situations, and conditions." They stood with rapt attention watching the three-dimensional image as followed the aero car weaving down the streets. It was like a car chase. Dom and Jack's aero car dipped and turned at high speed. When it came up to a long underpass, the aero car dipped down and went into the tunnel. It was dark, but the video feed remained on the aero car's tail, thankfully, due to the transponder red light.

"No low vision video in the tunnels?" Jackson asked.

Gal grimaced. "We had infra-red, low light, and even radar devices in our tunnels, but bandits kept breaking them, and we can't afford to replace them anymore. So, we've got certain dead zone areas. This tunnel is one of them." Just as he finished talking, the red dot disappeared in the darkness of the tunnel. Gal exploded. "We lost them!"

Hector blurted, "What happened?" Everyone looked harder into the dark void to see if they could see anything.

Gal said with exasperation, "Either they turned off the transponder themselves or they were captured and someone else who knows their way around an Authority aero car turned it off. The kill switch is a closely guarded secret for obvious reasons. So, either we've just seen an inside kidnapping job or our two friends have decided to jump to the other side of the law."

The desk jockey expanded the view so they could see an aerial of the entire area showing the entrance and exit of the tunnel. She clicked and swiped more. After a few minutes, the image in front of them moved to all views and fast-forwarded in time. "There!" she shouted. About four blocks away and a half hour later, an aero car matching the ID of the detectives' car appeared out of a building garage. Dru said with satisfaction, "These tunnel systems connect to various building systems underground. If you are patient enough and know how these systems interconnect, you will eventually find them escaping. They can't hide forever."

Gal exclaimed, "Okay! Great! Keep the trace on the aero car, and don't lose them again!" Gal gave Dru a high five hand slap.

"Will do, boss." She continued to work her hands at lightning speed on her terminal screen, and the two-dimensional aerial image danced, zooming in and out as other more detailed street scenes popped up to either side of the aerial map. Gal, Hector, and Jackson watched in rapt attention as Dru worked hard to keep up with the zigzagging movements of the aero car. Obviously, the detectives were looking for tails and trying to avoid the cameras so no one could do what they were now attempting to do—follow them using the ring security system. "These guys are good whoever they are," Dru remarked as she moved her hands on the screen trying to keep up with the aero car. Finally, the dizzying video screen images settled down, and they were staring at an aerial view of the aero car hovering in a darkened street with a large warehouse in front of them. It was an old beat-up building with a red brick exterior—the same as all the other warehouses except for a huge door like that of an aircraft hangar door that extended from the ground level to the roof of the warehouse. As she fast-forwarded the feed, they watched the metal door open and the aero car enter. They fast-forwarded the feed a few hours, but there was no further activity in or out of the building.

Gal motioned to Dru. "Get an identification on the warehouse company and owner's name." The screen in front of them changed to a series of documents as the desk jockey worked her monitor screen. "There it is," she remarked as a file popped up showing the company name, "Middle Eastern Imports/Exports. The owner's name is Bin Laden."

"Where have I heard that name before?" mused Gal. "No matter. I'm sure it's a fake name and a fake company. Continue to monitor the video feeds. They will have to make a move sooner or later. Gents, we'll get you the current movements of our two detectives."

Jackson said, "Great news! Thanks, Gal and Dru. Saul will be very pleased." That got big smiles from Gal and Dru.

"Come on to the back of our shop," Gal said, leading the way. "You two can rest and plan your next move while we locate your two detectives for you."

Hector enquired, "Thanks, Gal. Do you have coffee?"

"We have a full stock of drinks and food. Whatever you need." And with that, the head security officer ushered them into a spacious room that adjoined the command center.

About two hours later, Gal entered the back area room to find Jackson and Hector huddled together at a table tapping away at their clear pad devices. "Gentlemen, we have established all we can on the trace of the two detectives."

Jackson and Hector quickly stowed their devices and followed Gal back to the command center. Dru was there at the desk feverously swiping and typing away at her screen. As they walked up behind her, she spoke without turning away from her screen. "I've just finished compiling all the data feeds into a continuous stream. The data runs over a period of five days from the night the aero car entered the warehouse." The screen in front of them went from three dimensions back to two dimensions. The aero car hovered in the darkened street and then entered the warehouse. There was a date and time indicator on the bottom of the screen. The video fast-forward to the next day. At about noon, the aero car reappeared exiting the warehouse. It took its time traveling in heavy traffic to the outskirts of ring four. There it stopped at a rundown motel. The feed fast-forwarded two days, and the aero car once again took off in early evening and went to an old fire station at the edge of the fourth ring. About a half an hour later, all emergency vehicles shot out of the fire station. Dru narrated, "While the two detectives were at the fire station, there were a couple of major emergencies just minutes apart. One of the emergencies was a radiation incident alert from one of the old nuclear plants, and it just so happened that the special radiation team is located at that fire station."

"Interesting coincidence," Jackson mentioned, rubbing his chin. A few minutes later, after all the fire station vehicles departed, two figures emerged from the fire station hauling a bunch of duffle bags slung over their shoulders. They got into the aero car and departed swiftly. It returned to the same warehouse in ring five. The video feed continued in fast-forward speed up to the present time without the aero car leaving the warehouse. Transport trucks went in and out of the warehouse, which didn't seem unusual as it was an import/export business.

Hector asked, "So, our detectives took something from the fire station and went back to the warehouse and never left?"

"So, it appears," Gal replied.

Dru keyed up a feed from their tracking while talking. "I did come across this. The day after the aero car went into the warehouse, another aero car left. It's definitely not the same aero car, but there is an angle shot of two men in the car. I followed the aero car to ring three where it stopped at a motel near the TT."

"Whoa!" Hector exclaimed. "A ring-three motel near the TT must be pretty pricy." The aerial video image fast-forwarded again, and the next day the aero car left the motel for a quick trip to the TT. The time stamp on the video screen indicated that was one day ago. Dru typed and swiped her hands on the screen, and various views of the aero car and its occupants were on visual. The TT area had far better surveillance coverage, especially because it was in ring three. The two men got out of the aero car and were met by another man.

"Looks like they are passing off the aero car," Jackson said. As they continued to watch various angles, they saw the two men go to the TT station entrance as the other man flew away in their aero car. One camera had a good angle on the two men, and it zoomed in. It certainly didn't look like the two clean-shaven detectives with military-style short haircuts. The men had long hair and full beards. They wore earrings, and even their brown skin color was different than the light skin of the detectives. But their height and build matched the profile of the two detectives.

The video feed followed the two men to a ticket counter. Hector asked, "Where are they going?"

But the screen in front of them was already changing. It flashed a side screen showing the ticket terminal screen view. Gal replied, "They bought first-class tickets to the South America Ring Kingdom."

Jackson exclaimed, "Why on earth would they go to that dump of a ring kingdom? It's the armpit of the world."

Gal replied, "If you were running away, what better ring kingdom to get lost in?"

Hector nodded his head. "Good point."

Jackson asked Gal and Dru, "How certain can we be that these two men are, in fact, our renegade detectives?" The desk jockey continued to click on her screen and multiple images of the two clean-cut detectives appeared. These new images flashed on the screen beside the scruffy characters. Then the images melded together. A complex analysis of the combined images continued, and a percentage of probably went from zero percent rising to eighty-five percent and continued to tick upward stopping a few seconds later. "A ninety percent probably of a match," Dru concluded.

Gal did some calculations in his head. "If they took that high-speed TT, they would have made it to the South America Ring Kingdom by today."

Hector replied with frustration, "So, they are lost in the South America Ring Kingdom already. Ugh!"

Gal continued, "All is not lost. We know where they went. We have some contacts with the security officers in that kingdom, and we will see if they can follow their trail. Of course, nothing comes for free in that kingdom." Gal looked directly at Jackson and Hector, and they got the meaning. They would need some grease before they could get any information in the South America Ring Kingdom, and the grease would be in the form of lots of credits.

Jackson and Hector called Saul to relay the good news and bad news. They felt it was a high probability that they had found and tracked the two detectives, Simon Halos and Jack O'Leary. The bad news was that the trail currently ended at the South America Ring Kingdom.

"Good work, you two," Saul replied to the news. "Let's work on two fronts. First, we'll pay a visit to the warehouse and see what's inside. Ask our friend Gal if we could do this in a low-profile way— just ourselves and a couple of his men for back up. Second, we'll need a plan for a trip to the South America Ring Kingdom."

"We're going there?" asked Hector in a bit of a shaky voice.

"It's the only way," Saul returned. "Without the detectives, we have nothing. You know what nothing means in the eyes of our masters."

"You don't have to say it," Jackson whispered. "Failure is not an option to the Authority. Okay, we're going to the South America Ring Kingdom." Hector nodded his head.

"Good," Saul confirmed.

Four hours later Hector, Jackson, and Saul were in an aero car hovering in the same dark street that Hector and Jackson had seen at the security office earlier in the day. The old red brick warehouse with the large hangar door was about two hundred feet in front of them. A crackle came over the aero car communication system. It was Gal. "Our video feed shows no movement for the last few hours in or out of the warehouse. A bit unusual. Be careful. They may suspect we're onto them."

Saul said, "Let's do this quickly to gain as much surprise advantage as we can." He then called the other aero car that was beside them, which was transporting four operatives from Gal's security detachment. "On my word, move forward at high speed. Use your blasters to rip open the hangar door. We'll be right behind you. Remember—we need people alive to interrogate. Once we're in, move rapidly on foot and set your blasters to stun."

"Roger that!" came the reply from the other aero car.

A few seconds later, Saul announced, "Okay get ready." Then he shouted "Go! Go!" The aero cars streaked at high speed down the dark street. Two laser-like beams shot out from the lead aero car, and the hangar doors erupted in a huge explosion that blew them away in a red fireball. The aero cars raced inside and stopped toward the back of the cavernous warehouse interior near the dock area. Four operatives immediately jumped out of the lead aero car and ran to the back near the elevated dock and vault-like door that was off to the side. Saul, Hector, and Jackson were right behind them. Stopping at the foot of the elevated dock, they used the raised platform as a shield in case anyone came rushing out of the vault-like door. Just silence. No one was in the warehouse area, and no one came rushing out of the door. Saul whispered to Hector and Jackson, "I have a bad feeling that we missed the party." Keying the communicator strapped to the front of his vest, Saul commanded to the operatives, "Blow the door." One of the operatives stood up from the dock area, shouldered a massive blaster rifle, and fired. The vault door erupted and blew out nearly taking out Saul, Hector, and Jackson with it.

"Man, that's one big blaster!" Hector shouted over the deafening explosion. With the door on the ground next to them, the four operatives ran through the opening with the trio in close pursuit behind.

It was hard to see with all the smoke in the room, but it was clear that they were too late. The entire area had been wiped clean. Just empty rooms. The operatives moved forward to search all the other offices while Saul relayed to Gal that the area was clean. They'd been too late. Time to launch the next phase of the plan. Onto the South America Ring Kingdom.

CHAPTER 18

No Turning Back
(The Medical Examiners–
aka God's Quad Squad)

ohn, Matt, Sara, and Christie were up early the next morning eating breakfast by six thirty. As they were munching on their food, John recited the basics of the plan again to the team, but he was mainly saying it aloud so that he could remember it himself. "Our aero cab arrives at eight. It will take us straight to the ring-three TT. Using our fake ID chips and travel permits, we'll buy standard-class tickets to the South America Ring Kingdom. When we arrive, we'll get an aero taxi to the ring-five Chinatown to a restaurant called the Seven-Seven-Seven Lucky Duck Restaurant in the East Asian Mall. We'll ask the waiter for the back table number twelve. When we are seated, the waiter will serve us water. We will ask the waiter for the special plater twelve-twelve. He will say that's not on the menu, and we will reply, 'We preordered the twelve-twelve dish.'"

Just as John finished reciting the memorized plan, the doorbell rang. Christie went to the door. She checked the video monitor at the side of the door, but the hall was empty. She opened the door to find that someone had left a package on the doorstep. After quickly grabbing the package, she closed the door. "This must be our ID chips and travel permits," she said as she walked back to the dining table. She opened the package and distributed the contents.

Matt looked at his permit and chip. "I guess we're all set, then, for our journey. We'll have to commit our new names to memory." They all looked at their permits and announced their new names one by one so everyone could become familiar with at least their new first names.

Sara spoke up. "I don't remember what happens after we give the code phrase to the waiter."

John replied. "Mary didn't tell us what happens next. She just said to stay calm and go with the flow. Whatever that could mean."

Christie added, "Yeah, she mentioned that, above all, we must stay calm." That got a tense chuckle from the entire group. Christie continued. "We need a name for our team. You know all great adventure groups have names."

"Okay," John said. After thinking a bit, he said, "How about the Quad Squad?" That got good laughs.

Sara, getting into it, jumped in, "Okay. How about the GQS?" Everyone looked a bit confused. "Oh, come on, people. GQS— God's Quad Squad!"

"Yes! That's the one!" John replied. Everyone was all smiles.

"GQS it is then," Sara affirmed with a smile. Just then, the holographic Mary appeared at the table, and the GQS spent the next half hour in prayer with her.

The aero taxi was right on schedule at eight o'clock, and the four were ready to go, each carrying just a single backpack and a small duffle bag. Originally, they had been told they could take only a single backpack, but they had convinced Mary they also needed a small duffle bag so they could take some extra clothes and necessities. Mary reluctantly agreed but stipulated that they carry nothing of importance in the duffle bag. In an emergency, they would need to run at full speed, and lugging a duffle bag would slow them down. Each of them also wore a wrist band communicator that also served as a tracker so they could always find each other. It also could record and store data. They were able to upload the Mary hologram to each of the wrist bands so that she could be with them through the entire trip. Mary would also serve as a direct interface linking the four together in case of emergency or if they got separated.

It took a good part of the day to make it to the TT station in ring three. This was enough time for them to memorize all the cover identities. Everything was clicking like clockwork, and they had an easy time purchasing their tickets with no obvious suspicions on the part of the ticket agent or the guards at the station security checkpoints. On the train, they settled into their assigned seats. The train was configured like a standard-class train with a single central aisle and rows of double seats on each side. The team had chosen seats facing each other with a table between them. They felt it was important to stay together. Thankfully, it was not a full train, and the seats directly adjacent to them were all empty. There were a few other travelers in their car, but they were all several rows down. Nonetheless, they did not talk about anything of importance. "Walls have ears" was the motto everyone had grown up with. The Authority had eyes and ears everywhere to monitor all citizens. For the citizens' own protection, of course.

A voice came over a speaker announcing that the train was departing. Immediately, the foursome felt the force of acceleration as the train sped away from the terminal. They had just crossed the point of no return. As directed, they had not notified their employers of their absence. After a few days, they would become missing persons, and then labeled as fugitives by the Authority at some point. Their identities would be put on a wanted list. Everything was truly in the hands of the Lord now.

As the train gained speed, Mary sensed their unease and sang a song she had learned a long time ago. The group heard it through the micro earphones that had been embedded in their ears so they could communicate with each other and with Mary. Closing their eyes, all four listened to Mary's soft voice singing in a sweet country music tone "I Have Decided to Follow Jesus," which had been written long ago by Sadhu Sundar Singh:

> I have decided to follow Jesus;
> I have decided to follow Jesus;
> I have decided to follow Jesus;
> No turning back, no turning back.
> The world behind me, the cross before me;
> The world behind me, the cross before me;
> The world behind me, the cross before me;
> No turning back, no turning back.
> Though none go with me, still I will follow;
> Though none go with me, still I will follow;
> Though none go with me, still I will follow;
> No turning back, no turning back.
> My cross I'll carry, till I see Jesus;
> My cross I'll carry, till I see Jesus;
> My cross I'll carry, till I see Jesus;
> No turning back, no turning back.
> Will you decide now to follow Jesus?
> Will you decide now to follow Jesus?
> Will you decide now to follow Jesus?
> No turning back, no turning back.

The members of God's Quad Squad became lost in a moment of bliss as Mary's soothing voice encouraged them to get a bit of rest. This rest, which seemed like a few minutes but actually lasted for hours, was rudely interrupted by a loud siren-like shriek over the speakers. The blaring sound was followed by a prerecorded announcement that the train was approaching the Central Africa Ring Kingdom and would arrive in the next fifteen minutes. The high-speed TT rocketed along at a speed of just over seven hundred miles an hour making the 3,200-mile journey time from the Middle East Ring Kingdom in Baghdad in just under five hours.

Wiping the sleepiness from their eyes, John, Sara, Matt, and Christie took turns going the restroom to freshen up. They made sure that two of them always stayed with their backpacks and duffle bags at all times. A lot of things tended to walk away when left unguarded, and a train was no safer than the streets or restaurants or any other public place.

Once they transferred to another train, there would be no more checks until they arrived at their final destination. They had an hour to make the short, ten-minute walk to the platform where they would board the South America Ring Kingdom train. The key was not to look tense or suspicious. Easy enough said, but hard to do when they had the feeling of being absent without leave from work and knowing that soon they would be fugitives on the most dangerous mission of their lives—the Quest. As the foursome walked to the transfer train, a voice came over their earpieces. The soothing voice of Mary reassured them. "Just relax. You all have authorized permits and tickets. You are just normal travelers walking and looking for your connection. It's natural to look a bit uneasy and confused as you walk in the large transit station, but it is another thing to look paranoid and to look around too much. Relax. Jesus is with you."

Thankfully, there was a coffee shop where they could wait in sight of the platform and try to not look suspicious. There weren't many customers. John and Sara sat down with their gear as Matt and Christie went to order some coffee and pastries for the four of them. John made some tourist-type conversation with Sara. He looked at his clear hand-held screen device as he spoke. "There is so much to see in the South America Ring Kingdom. Such an exotic place."

"Yes, you are certainly right about that," Sara replied thinking to herself, *Well, I wouldn't say* exotic *is the right term.* Looking at her clear screen device all she could see on the "tourist" write-ups were a bunch of negative reviews about the kingdom. Reviewers referred to it as the armpit of society and the most dangerous place on Earth. And these were reviews from seasoned travelers who had been to all ten ring kingdoms. Sara continued, "Yes, the reviews say there are many very exciting places. Just read the vivid stories they tell! Sounds like an adventurous, once-in-a-lifetime trip." They looked at each other and had a hard time not laughing out loud because their conversation was so ridiculous.

"Now, now." The voice of Mary came over their communicators. "Let's not exaggerate your conversation too much. People may think you have lost your minds." She chuckled. "Nice to see you two still have your sense of humor. You will need it." That sobered John and Sara's mood back from laughter to reality.

Matt and Christie returned with cups of hot coffee and delicious-looking assortment of pastries. "Wwooooo! Yahh! Steaming hot coffee and pastries! You two are angels," Sara exclaimed as they sat down. The three of them just stared at Sara, giving her a slight frown and a lift of their eyebrows as a silent admonishment. Sara, realizing what she had said, covered her mouth. "Ooops. Sorry, guys." Her remark was returned with smiles. They all did it from time to time. Saying religious words such as *angel*, *God*, or other names was forbidden. Those types of words attracted attention from the ever-listening walls and super computers that received, logged, and analyzed all conversations. Key words attracted additional scrutiny—something they wanted to avoid now.

The four of them took a moment of silence before diving into their treats: a short, silent prayer. They had been taught to not speak or bow their heads in prayer in public. Instead, they thought their prayers in their minds—a short thank you to Jesus. Each prayed the short prayer that they had learned: "Lord, we thank you for this food before us. From your Word, all things come to be."

They shared a tranquil moment of bliss as they ate and drank. Sara told them of all the "exciting" things to see and do they had read about the South America Ring Kingdom. "Sounds like a real blast," Matt commented. "So glad you invited us on this trip."

He raised his hot cup of coffee up, and they all clanked cups together as John exclaimed, "To our adventure!" And, in their minds, they toasted "To our quest!"

About fifteen minutes later, the announcement came over the speakers that the South America Ring Kingdom train was arriving. After finishing up their snacks, the four headed back outside and waited on the platform. A loud siren blared as the train came shooting into the station. It was a good thing that the horn was blaring because the train itself was so fast and silent, no one would even know it was approaching. Levitated on magnets and powered by electricity, the train didn't make a sound as it approached. Standing on the platform, the travelers felt a gust of air as the approaching train pushed a huge volume of air in front of it in the tightly spaced tube as it neared the open platform area. This was called the piston effect. In the newer stations, there were ventilation shafts that absorbed this air. In the older stations, the platform served as a ventilation shaft. Anyone standing too close to the edge of the platform could be blown onto the tracks. Not a pleasant thought.

Boarding the train and finding their seats was easy. A chip embedded in their tickets was read and recorded as they boarded the train. Thankfully, their seats were arranged the same way their seats on the first part of their journey had been arranged—facing seats with a nice table in between them. Also, as it had been on the train from the Middle East Ring Kingdom, there were very few people around them. Several rows ahead of them sat two men in wrinkled suits looking a bit worse for the wear. Further down was a lone Chinese man hacking away at his screen, obviously a techie. All appeared to be normal, which enabled God's Quad Squad to relax a bit. Wearing casual clothes and carrying backpacks and duffle bags, they looked like a pair of couples on a quick tourist trip. As unlikely as it was for anyone to go to the dangerous South America Ring Kingdom for a vacation, its notorious reputation was known to draw adventure-seeking tourists once in a while. It was everyone for themselves, and most kept to a low profile, not wanting to draw any attention. Especially because those doing business in the South America Ring Kingdom often carried off-book, untraceable credit transaction–type work. This was even more reason for travelers—especially the GQS—to stay to themselves and away from the prying eyes and ears of the Authority and even fellow citizens.

The distance from the Central Africa Ring Kingdom in Nigeria to the South America Ring Kingdom in Brazil was approximately 3,700 miles, only a little longer than the first leg of their journey, which meant about the same amount of time—about five hours. With time to spare on the train, the foursome checked and repacked their backpacks and duffle bags, memorizing what they had brought and where they had stored each item for an easy grab, especially of the most important items in case of an emergency. This was one of Mary's many training drills. If they had only five seconds and had to leave their backpacks and duffle bags, they had to know where the most critical items were so they could grab them and run. Thankfully, most of what they absolutely needed they were wearing. Their wrist bands, which had team locators, communications, and Mary's artificial intelligence program, were stored away. They all had black chips glued onto the skin of their right wrists; they were packed with untraceable credits. It wasn't a lot of money, but enough to see them through the mission— about sixty days' worth of credits for meals, hotel rooms, local transportation, and a little extra for clothing and other sundry goods in case they lost their backpacks and duffle bags. They marveled at Mary's deep pool of resources. The black chips and a chip glue gadget had arrived the morning they departed along with their transit train travel permit papers, which were actually clear plastic wallet-sized cards with their names etched into the plastic. Mary had walked them though how to glue their chips onto their wrists.

The most important item in each of their backpacks was a small survival pack that would keep them alive for up to five days if they couldn't find sources of food or clean water. The pack also contained a small medical kit; all-weather, micro-thin protection overalls; and eyeglasses that enabled them to see in the dark. The eyeglasses were also linked to their mobile clear devices and could display locations and mapping. There was even a small one-hour oxygen canister with a mouthpiece and several micro explosive charges with enough blasting power to blow out locked doors. The survival pack, while comforting, was also a source of apprehension because they had to wonder why they would even need such items.

The hours passed as they took naps and read up on their next destination trying to memorize the layout of the South America Ring system and place-names. In case they got lost or separated, they designated a location in each of the rings where they would rendezvous; that would be rings three, four, or five. No information was available on the inner rings one and two, and it was highly unlikely that any of them would end up in ring six—the agricultural ring. For now, their contact was in ring five, and they spent most of the time trying to memorize the ring-five layout, knowing their very lives may depend on it.

When they finally arrived in the South America Ring Kingdom, John rallied the group. "Remember—stay close to each other, within eyesight at all times. If you lose sight, stop and call in with your wrist communicator, and then we can come for you using our locators."

"We are in the hands of Jesus," Sara whispered to the group.

She received a soft reply from the three others: "Amen."

Reaching the outer doors of the TT station, they stepped out into ring three. If they thought it would be at least somewhat similar to the Middle East ring three, they had a rude awaking. "Oh, man!" Matt blurted out as they breathed in the air. "This place smells like trash and burning fuel oil."

"Uuggh!" Christie chimed in. "And what is with the heat and humidity? Feels like they turned off all of the climate control systems."

"Welcome to the South America Ring Kingdom," Sara announced.

Matt followed up: "And this is ring three. Can't wait to see what ring five looks and smells like!" "Good thing we have that little backup oxygen canister in our survival pack," Matt mused, and everyone laughed.

John added "Yup, Matt, looks like we're going to need every bit of our gear. Let's head toward the street and hail an aero taxi." It was tough walking as there were people everywhere on the sidewalks maneuvering in all directions. The street area was just as congested with land vehicles and, just above them, low-flying aero cars. The ground vehicles belched out black smoke.

"Wow! Take a look at those land cars!" Christie pointed as they walked. "I thought they got rid of fossil fuel cars centuries ago. It's like going back in time."

Sara added as they all looked around in amazement, "Looks like we just stepped back in time hundreds of years. Incredible! If it weren't so dangerous a place, I can see the allure for travelers." The smog-belching old-style cars stood in sharp contrast to the gleaming mirrored high-rise buildings that lined the streets. The glass of the towering buildings was streaked with brown stains and mold from the humidity and the vehicle exhaust.

"It's a cool scene for sure," Matt noted. "But very dangerous. Let's keep our wits about us and stay close."

Stopping close to the curb, they waved their hands and hailed a low-flying aero taxi that looked big enough to carry the four of them, their backpacks, and their small duffle bags. The aero cab was a bit beaten up, and its color—probably once bright yellow—was a faded beige brown with some yellow on the parts that were not dented. When they clambered aboard, the cabbie asked them with an Asian accent, "Where you want go?"

John looked at the group and assumed an expression that implied, "At least he should know where to go! And then he told the cabbie, "Take us to ring-five Chinatown."

The cabbie shot back excitedly, "Oh, man, I just take white men this week to Chinatown. Big problems. Real dangerous. Going to cost you extra one hundred credits."

Sara heatedly responded, "That's robbery!"

The cabbie just said, "Look my car! All damage from ring five. Ring five dangerous. You no like, you find another cabbie. Maybe he not even take you."

John said with exasperation, "Okay, okay. One hundred credits no more."

The Chinese cabbie was all smiles. "Good. Good. Where in Chinatown you want go?"

John hesitated before answering. "Take us to the East Asian Mall."

They all thought the cabbie was going to have a heart attack! He mumbled a few phrases in Chinese. "Chinatown bad place! One of worst places in ring five. Men I pick up went to same East Asian Mall. Big gangs there. I almost get killed. Fifty more credits it cost you!" He then started to blabber on in Chinese.

Christie jumped in. "No way! That is highway robbery!"

John replied with defeat in his voice, "What else can we do? You heard him. He almost got killed there the other day."

"And you think he is telling the truth?"

"I don't know, Christie. But from his expression, it sure looks like he meant it."

Matt said in a low voice to John, "Okay. Just pay the man, and let's get on with it. We don't need to save the money for anything long term." He was right. They were now officially living moment to moment.

John turned his head back toward the cabbie. "Okay. Fifty more credits, and that's it. Not a single credit more."

"Good. Good." The cabbie shot back. "Relax. Ma will take you safe. Ma know the way." The cabbie immediately put the throttle down, and the cab shot upward. The massively tall, mirrored skyscrapers cast deep shadows into the narrow canyons of intersecting streets. At the edge of ring three, Ma dived back down to street level and entered a tunnel. All the while he narrated, "We take bypass tunnel. Avoid ring-four checkpoint. Tunnel go from ring three to the checkpoint at ring five. Ma know security man. No problems."

True to his word, Ma raced through the tube and exited right at a ring five checkpoint station. Ma slowed down but never completely stopped. The guard, another Chinese man, looked at Ma, and they clicked hands. Ma passed on a few credits as "express payment," and the cab slipped though into ring five.

The four got a glimpse of the grim scenery of ahead of them. It looked like a throwback to the twentieth century with no improvements made in the last four hundred years. The buildings were crumbling. There were some newer areas that stood out like sore thumbs amongst the older neighborhoods. A thick haze lingered at the tops of the buildings, and the height of the dome ceiling was claustrophobically low. The squat, low buildings continued on for miles and miles. South America ring five was a massive place. After what seemed like hours, they saw on the horizon two monster-sized buildings. As they approached, Ma reduced speed, and the two buildings in the distance took shape. The tall buildings were actually two enormous terra cotta soldiers that stood at either side of a wide street intersection.

"Welcome to Chinatown," Ma announced, looking back at the four. "Okay. Now strap in. We go low fast now to avoid bandits."

Christie gulped. "I thought you were already going fast, Ma."

Ma replied, "That patty cake. Now real speed." Ma put on his game face and rocketed the aero car forward. The four felt a few Gs as they were pushed back into their seats.

"Hang on for the ride!" John called to the group as the low red brick buildings became a blur. After a few nauseating minutes of zigzagging low to the ground along various streets, Ma slowed down the aero car.

"Thank you, Lorrr ...." Sara caught herself before she finished the word *Lord*. "Thank you, Ma. Great driving."

"You welcome, young lady," Ma replied.

"So where is the East Asian Mall?" Matted asked Ma.

"Right in front of you. You looking it now."

Matt strained forward to look in the direction that Ma was looking at. "I can't see anything." They were expecting a huge open area mall or at least a large single building that looked like a mall. All they saw were the same ugly old ten-story-high brick buildings.

"Right there!" Ma pointed.

Matt exclaimed, "You mean that old half-broken sign above the door?" Flashing in front of them, flickering on and off above a double steel door, was a sign: Welcome East Asian Mall. It had all been just words until now: Be careful. Danger. Reality hit the four of them hard. This was dangerous!

"You sure this is the East Asian Mall? There is no other mall with the same name?" John asked Ma.

"Friend, one mall in Chinatown call East Asian Mall."

"Okay," Matt replied reluctantly and clicked hands with Ma to transfer credits.

"Nice do business with you four. You have my contact. You need ride, you call Ma."

Matt replied, "Thanks, Ma. We'll keep that in mind." And he turned to the group. "Okay, gear up. Make sure you have everything. Let's go to the East Asian Mall."

CHAPTER 19

The Tube (The Detectives)

Night was approaching fast, and there was a lot to accomplish to finalize the plan with the two outer shell maintenance crew members who were giving Dom and Jack a ride with them on their maintenance task. There was an emergency problem with a circuit located about ten miles from the Venezuelan Post in the outer TT ring. The transit system consisted of an inner tube and an outer tube. The inner tube housed the train itself, and the outer tube contained all the power, ventilation, and other utilities needed to run the train. It was just good timing that the workers on the Venezuelan side had been killed that morning making the South America Ring Kingdom crew the only crew available to fix the problem. Dom and Jack didn't want to ask what other "luck" they might need to accomplish their mission. It seemed as if Fast Eddie and Crypto were pulling out all the stops to make this journey happen.

The two service men were right on time, meeting Dom and Jack as they exited the secret tunnel that ran under the wall separating ring three from ring two. After Dom and Jack changed into standard uniforms, the four looked like a proper group of tube service men on their way to work.

They timed their arrival to the ring maintenance entrance just as the entrance security system encountered a power down and reboot, compliments of Crypto, giving Dom and Jack the few precious minutes they needed to enter the service door with the two maintenance men, Aetus and Caeso. Aetus was a big, dark-haired, burly Eastern European man who stood over six feet and weighed over three hundred pounds. Caeso was shorter, black haired, and brown skinned—a local with a trim physique. Both were wearing service overalls in the fashionable Authority dark-red color.

There was no time for long introductions, and they didn't want to know who Dom and Jack were or what they were doing. The two maintenance men were being paid well, and that was all they had to know. Quickly walking through a short corridor, the four men entered a fire escape stairwell and went down three flights of stairs. Before opening the door at the bottom, Caeso gave a signal for Dom and Jack to hold back as he went outside. It was a tense minute of waiting. Although the air was cool in the stairwell, the three men were perspiring from the adrenaline rush. The door opened. "Okay. It's all clear," said Caeso. "Sometimes there are maintenance people serving the train in this area. We have to be fast. Follow me." With that, Caeso turned and moved rapidly.

Beyond the stairwell door was a wider corridor with floor-to-ceiling glass walls. The rooms behind the glass walls were workshops equipped with heavy machinery equipment. Most were run by robotic machines that fixed or built parts for the transit train. Alongside the robots, engineers sat at a series of desks and clear screens monitoring and directing the robots. The foursome moved quickly down the corridor until they came to a large, shiny steel double door. Caeso quickly punched in a code, and the door silently and rapidly opened to a small room. Full-body space suits lined the walls. "Get into the suits quickly," Caeso ordered. Luckily the suits were large and made for a range of heights. Once they were all suited up, Aetus checked to make sure Dom and Jack's were tightened up.

Aetus turned to Caeso, "Ready to go." Caeso turned to a black door and punched a code into the keypad. A high-pitched hiss sounded as the door opened, and they all felt a sudden pull. Aetus quietly narrated, "The outer tube is vacuum sealed to keep all dust and other elements clear. Essentially, it's a super clean room. The air from the room we were in was just sucked out through the tube system. That's why we have to wear the suits. There's no air in the outer tube, so don't let your suit get damaged. You will suffocate and die. We were told we get a bonus if we deliver you to the other end alive." Aetus ended his pep talk with a huge smile.

Caeso added, "We're getting paid well even if you two die, so don't cause any trouble. Do as you are told. No questions."

"Don't worry about us," Dom replied. "Jack and I want you two to get your bonuses." That got a laugh out of everyone.

"Okay. Let's do this," Caeso replied, and he went through the door.

The outer tube area was very narrow. The distance between the inner tube and outer tube was about twenty feet, just enough room for a single-service-way rail track. The service cart looked like a small boat. It was about fifty feet long and fifteen feet wide and filled with the appropriate equipment and gear to fix almost any problem. About one-third of the cart was open, and the other two-thirds was enclosed. They entered the service cart airlock room. After closing the outer door, Aetus punched a code into a keypad, and the room hissed with flowing air and pressure. A red status light over the door turned to green, and Aetus and Caeso took off their headgear and then helped Dom and Jack out of theirs. They stowed their suits on four empty hangers on the wall.

Opening the inner door, Caeso announced, "Gentlemen, welcome to the *Nebuchadnezzar*. Ant, show our two guests around while I get our cart ready to go."

Dom looked at the Giant. "Ant?"

The big man laughed and then replied in a thick Russian Accent. "That is my nickname. You may call me Ant as well, my two new best friends." Dom and Jack looked at each other and shrugged their shoulders. The money must be really good if they were the big man's new best friends.

There was a wide-open area in the enclosed portion of the service cart where detailed equipment repair could be performed. The cart was controlled from a small cab in the front section. There was also a bathroom and a small break room with a small kitchen. A set of stairs led to a small upper room area with a double bunk bed sleeping area. The setup was good for a service call that could last for days.

After Ant gave them a brief tour, Dom and Jack arrived in the front control area. There were two chairs. Caeso was sitting on one of them and was just powering up the cart. On the side walls there were two small jump seats. Caeso looked back as he finished typing on a screen. "Buckle up. It's time we got this show on the road." Ant took the seat next to Caeso, and Dom and Jack strapped into the jump seats.

"How long will it take us to get to the service point?" Dom asked.

Caeso punched in the display and replied. "It's approximately twenty-seven hundred miles to the Venezuelan Post, and the repair site is ten miles from the transit train stop. We'll average about one hundred fifty miles an hour. So just under eighteen hours."

Jack murmured. "The slow boat."

Ant replied, "Gents, this is a service vehicle. We go slowly and take visual thermal radar and other scans along the way. If we encounter other places to repair, it may be a lot longer than eighteen hours. So, take it easy. We'll walk you through the instructions Casanova gave us for the next leg of your journey. I'm not a man used to fear, but I've got to say that I'm glad that I am not you two. From what we've heard about the Venezuelan Post, it's a nightmare. Makes our South America ring five look like a seven-star resort.

That gave Dom and Jack pause. Ant was a huge man. If he was scared, they should truly be worried. Jack asked, "You two have never been to the Venezuelan Post?"

Ant answered, "We work sometimes with the two Venezuelan service men if there's an emergency that can be fixed faster with four of us. They have the same service cart we do, and we can operate both together. There are bypasses along the route as well in case there's a problem with one of the service carts." After a brief pause, Ant looked at Caeso as if to ask if he should tell them more. Caeso just shrugged his shoulders, and Ant continued, "They tell us about the post life, and we tell them about the ring kingdom. Living in the post sounds like a combination of living with today's technology in living conditions like they were just after the Great Conflict. The Authority officials live well along with about half the population, which is made up of soldiers.

"Whoa!" Jack whistled. "Half the population are soldiers? Must be big troubles out there."

Ant continued, "Everyone else lives in poverty. The two servicemen make out a bit better because they are or were essential workforces. There is no law there. The Authority personnel and soldiers make it up as they go. There's even a slave population. They wouldn't say more except that it is nothing like you would imagine in your wildest dreams or nightmares."

Caeso looked back at Dom and Jack. "Your mission must be pretty important. You realize it's most likely a one-way mission."

Dom looked at Caeso. "Never heard of one-way or impossible. Jack and I have been through some tough missions. This is just one of them. No one lives forever."

Caeso replied. "You got that right. No one lives forever. With this payday, the Ant and I may just find a way to escape and live it up for a while. There's food and drink in the kitchen area. Rest up. We have a while to go. Once we make it to the repair point, we'll still have another eight hours or so."

Taking the service man up on his invitation, Dom and Jack unbuckled and headed to the kitchen. They passed the time eating and taking in a couple of naps. In between, they planned their next move as Eddie guided them. They were concerned that the farther down the tube they went, the harder communications might become, so all planning had to be done immediately. Ant and Caeso had been told a different plan just in case they changed their minds and decided to turn in Dom and Jack. One could never be too careful. It appeared a bit strange with Dom and Jack sitting at the small dining table in the kitchen as they went over maps on their clear devices while seeming to talk to a third person who wasn't there. They had to be careful. When Ant or Caeso checked up on them, they had to remember not to talk to Fast Eddie.

In their heads, an excited Fast Eddie rambled on. "Okay, we knew that the Authority ruled with an iron fist in the Venezuelan Post and had soldiers to help keep the peace, but half the population are soldiers? Now that is something new."

Dom reasoned, "That many soldiers are not for keeping the peace. There's something else out there that requires that type of force."

"And what about that talk about slaves?" Jack asked. "The people already do as they're told. Who would the slaves be?"

"Lots of questions with no answers. I am so excited about this mission, guys!" Eddie's voice was giddy as he anticipated what was yet to come.

"Like we said before," Dom responded to the voice in their heads, "I'm glad that at least you're having fun Eddie. From our point of view it's more apprehension and fear than excitement. I keep thinking to myself how we came down this path." Eddie answered Dom, "Hey so you two are outlaws and by now the Authority probably has a kill order out on you two. But cheer up. You find the story behind that woman's mark, find the two medical examiners, and bring them back to the authorities, and you will be heroes. They will restore you back to service and probably give you both promotions. On top of that, you'll keep all those black chip credits because no one will know what happened to your aero car. A win-win for everyone!"

Jack replied, "Sounds great, Eddie. Just as you said, it's an easy walk in the park. Dom, why are we so anxious? You heard Eddie. No problems!"

Eddie continued, "Okay. Okay, gents. I may have left off a few concerns." They all laughed.

Time passed slowly on the service cart for Dom and Jack. Finally, Ant came back to get them. "Gentlemen, we have arrived at the repair site. Looks like the job will take about four hours. We can do it in less time if you two helps us out."

Jack replied, "Definitely. Always willing to learn something new."

Ant smiled, pleased for the extra help. "Good. Let's get back to the airlock and suit up."

As they were all suiting up in the airlock, Dom asked. "What's the problem?"

Caeso replied as he was fitting his gloves on. "There's a leak in a high-pressure air pipe. We need to find the leak and perform a hot patch without any shutdowns. Normally, we would isolate the line by shutting off valves on either side. Then we'd cut out and replace the section of pipe. But there's some type of action going on in the post, and the higher ups won't let us take the TT offline. Must be some big turmoil brewing. Anyway, it doesn't matter. We're prepared for all types of repairs."

When they were all suited up, Ant typed a code into the outer door keypad, and they heard the hissing sound of evacuating air from their small airlock. Slight suction pulled them toward the door. Oddly, the hissing sound did not stop. Ant, seeing the confusion on Dom's and Jack's faces, responded. "The hiss is the sound of the micro leak. We don't have the exact point of the leak determined, so follow behind Caeso and me. Do not deviate. The micro leak is invisible to the eye, and the pressure is so high it could cut you in half."

Jack responded, "Don't need to say another word, Ant. We are following your lead."

Satisfied that the detectives wouldn't do anything dumb, Ant started forward. It took about fifteen minutes to gather up the equipment and pack it in sealed containers on the open deck area. Ant carried a small box and gave Dom and Jack a footlocker-sized box with handles on each end for them to carry between them. Caeso carried a small case in one hand and a gun-like device in the other. "Looks like we have everything," Caeso announced.

An affirmative came from Ant. "We have all the gear. Let's do it."

Ant and Caeso started walking down a metal ramp on the inner side of the transit tube shell followed by Dom and Jack lugging the footlocker. The entire side of the curved inner tube was lined with a maze of large and small pipes. Blinking boxes with data keyboards were arrayed in a glowing patchwork between the pipes. Caeso was holding a device that shot out a spread of red laser light in front of him, scanning in all directions. The light level was very low. Thankfully, the suits were equipped with infrared visors that illuminated the tube in an eerie green color.

After they had walked for about ten minutes, Caeso's voice came over the headsets in their suits. "Hold up. We're getting close." Caeso moved forward alone with his scanner. Setting the scanner on the ground, he depressed a key, and the scanner's red laser light changed to a wide-angle single beam spread. "There!" Caeso announced as the trio behind him approached. In the red wide-angled beam, there was a thin dark line.

The leak! Ant ordered, "Dom, Jack, set the box down. Open it up and get out the large clamp." Doing as they were told, they opened the box, and Dom picked up the clamp. It was made of heavy-duty alloy and was about three inches thick, shaped like two half tubes with two bolts on each end. The idea was to place the clamp around the tube and then slide it over the leak and tighten the bolts to seal the leak. Seemed simple enough. It took another ten minutes position the clamp around a maze of pipes. It was about one foot from the leak.

"Okay. Here's the tricky part," Caeso lectured. "The pressure of the leak is so high we can't simply slide the clamp over it and then tighten the bolts. As soon as the clamp goes over the leak, it could be deflected toward us and kill us all. I'll use this laser weld torch to heat up and melt the pipe at the leak. This will stop the leak for a minute. That's all the time we have to slide the clamp into position and tighten the bolts. Any delay, and we are all toast. Understand?"

The replies came back in unison: "Understood."

Caeso continued, "I will seal the leak. Dom and Jack will slide the clamp over the leak. Then Ant will use the tightener to seal the clamp tight. We have one chance at this. Ant, if you start to hear the hiss as you are tightening the clamp, get out of the way."

Ant acknowledged, "Gotcha, Caeso." Just to make sure, they went over the plan two more times.

Caeso breathed out heavily. "Okay. Here we go." He moved forward and pointed a sticklike device in front of him. A red light glowed at the end. A high-pitched hiss sounded, and smoke filled the tube space as the pipe started to melt. Then all went silent. "Go! Go!" yelled Caeso as he stepped away. Dom and Jack immediately jumped into action. They slid the clamp over the glowing spot of heated pipe. When it was in place, they stepped away, and Ant moved forward and rapidly began to tighten the fours bolts. He had to use even pressure. Tightening one all the way down would offset the clamp. He had to tighten the first bolt only so much and then tighten the others to the same pressure. Then he had to repeat the process until all the bolts were sufficiently tightened. It seemed as if it was taking him forever.

"Done!" Ant finally announced after a furious minute. He stepped away. Caeso fiddled with the beam device and scanned over all areas of the clamp. Satisfied that it was perfectly installed, he turned back to the team. "Well done. The clamp is holding, and the leak is fully sealed." Sweat was pouring down over the faces of Ant, Dom, and Jack.

After they returned to the *Nebuchadnezzar* and got out of their suits, the four men sat down at the table in the kitchen. Caeso got up and typed into a keypad on a cabinet high on the wall. The small door popped opened, and he reached in and pulled out an old-looking glass bottle. He retrieved four short tumblers and brought them to the table with the bottle. Then he poured each of them a drink. "Gents, you will not find a better bottle of whisky in the South America Ring Kingdom. Over two hundred years old and perfectly sealed."

"Whhooaa!" Dom came back.

"Wow, I've never even seen a bottle like this," said Jack.

After they clinked their glasses together, Caeso said, "A toast to a dangerous repair well done! Ant and I salute you two and wish you well on your continued journeys!"

They all shouted "Here! Here!" and slowly savored the smooth liquid as it poured down their throats, warming their bodies. Each man was lost in his own thoughts. Caeso and Ant were dreaming of their payday and bonus for getting their new friends to the Venezuelan Post alive. Jack and Dom were contemplating the unknown horrors that awaited them on the other side of the next door they crossed.

CHAPTER 20

Following the Trail to the South America Ring Kingdom (The Authorities Three)

T he smoke from the warehouse breach finally cleared, and the team made another sweep just to make sure there were no hidden rooms. Finally, they confirmed that the warehouse was empty. There was no sign of the two detectives or their aero car or anyone or anything at all in the warehouse belonging to the Middle Eastern Imports/Exports and its owner, Bin Laden (Fast Eddie's warehouse and his alias).

With no more tangible leads in the Middle Eastern Ring Kingdom, there was only one alternative left. Earlier, with the help of the Authority security officer, Saul, Hector, and Jackson had traced the two detectives—Dom and Jack—to the TT where they discovered that they had bought tickets to the South America Ring Kingdom the previous day.

Saul shouted to Jackson and Hector, who were off in the corner of the warehouse talking to the security team that had helped them make the breach into the warehouse. "Hector! Jackson! Hustle up here! We have to make our next move to catch up with the detectives. We're already a day behind, and if we don't hurry, we'll fall even further behind them!"

Jackson and Hector ran to where Saul was. Jackson asked, "Okay, boss. What's the plan now?"

Saul replied, "We need to head back to the security office and download the search data on the two detectives to our mobile devices. Let's spend some time with the head security officer, Gal, and get his help to coordinate and link us with his contacts in the South America Ring Kingdom."

Jackson nodded, adding, "Saul, I remember Gal mentioning that his contacts will require some grease to help us out."

"Good point, Jackson. We'll need to ask Gal for some big money as well. I'm sure those Authority security guys have access to a lot of credits." Saul continued, "If all goes well with Gal, we can get everything we need to move fast. We'll pack light and head to the ring three TT." Looking at the time, Saul grimaced. "It's too late in the evening now. Let's head back to the hotel and get some rest. We'll reconvene at eight in morning at our usual café for breakfast. Then we'll head out to see Gal and his security team." It had been a long day, and no arguments came from Hector and Jackson. They were ready to get some rest. They all felt that they would need it for what was to come next.

Back at the café the next morning, they all experienced a bit of déjà vu. Saul came dragging in. Both Hector and Jackson were already there in their normal booth at the back of the restaurant. Like clockwork, Hector bellowed, "Saul! We thought you'd had a stroke or something!"

Saul joined them in the booth and replied, "Yeah, well even if we didn't hit it hard at Pete's Italian with food and drink, my body feels the pain of age. You two just wait a few more years, and you will understand."

Hector looked at Saul and flexed his biceps. "Not from this chap. Look at these rocks." He flexed even more. "These big guns will never wear down."

Jackson patted Hector's stomach. "Well, those guns are seated on a few big tires, my friend." That got a round of laughs.

"Well," Hector went on, "the tires do present a bit of a problem. Need to cut down on the beers."

Saul, sitting across from them in the booth, chimed in, "And cut down on the pasta, burgers, fries, and four meals a day ... Shall I go on?"

"Okay. Okay, boss. Got the point. I'll start the diet after breakfast." A huge plate of sausage, bacon, eggs, and toast was sitting in front of Hector. "Waste not want not goes the saying."

After breakfast, the trio headed directly to the security office. Gal, the Authority security manager, had already been working away on their next steps. Meeting them at the front desk, he hurried them to the command center. They entered the amphitheater-sized command center with its massive screens. It was a sight to see. The Authority spared no expense in tracking its citizens and hunting down those who disobeyed Authority rules. Sitting in her place in the row of desks in front of the video wall, Dru was the only one in the room, and she was typing away at her clear screen monitor. Gal walked quickly to her with Saul, Hector, and Jackson close behind. As Gal got close, Dru swiped her hands at even faster speed while talking to Gal without turning away from her screen. "Sir, we've inputted all the data we received from your contacts in the South America Ring Kingdom and obtained sporadic identification traces of the two perpetrators. Oops ... I mean the detectives in question. They got into an aero cab and went to the fifth ring. Once there, they went to Chinatown to a place called the East Asian Mall. The contact said they are still checking additional details and that the situation would need to be discussed in person."

Gal replied with a big smile, "Great work, Dru!" How many credits did that information cost me?"

"Fifty thousand, sir," she replied.

Gal crinkled his nose. "And I am sure it's going to cost a lot more to get more information in person. Oh well, we must do what we must to solve this case and get our fugitives. Make no mistake, Saul. The Authority will do whatever it takes to capture and bring to justice anyone who defies the Authority. What people do to themselves is of no concern to us, but if it affects the Authority, there is nowhere anyone can hide."

Saul replied, "We appreciate your support in this matter, Gal. You have the best team in the world, and you are a true patriot!"

Saul's enthusiastic response did the trick to elevate Gal's already inflated ego. "Thank you. Thank you, Saul. We'll get you and your team to the South America Ring Kingdom and put you in contact with our partners there. They should be able to help apprehend the two detectives. And don't you be concerned about the expenses. We at security have ample funding to make sure our contacts will keep you on track in your pursuit." He cleared his throat. "There is one point …" Gal hesitated for a moment. "Saul, I would like to ask you for a personal favor."

"Sure, Gal. What is it?"

"When you get close to finding the two detectives, I would like to be a part of the capture. I have become intrigued with the pursuit over the past couple of days, and I'd like to see this through to the end. Also, I have never actually been to the South America Ring Kingdom, but I've have heard so much about it. We have our video and holographic feeds, but it's not the same as being there and taking it all in."

Saul responded, "Well, of course, Gal. We're thankful for all of your support, and your continued help is much needed and appreciated." Jackson and Hector nodded enthusiastically at Gal; they all truly appreciated the efforts that Gal and his team were putting forth. Saul thought to himself that Gal's enthusiasm at having a chance to go to the South America Ring Kingdom had nothing to do with apprehending the two detectives. He figured it was more to take in the brutality of the most dangerous ring kingdom. He was just that kind of guy—death and destruction were what made him excited. Saul made a mental note: Gal just may be the most ruthless and dangerous man he had ever met.

"Gentlemen," the desk jockey said, "we have just completed compiling the potential route the aero taxi took from the South

America Ring TT station to the ring five Chinatown East Asian Mall. It's based on a hit-and-miss capture of the aero taxi. Would you like to view what's in store for you? All the data are compliments of our friends from the South America Kingdom, and Gal's fifty thousand credits."

Gal turned to face to the three men. His wild-looking eyes were blazing with excitement at the prospect of seeing the South America Kingdom. Saul, Hector, and Jackson looked at Gal and then at each other. Of course, the trio were also curious, but more out of dread at having to see what was in store for them, as opposed to the sheer excitement Gal was experiencing at seeing a war zone. Saul spoke for the trio: "Gal, thanks so much for assembling and compiling all this great information. Of course, we're excited to see where this will take us next."

Gal immediately turned to Dru. He did not even have to say the word as she turned to her screen, swiping and taping at a furious speed. Moments later, the room in front of them came to life as the three-dimensional holographic image of the South America ring three came to life. It was a closeup aerial view of the outside of the TT station. The scene unfolded with a mass of people walking on a wide sidewalk. A red circle wrapped around two figures just coming out of the TT station doors. Dru explained, "I've attached red circles to our two detectives. They're just coming out of the station, and we can follow them in the crowds. You can't see their faces, as this is an aerial view, but internal station video cameras confirm its them." They watched intensely as the detectives made their way slowly, moving through the mass of people toward the street.

Jackson commented. "The combined aerial view and three-dimensional imagery are amazing. But why is the image a bit hazy? Are the video camera lenses old or damaged?"

Dru replied, "One moment. I'll check the equipment and try to sharpen it." After she typed furiously for another minute, the red-circled men continued to walk across the wide sidewalk area toward the street. Finally, she stopped and turned to the four men. "I've checked the equipment functions and the settings. The video feed equipment is fairly new. I scanned the area using the atmospheric instrumentation sensors that come with the video equipment, and it is as I suspected. The equipment is fine. That dark haze is a combination of petroleum oil fumes, carbon monoxide, carbon dioxide, sulphur, and a mixture of heavy metals."

Saul replied, "Ugh! In short, all that haze and smoke is just pollution on a huge scale."

The woman swiped some more on the clear screen. "From the historical readings, I can see that the levels you are seeing right now make this actually one of the better days. The blocks of high buildings, the relatively narrow street corridors, and the heavy use of old combustible engines makes the street level a virtual smog cloud twenty-four hours a day seven days a week."

"Lovely," remarked Jackson.

"Yes! Yes!" Gal said enthusiastically. "The smog! The awful stench it must give! I can almost feel the despair of those poor inhabitants! If I weren't so needed here, I would so much like to join you three on your quest to find our adversaries. What a glorious time it would be!" Saul looked straight at Gal's blazing eyes and had to look away. Jackson and Hector were equally mortified at Gal's sheer joy gazing at the misery of the millions of people in the South America ring three.

Saul replied, "Yes, what a shame." Saul tried to put on a sincere face. "Your expertise will be missed, Gal. However, rest assured we will keep you informed of our progress every step of the way, and we'll check back with you with video feeds. Of course, due to the sensitive nature of the mission, we can send in data only sporadically. We'll endeavor to check in frequently with imagery, even if it's delayed. But you will feel as if you are there. Have no concern about that."

Gal smiled and replied, "Thank you! Thank you! Rest assured you will have my full support."

After thinking a bit, Saul motioned Gal to the side for a quiet chat. "Gal, this is a most sensitive mission. Those two detectives have information that the Authority must keep very quiet at the highest levels. I dare say this comes from the highest ring-one Authority. No one must speak of this mission, even to fellow Authority personnel. At the end of this mission, we will make sure to let those in power know how instrumental you and your crew were to its success."

Gal replied with enthusiasm, "Yes, yes! I understand of course! As they say, loose lips sink ships." Gal's eyes glazed over as he thought of the notoriety he would receive at the success of a critical ring-one-sanctioned mission. The added power he would have. Then, as he thought about it more, a frown came over his face. *What if the mission fails? There's a good chance of that happening. The higher Authority will not take kindly to a high-level mission failure.* Normal protocols would be enforced—the PAP code: Purge All Parties. Anyone and everyone involved with the failed operation would be tortured and killed to serve as a reminder that failure is not an option.

Clearing his throat, Gal spoke to Saul in a whispered voice, "And if you ... I mean we ... are not successful in apprehending the detectives?"

Saul looked directly into the eyes of Gal. The fire and excitement had drained from Gal's eyes and had been replaced with an expression of concern. "Gal, that is the other reason this mission must be a close secret. If we fail, then it will be only on Jackson, Hector, and me. We will be held fully responsible for failure as long as your staff keeps it a secret.

Gal replied as he thought it through, "Of course. Minimum collateral damage is best for everyone." Gal looked straight in the eyes of Saul and saw that Saul meant what he said. Gal's expression turned from concern to calm. A determined look came over his face to help his newfound friends. The upside was enormous for Gal and the downside now minimized. Internally Gal was thankful that he chose Dru to be the only one besides himself that knew about the trio's mission. She and Gal went way back, and he could count on her to keep secrets.

After returning from their private conversation with Gal, Jackson and Hector talked to Dru about how she put together all of the pieces to create the holographic image. Gal jumped into the conversation. "She's the best at it. Fascinating technology. Let's press on to see where our two detectives are going." Dru immediately swiped her clear screen, and the frozen three-dimensional image came back to life. The two men were once again highlighted by a red circle as they continued to walk through the masses to the edge of the street.

Everyone watched, enthralled by the scene before them; it was such a different place. The detectives got into an aero taxi, which shot off down the street with towers of brown stained mirrored glass buildings on each side. The scene skipped forward. Dru narrated as they watched. "We lost the aero taxi as it went through ring three, but we picked it up again at the security entrance to ring four and then again at ring five." The three-dimensional image jumped a bit. There was disappointment on the faces watching because they were not able to see what ring four looked like. Dru saw the disappointment on everyone's faces. "Unfortunately, we didn't get any video feed for ring four. But our contacts did give us a tour of ring five. They took a couple of snapshots of the aero taxi the detectives were in, and then they flew the same route using one of their aero cars from the ring-five checkpoint to Chinatown.

The holographic image zoomed in at the ring five checkpoint and expanded to a larger view as if they were in an aero car looking at the ring-five scene in front of them as it skimmed at the top of the low buildings. In front of them was a super grid of ten-story buildings extending all the way to the horizon in all directions. The horizon itself was hard to see amidst the haze of pollution. The top of the dome that protected all from the deadly radiation and toxic air of the outside world was so low they could see it. They could even feel the claustrophobic effect of the low ceiling.

The speed of the three-dimensional image increased as Dru continued her narration. "Chinatown is a good distance from the checkpoint, so we are speeding up the image for the sake of time." As the scene continued to move away from the ring-four border, the horizon in front of them became fuzzier, and then they were able to see only a few hundred feet. The air swirled in front of them.

"Is the aero car in a cloud?" Hector asked as they watched the air in front of them swirling like a cloud or thick fog.

Dru replied, "Unfortunately, for you three, what we are seeing now is what they call in the ring-five area a smog bank. From time to time, the air scrubbers are shut down for maintenance or they break and need repair."

Hector asked, "How often does this happen?"

The desk jockey typed in a few more keys. "From the information we received, it looks like there is some type of environmental system repair somewhere in ring five approximately two thousand times a day, and the resultant smog bank covers approximately twenty five percent of ring five at any one time.

"Oh my!" Gal exclaimed. "This is incredible footage. I can't see anyone in ring five even living to the ripe retirement age of forty-four in these conditions." His lips smacked at the thought of their misery. Saul just rolled his eyes at Gal's words. Dru cracked a knowing smile at Saul. She knew what Saul was thinking about Gal. He was quite a wild man.

Saul replied, "Well, fortunately for us, we'll be in and out of ring five with our two detectives in a short period of time."

The three-dimensional image continued, and they came out of the smog bank just in time to see two huge objects rising above the low-lying buildings. "What in the world is that?" Saul asked.

Dru replied as she continued to swipe at her screen, "That is the entrance to Chinatown." The view in front of them moved closer. What they had assumed to be two large buildings were revealed as two huge Chinese terracotta soldiers. The moving image passed through the two giants and then headed down to street level. The three-dimensional image briefly disappeared and then reformed as an aerial view of a street scene at ground level. In the foreground was an old building that looked to be hundreds of years old. The street was scattered with garbage, and people who looked to be homeless wandered on the sidewalk. In the corners of the building at the street intersection they could just make out shadows of a few people lurking like a pack of wolves waiting for prey to cross their way.

Jackson asked, "A lovely scene, Dru. Just what are we looking at here?"

She swiped a few more times, and then the image moved and zoomed into an old metal double door. Over the door was a half-broken sign: Welcome East Asian Mall.

The expressions of Saul, Jackson, and Hector said it all. Their ashen faces were grim with concern. Dru said, "And that, gentlemen, is the end of the feed provided to us. As promised, you are looking at your next stop, the East Asian Mall. Our South America Ring Kingdom contacts said they will provide instructions on how to contact them once you enter the mall." Looking at her screen she continued, "The contacts require an upfront payment of one hundred thousand credits for the next 'phase' of their assistance."

Saul thought out loud: "I wonder how many phases our contact has in store for us?"

Gal replied, "Think nothing of it, my friend. We will make sure your mission continues as planned with our contacts." His anticipation soared as he imagined the power he would have if this was a successful mission that received the favor of the elites of ring one.

CHAPTER 21

The South America
Underground
(God's Quad Squad)

S till shaking a bit from the wild ride, and having said good-bye to the taxi driver who called himself Ma, John, Sara, Christie, and Matt—the self-named God's Quad Squad—walked a bit unsteadily from the sidewalk to the double doors over which hung the flickering, half-broken sign: Welcome East Asian Mall. Thankfully, they were dressed in old and shabby clothes in muted colors so they wouldn't draw any attention. Their staggering walk helped to give them that worn-out and on-medication/drugs look.

As they came up to the door, John whispered to the group. "Here we go, team. We need to head toward the center of the mall." The soothing voice of Mary, their artificial intelligence (AI) derived from the woman who had passed away but who had started this entire adventure, talked through small devices embedded in their ears. "Take it easy, you four. As John said, walk toward the center of the mall. I don't have any information about the layout, so just keep an eye out for the Seven-Seven-Seven Lucky Duck Restaurant. No harm in asking for directions. After all, you four are supposed to be tourists."

Sara joined the conversation. "Okay. We'll be on the lookout."

Mary came back immediately: "And remember what we talked about. When I talk, don't respond. It sounds weird—as if you are talking to yourself. Conversations between you four only. Not with me in public."

Sara was about to reply to Mary again but caught herself. Everyone looked at her with a smile because she had a guilty look on her face.

After a few minutes of walking in the mall, Matt signaled, "Hey guys, farther up I see a sign. Can't read all of it but there are numbers, Seven-Seven-Seven. Let's head that way."

Christie replied. "Great. Lead the way." And with that, the four started moving toward the blinking Seven-Seven-Seven numbers with Matt in the lead. John brought up the rear for safety.

The mall was fairly open in the center and set up as a food court with lots of small food kiosks. People ordered their food at the kiosks and ate at tables located in the open area. There were a few small restaurants in the middle area with limited seating inside; the larger restaurants lined the walls of the food court.

It was midday, and the area was busy with people eating lunch. It seemed to be a good time to be there because it was easy to get lost in the crowd. Walking slowly and together, they were trying to act casual but keep on high alert. There were thieves everywhere, and someone could easily steal something from their backpacks or their duffle bags—or worse, steal all their gear. As they made their way through the crowds, a woman screamed about twenty feet in front of them, and they watched as a young man ran away while the lady frantically pointed and screamed. They man had grabbed the frantic woman's bag. In the corner, a couple of security guards stood near the unfolding scene. They were close enough to chase and grab the man, yet they did nothing. The guards were talking to three high-ranking Authority types, and all their attention was on them. They briefly looked at the screaming woman and the man running away. The altercation seemed to them more like an annoyance, and the three Authority officials acted as if their business was a lot more important than a petty crime.

The woman settled down, took an empty seat at a table next to her, put her hands over her face, and sobbed. No one was helping her, and it was obvious to the newcomers that the place was run by corrupt security and an unseen mob. That young thief was just one of the mall "workers" doing his job for unseen forces. As the four of them passed, the woman looked up at John with red swollen eyes. There was something about that woman that John could not shake off. He had a feeling that she was one of them—a Christian. Words came into his mind: *Help her, my son.*

John bent down and took the sobbing woman's right hand in his. Very softly John whispered to her, "Be of good cheer, Sister, for there is one who looks after us all." Then he whispered, "Transfer two hundred credits." His wrist lit up briefly and the woman's wrist also lit up. She looked at her wrist in amazement. Her sobs turned to a look of confusion and then to a tearful smile. She looked back up to thank the generous man, but John and the group had already gone; he and his companions were lost in the crowd.

They stayed close as they walked. Matt pointed ahead casually. "Hey there, everyone, I'm hungry. Let's get a bite to eat. I heard good things about that restaurant." Matt pointed to a bright neon green sign up ahead. The top row of lettering read Seven-Seven-Seven. The bottom row read Luck Duck.

They all nodded in agreement. Christie remarked. "Sounds like a great plan, Matt. Let's go."

It was one of the smaller restaurants that lined the walls of the food court area. The host was a short, pudgy Chinese man. He greeted the four visitors with a warm smile and spoke in broken English: "Welcome Luck Duck. Best China food here. Wang make sure you have good lunch."

Sara spoke for the group. "Thank you, Wang. We've heard a lot about your fine restaurant." She looked around at the tables. "It's just four of us today for lunch." Pointing to the back of the restaurant Sara continued, "We would like to sit at table twelve please."

Wang didn't say anything for a few seconds. He just looked at the four. His warm smile faded and was replaced with a more inquisitive look. "Yes. Wang take you table twelve." Wang grabbed four menus from the front desk. "Follow Wang." And he turned and walked to the back of the restaurant. The restaurant was a small place with only twelve tables. As they sat down Wang continued, "Twelve lucky number. Wang come back with hot tea." John tried to speak up to give their coded order, but Wang was already gone.

Matt said, "Seems like a nice enough fellow."

Christie replied. "Yes, I do like his smile. He has a warmth about him. Not sure how to describe it."

John remarked, "I had the same feeling. The same good feeling I had about that Asian woman whose purse was stolen."

A couple minutes later, Wang came back with four teacups, a shiny steel pot of hot tea with steam coming out of its little spout, and four plastic cups of water. He looked with obvious curiosity at the four sitting there because none of them was looking at the menu.

John and Sara were seated closest to Wang. John said, "We would like to order the special platter twelve-twelve."

Wang, now very intrigued, glanced over the group again looking at each face. Then he looked back at John. "That dish not on menu."

Sara responded as planned. "Sir—Wang—we preordered the twelve-twelve dish."

Wang just stood there looking at Sara for a few seconds trying to take in what he had heard. "Okay, Wang get special platter." With that, he abruptly turned and headed to the kitchen.

"What now?" Matt asked.

John responded. "Let's drink our tea and wait for lunch." A few minutes later Wang came back with a helper who was holding a big lazy Susan. He set the round wood disc on the table, and Wang put on top of it a large bowl of soup, four small bowls, and four soup spoons. "Special platter twelve-twelve first dish wonton soup." Wang and the server both clapped their hands, made small bows, and then quickly departed.

A bit of confusion came over the four. They had been expecting some type of coded reply from Wang. They thought he would, perhaps, take them to a back room or do something spy like. Instead, in front of them, was a steaming hot bowl of soup. John asked. "What should we do?"

A soft voice came into each of their heads. "You eat it of course. You all ordered food, didn't you?" It was Mary's voice.

There were only a few other people eating lunch in the restaurant, and they were sitting at the front near the entrance. John saw that no one was looking, so he nodded. Quickly, they all joined hands and bowed their heads. John whispered, "We thank you, Lord, by whose word all things come to be."

When they started to eat the soup, they realized how famished they were, and they finished the bowl in just a few minutes. Just like clockwork, Wang and his helper came back with several more dishes, enough of each so that they all got a little taste. The four realized that the special platter twelve-twelve consisted of twelve different dishes. Kung pao chicken, mushroom chicken, and stir-fried beef were just some of the dishes, and they were all great. Over the course of the next two hours, the four were treated to a fabulous meal. Each time Wang served a dish, he politely announced the name of the dish. Saying no more, each time, he quickly departed to let them eat. The twelfth dish was the best one. It was an entire duck roasted Peking style with plum sauce and steaming Chinese pancakes in which to wrap the crispy duck.

It was a true feast, and the four ate until they were utterly stuffed. About fifteen minutes after the four had finished the last dish, Wang came back to the table. "Wang tell you Wang would give you best lunch."

Christie remarked, "You truly outdid yourself, Wang. A huge compliment to you and the chef. We've never had a better meal." The other three nodded their heads and smiled in agreement. All three added their compliments, but not just to make Wang feel good. Several hours had passed, and with lunchtime over, there was no one else left in the restaurant. One of the servers, a young woman, went to the front door, flipped the open sign to closed, and locked the door. She walked back to the table where she and Wang pulled up a couple of chairs and sat next to the four.

The young girl, who looked like she was in her early twenties, spoke: "We are so glad to meet fellow brothers and sisters from a different ring kingdom." Her voice was soft and soothing and was strangely familiar. She was wearing a net over her hair because of working in the kitchen. When she removed the covering, a full head of pure blonde hair came rolling down over her shoulders. The group was in shock. "You may know me. My name is Mary." The woman was the splitting image—although a bit younger—of their holographic Mary. John's wrist device vibrated for a second, and a holographic image formed in the middle of the table. The older Mary's head and shoulders appeared.

"Hello, Mary. The last time my eyes gazed upon you, you were just a small child."

The young Mary replied, "It's so good to see you! As you are not here in person that can only mean you are with our Father in heaven now." A sadness came over young Mary and Wang.

Wang spoke. "Mary, we owe so much to you over the years. We pray you are finally at peace now."

Seeing confusion in the eyes of foursome, Wang spoke. "Young Mary is a clone of the older Mary that you know. But not a test tube clone; she was born of Mary in her womb." Wang's Chinese accent was gone, and he was speaking perfect English.

Christie smiled "And, Wang, it's a miracle that you learned perfect English in the last hour." They all laughed.

Wang replied, smiling, "Yes, one must not only look the part but speak the part so guests believe they are getting authentic food."

"Come." Wang got up and so did young Mary. "We have much to do and little time. The fact that Mary sent you means that we are close to the truth." The four got up and instantly felt the effect of sitting and eating for several hours.

Matt patted his full belly "Ugh. My stomach."

Sara replied, "You got that right. When I stood up, I realized how much food we ate."

Wang looked over his shoulder as he walked toward the kitchen and waved his right hand to indicate they should follow him. "Nothing but the best for our guests. We haven't served special dish twelve-twelve since the last time we saw your Mary."

They walked through the small kitchen past four gas burners side-by-side with enormous woks sitting clean and ready for the next group of customers. A standing oven held two rows of ducks and two rows of chicken slowly turning on skewers. They inhaled a nice fragrance that normally would make their mouths water, but the four were so full, just thinking about more Chinese food was enough to give them heartburn. At the back of the kitchen was a supply room. Wang entered it with young Mary, and the light automatically came on. It was a fair-sized supply room. Shelves lined the walls and were filled foods in cans and jars, bags of flour and rice, and jars of all sorts of spices. Matt, Sara, Christie, and John followed their new friends. The room seemed a lot smaller with six people in it. Wang motioned to Matt who was the last one in the room. "Close the door." After Matt closed the door, Wang, standing at the back of the room, stuck his hand in a tub of dry rice and pulled out a small keypad into which he typed in a sequence of numbers. A few seconds later, a series of laser-like lights scanned each person; taking a few seconds for each. After the scans were complete, the lights in the room turned from white to green. Young Mary pronounced, "All clear." Seeing their confusion, she said, "We have to be cautious about tracing devices. Any of us could have one planted on us without our knowing by Authority spies." Wang then punched in another series of numbers in the keypad and then buried the pad back in the rice bin. The shelves at the back of the room then started to swing in. A secret door! John looked back at group and gave them the "now this is the type of spy stuff we were expecting" nod while raising his eyebrows.

They walked through to the next room, which was a lot larger than the supply closet. It was about the size of the restaurant dining area. They noted a couch, two tables with clear screen devices on them, and a larger clear table in the center of the room with chairs around it. On one wall there was equipment that looked like data server storage devices. Blinking lights showed that it was active. At one end of the room was a small kitchen and a couple of dining tables. There was also another couch in another corner of the room. The walls were painted a light brown, and the floors were covered in tan tiles. The lighting was nice and comfortable—not too intense or too dim.

A woman was sitting at one of the worktables swiping away at the clear screen. Looking intensely at her screen, she didn't even notice Wang, young Mary, and the four others entering the room. Wang moved toward the woman, and the rest followed. As they approached, she finally looked up from her screen and got up to greet the new guests. As she looked at the group, her eyes locked on John and got really wide. John, too, was shocked. She hurriedly approached him and gave him a big hug. Wang and young Mary were very confused. Wang asked, "You two already know each other?"

The young woman proceeded to shake hands with Christie, Sara, and Matt. Turning back to Wang and young Mary, she said, "Wang, the man I hugged was the man I told you about earlier who was so kind and gave me two hundred credits when my bag was stolen. I thought I'd never see my good Samaritan and his friends again."

Wang looked again at John and the others with new appreciation. They were true Christians.

"Well then," Wang continued, "let me formally introduce you to our top computer expert and the recipient of your good deeds, Rui." They made introductions all around. Christie, who worked in the IT department of the company that Matt worked for, instantly bonded with Rui because of their common interest in computers and technology systems. Matt found out that Wang was a handy man with all kinds of equipment. Being a mechanical engineer at a manufacturing plant, Matt got along well with Wang, and they sat down and started to talk shop as well. This left John and Sara to talk more with Young Mary. She was just like their older Mary, wise beyond her years, and she had a glow about her that spoke to her calm demeanor.

The hours passed quickly, and the four begged forgiveness at suppertime. They ate very small amounts of food because they were still full after the huge twelve-course lunch. Later in the evening, Wang turned to the group. "I feel so blessed to have our brothers and sisters from the Middle East Ring Kingdom join us here. We have ample room here with several bedrooms with bunk beds for you all to sleep in. We also live here as well. It's much safer not to travel around the fifth ring. As you have seen, even in this open mall there are crooked security personnel and bad elements. Outside of this mall, the streets are much worse. It's a difficult life, but we praise Jesus every day for His blessings upon us. We are a small family but one full of love for each other and of the Lord. What more could anyone ask for?"

A big round of "amen" came from the group of four.

Wang continued, "Rui will show you to your rooms. Get some rest, and tomorrow we will talk about what you are doing here and what you need."

CHAPTER 22

The Nebuchadnezzar
(The Detectives)

T he night's festivities continued with food and drink. Earlier in the day, the repairs in the outer transit tube had gone well, and the two transit service men, Caeso and Ant, were sharing a hearty meal and drinks with their passengers, Dom and Jack, on board their service vehicle, the *Nebuchadnezzar*. Caeso and Ant were being well compensated for taking the duo to the Venezuelan Post. Not to mention that Dom and Jack had been instrumental in helping Caeso and Ant with the repairs. As the night dragged on and the flow of drink continued, the group became merrier. At least Caeso and Ant were savoring the moment and dreaming of their big payday to come. For Dom and Jack, this was the easy part of the journey. From what they had heard of the Venezuelan Post, their dreams of what lay in store for them were more like dreadful nightmares. But that was tomorrow. Today they were alive and supplied with good food and lots of drink.

Shaking off thoughts of what was to come, Dom raised his cup and offered a toast: "To the crew of two on the *Nebuchadnezzar*! She's a fine ship, and we are much obliged for the ride to the Venezuelan Post!"

"Here, here!" they all shouted as they clanked their glasses. As they drank up, Dom continued, "Now remember, my two friends, about your extra bonus if you get us to the Venezuelan Post *alive!*"

Caeso replied, "Ant and I can think of nothing else but to get you all there without the slightest scratch on our new best friends!" Laugher roared all around, and it was comforting to the duo that Caeso and Ant appeared to really think them as friends and not just tickets to a payday. Caeso continued, "We're actually ahead of schedule, so continue to eat and drink. Tomorrow we can spend the day in rest so we'll be ready in the evening to finalize our plans for arrival the following day."

Jack roared with a huge smile, "Now that sounds like a sound plan!"

The next morning, déjà vu hit Dom as he woke up with a splitting headache and sore body. Luckily, he remembered where he was—on the upper bunk; otherwise, his first step off the bed would have been a doozy. Jack was on the lower bunk bed snoring like a train. After easing off the top bunk, Dom went down the narrow stairs to the lower level and headed straight to the bathroom to take a quick shower. The *Nebuchadnezzar* was a small work platform on wheels, and everything was tiny, compact, and utilitarian. But Dom had to admit it provided just enough accommodation to keep a crew working and living with the basic necessities for prolonged assignments. Not wanting to waste water, Dom showered quickly. The hot, steaming water felt good on his tired muscles and throbbing head. After performing his usual bathroom routine, he headed for the next necessity—a steaming hot cup of coffee in the kitchen. He didn't have to walk far because the kitchen was next to the bathroom. Caeso and Ant were already awake and sitting at the small dining table.

Caeso called out to Dom as he was pouring a cup of coffee, "How's the head?"

Dom wearily replied, "My head feels like I look, guys—old, worn out, and throbbing with pain."

Ant replied, "Ahh. Then it was a good night for all of us. I feel the same way. Above the coffee pot in the cupboard there is a bottle of pain pills. Take a couple. They'll do you good."

Dom said with a smile, "Don't mind if I do. Thanks, Ant." Dom took out a couple of the pills and washed them down with the black coffee.

Sitting down next to Caeso and Ant, Dom looked at a schematic on the clear screen tabletop and asked, "Is that the door and passage from the outer tube to the outside of the TT station?"

Caeso said, "It is. Ant and I were just reviewing the station schematics. We've both been in the post TT station a couple of times, but that was years ago. Normally they don't allow anyone other than the high Authority officials or the military in or out of the post, so just being in the station requires special permission. Ant and I have both had to fix problems associated with the TT system in the post TT station. We were just looking at these plans to see how current they were."

Dom, hunched over with interest and asked, "How old are the plans?"

Caeso hesitated a second before responding. "These plans are over two hundred years old. That's the best we could do."

Ant added, "And it cost your benefactor a huge number of credits just to get these old schematics." Ant looked back at the clear screen tabletop and started tracing with his hand on the map. "From what I remember, it looks like the main corridors are the same as they were when I was there about five years ago, but I recall a lot more doors and hallways branching off from the main corridor than what are shown on these plans."

Caeso nodded. "A lot has changed over a couple of hundred years. I also remember a lot of other hallways."

Dom looked at the map and then at Ant and Caeso. "A two-hundred-year-old map and a couple of trips by both of you in just a few areas of the vast transit station is the best we've got? I think my headache just got worse. So, what's the plan to get us to our next destination?"

Caeso replied, "Ant and I were just going over some initial thoughts and backup plans. We just got word from your benefactors about your next destination. After you two make it out of the Transit station, you are to make your way via local transport to a place called the Roundup Hotel. Apparently everyone knows about it as there are only three hotels in the entire post. Not many people visit the post, I guess. At the hotel there will be a room reserved for each of you. Once you are checked in and go to your rooms, you'll get a message about the next step for making contact."

Dom thought out loud scratching his throbbing head: "Seems like a lot of cloak and dagger business just to make contact."

Caeso replied, "From what I understand, keeping information in silos is safest for all. If you get caught or captured, you won't know anything about your contact. I heard there are bets on whether or not you two will even make it to the hotel."

Dom hesitated before asking, "What are the odds?"

Ant and Caeso looked at each other. Ant replied, "Tell him, Caeso. He might as well know what they'll be up against."

Caeso looked at Dom directly and answered with a grim look, "The odds are fifty-fifty that you and Jack will make it to the hotel alive."

Dom was about to laugh at the joke, but when he looked at Caeso's deadpan eyes, his smile turned into a frown and sweat beaded on his forehead. Dom replied, "Are you joking, Caeso? We only have a fifty percent chance of making it to the hotel? Who's taking bets that we'll make it?"

Caeso answered, "I heard that your benefactor, who is paying your way, is on your side. He believes that you two will make it."

Dom asked, "Are you two in on the bet?"

Ant replied, "Oh, no. Caeso and I get our pay and bonus for just getting you two alive through the exit door from the tube to the TT station. We don't need the bet, and besides the betting was finalized before you two even started your journey with us."

Dom replied with a smile, "Well if you still can, bet in our favor." He then promptly got up and went up to the bunk bed area and came back with his duffle bag. Caeso and Ant were looking at Dom curiously as he unzipped and dug into his bag, lifting out a set of clothes. Ant exclaimed, "Woooeeee! Where in the world did you get those?" Dom displayed an Authority soldier uniform. It was an officer's uniform—that of an army major, a solid rank that was high enough to keep the enlisted soldiers in line but not so high that his and Jack's presence would draw too much attention. The last thing they needed was a detail of soldiers surrounding them to protect them. They didn't want any activity that would call people's attention to them as celebrities, which might happen if they were high-ranking officers. If they were disguised as low-ranking soldiers, like corporals, they could be detained and questioned about where they were going or what they were doing. Those low on the military organization chain did not have much freedom and were subject to commands by anyone who outranked them. A rank of major indicated enough authority to keep other soldiers away so they wouldn't be inspected or brow beaten for whatever job they were doing or not doing.

Caeso and Ant inspected the uniform and held it as if it was some kind of treasure. Ant whistled. "Amazing. The uniform is not only an Authority military uniform, it also looks like the type I saw that is specific to the Venezuelan Post." Caeso touched the shiny cloverleaf on the shoulder bars and a few medals on the front jacket. The circle patches on the shoulder were unique to the Venezuelan Post; they were decorated with the letters VP and an image of an armored tank. The color of the uniform was a dark red, which was standard for the Authority Army.

Caeso asked, "Dom, what else do you have in your bag of surprises?"

Dom replied, "Glad you asked." He pulled out the military battlefield fatigues in a camouflage pattern appropriate for the South American jungle. These were for the same rank. Dom also pulled out military identification cards.

Caeso whistled and said, "Amazing is all I can say." He sat back in his chair with an impressed look on his face. "Your benefactor must have paid a hefty price for all this gear." Caeso and Ant looked at each other as if to say, "Maybe we should have asked for more money."

Looking back at Dom, Ant mused, "Well at least the uniform increases the chances that you and Jack will make it to the hotel." He rubbed the stubble of hair growing on his chin after a few days of not shaving. Smiling at Dom, Ant continued, "I give you a seventy-five percent chance of living."

Dom smiled and bowed his head. "Well, thank you for the confidence. Ant." They all laughed.

Caeso jumped in. "I tell you what, if you and Jack survive your journey and we meet again for your return trip to the South America Ring Kingdom, Ant and I will serve you two a full-course meal with unlimited drink."

Dom replied with a big smile, "Thanks, Caeso. Now that is a deal we will take!"

About an hour later, Jack came rumbling into the kitchen area. Dom, Caeso, and Ant were still sitting at the dining table chatting away, telling tales of past adventures. Jack made a beeline to the coffee pot and poured a large cup of steaming brew.

Sitting at the table, Ant looked at Jack with a smile, "You're looking a bit rough this morning."

Jack rubbed his throbbing head and replied, "I look just like I feel."

Caeso slapped Jack on the back as they all laughed. "Whhoaa! That is exactly what your partner said earlier." As Jack sipped on his coffee, he listened as Caeso and Ant gave a brief overview of the Venezuelan Post TT station on the clear screen table map and outlined the plan for getting the detectives to the hotel. There wasn't much to tell as there wasn't much information. Basically, somehow, they had to get through the TT station, get a cab, and make it to the hotel.

Jack replayed what Caeso had said. "So, the odds are fifty-fifty that we'll make it to the hotel. If I knew that, I would have bet that we *would* make it! And not just because it's self-serving that we stay alive. I really think we *will* make it! Dom, did you show our two friends our uniforms?"

Dom nodded. "I did, Jack. And they definitely swing the odds in our favor."

The four men spent the rest of the day talking about what little Ant and Caeso remembered about the Venezuelan Post from their talks with the two service men from the post that they had worked with before. They also recalled any conversations they'd had with the military personnel in the post transit station the few times they were ever allowed in the station.

Late in the afternoon, all four roughed out a meager plan of action. Caeso timed their speed to arrive at the Venezuelan Post TT station in the morning at about seven o'clock. From the outer tube maintenance door, Dom and Jack would navigate through the underbelly of the station using a map on their hand-held devices and the additional descriptions that Ant and Caeso had given them. Their one goal was to connect to the main TT public area and just follow the crowd to the outside street area. Most of the people in the station were military; they were the only regulars that came in or out of the post. From what Caeso heard, it was mostly inbound traffic.

Jack asked, "So over all the years, the Authority keeps sending in troops, and very few ever leave? You would think there would be a limit to how many people can live there. After all, it's just a post. It must be extremely small compared to a ring kingdom."

Caeso replied, "Good points, Jack. From what little we know from our talks with the Venezuelan service men, troops continue to come in regularly. They go outside the ring post to do some sort of patrols, and many times they don't return or only a handful return. There is something bad out there that requires the military to constantly send troops on one-way missions. Perhaps it's the high levels of radiation we hear so much about. But if it's that, why the need for patrols outside the post? The post TT service men told us that to talk about it or even question what's out there results in an instant death sentence. So, no one questions what is happening. And the influx of solders also happens to be great business for the people. The solders spend all their credits on whatever they can get their hands on—liquor, gambling, women, racing. The soldiers who are assigned to the post hear the rumors, and money doesn't mean anything when you most likely will not live long enough to spend it all. The soldiers come in for their one-way assignments, spend all their money, and everyone is happy. Except for the poor soldiers, of course, who never make it back."

Jack replied as he headed back to the kitchen for one more cup of coffee, "Well at least our uniforms will help us blend in—both inside and outside the TT station." Swirling the black brew in his cup, he decided not to drink it. The caffeine might keep him up, and they needed a good night sleep for an early morning. Jack and Dom would need one hundred percent of their wits to get them through to the hotel alive. Spilling the coffee into the sink, Jack replaced the contents with water and returned to the table.

Ant put his hand on Jack's shoulder as he sat down, "Smart move, Jack. You two will need a good rest tonight for what is to come tomorrow."

The next morning came quickly, and all four were up by four o'clock. Dom and Jack got ready. They put on their uniforms and memorized their new identities and the layout of the transit station so they would not have to look too much at their handheld devices. Jack spoke as they were finishing repacking their duffle bags and backpacks: "It would be good to have our internal friend, Eddie, to help guide us through the TT station."

Dom replied, "That would be very helpful. From inside the outer tube, we are only able to send sporadic messages back to Eddie through transmission bursts. They had lost real-time communications with the voice in their heads during their journey and were now in a communications dead zone. Dom continued talking, "From what Caeso said the other day, the TT station has a communications jammer to prevent terrorist activity. I am sure

Eddie will be happier when he can join us again as our full-time voyeur partner."

Jack replied, "Now, now, Dom. Be nice to Eddie. As Caeso and Ant so aptly put it, Eddie is our generous benefactor. He's paying for this trip."

Dom smiled at the remark and replied, "Our payback to him is giving him an adventure of a lifetime."

Jack thoughtfully added, "We've sent regular status reports to Eddie and our finalized plan to get through the TT station and to the Roundup Hotel, so he's up to speed on where we are and what we're doing. That's how we pay the bills, Dom."

Time moved slowly as anticipation built up within the *Nebuchadnezzar*. Ant and Caeso were busy with last-minute preparations for docking at the station. There should be no one there as it was a highly restricted area. But one never knew what would happen, and the two TT service men wanted to access the door, see their guests through, shut the door, and make their way back to the relatively safe haven of the South America Ring Kingdom as soon as they could. Dreaming of what they would do with their payday and bonus for getting Dom and Jack through the tunnel door alive also increased their level of anxiety.

Dom and Jack were also anxious but for an entirely different reason—sheer dread for what was in store for them beyond the metal door. Their brief respite of safety on the *Nebuchadnezzar* was soon to end, and their real journey was about to begin.

CHAPTER 23

Following the Trail to the South America Ring Kingdom (the Authority Three)

The holographic image of Chinatown in South America Ring Kingdom ring five was frozen in front of them hovering in midair. The image was focused on the half-broken sign of the East Asian Mall above the double steel doors and the depressing street scene around the building.

Saul, Jackson, and Hector were still in a bit of shock after witnessing the three-dimensional fly-by presented by the Authority security computer jockey, Dru. They couldn't believe how bad the South America Ring Kingdom was, and they were filled with foreboding that it was to be their next destination. The only person in the command center with a smile on his face was the Authority security director, Gal. His lust for devastation and human suffering burned in his eyes. Saul had also pumped Gal up about how secretive this mission was, and that it had the visibility of the high Authority officials of the Innermost ring one. Gal could hardly believe his good fortune at such an opportunity to get his name on a successful mission of this importance. Saul had promised to tell of Gal's role only if the mission was a success to ensure no blowback in Gal's direction if it failed. Failure of a critical mission for the Authority resulted in death for everyone involved with the failure. It was a no-risk, all-reward scenario for Gal.

Gal slapped his hands together, diverting the trio's attention away from staring at the holographic image. "Well, gents, let's get this show on the road. All is set for you three with permits and tickets to the South America Ring Kingdom. From there you will need to take an aero taxi to the East Asian Mall in ring five. Once inside the mall, use Saul's handheld device to call this number." Gall swiped his hand on his handheld clear screen device, and the details transferred over to Saul's device, as he was standing closest to Gal. After checking to make sure it had transferred, Saul gave Gal a thumbs up. Gal continued, "Okay, if all goes wrong and you can't call, plan B is for you three to go to one of the security guards in the mall and ask for Sir King. We will give you high-ranking Authority uniforms, so they will get the message not to mess with you. The security guards will take you to an intermediary person. Everything there is cash on hand, so they may do a little shakedown for credits at every step. Two hundred credits is about the right price. Your code phrase to the intermediary is *quaero notitia*—looking for information."

Saul replied, "Sounds easy enough." Hector and Jackson nodded their heads in agreement. Gal continued, "Should be easy. Sir King will help you three find your detectives. One item of note, our—or should I say the Authority's—reputation is well known throughout the world, and we are especially forceful in the South America Ring Kingdom to maintain some semblance of an orderly society. Our order to kill first and ask questions later is taken to the next level in the South America rings, and there are rogue elements that would love to take out their frustrations on high-value targets. The high-ranking Authority uniforms will keep most people far away from you. However, be warned that there will be those who look upon you as targets of opportunity."

Jackson asked, looking directly at Gal, "What do you suggest?"

Gal replied, "If I were you, I would pack lots of firepower. At any sign of trouble, lash out and kill anyone and destroy everything.

That will make them think twice about messing with the Authority." Gal's eyes had that wild look again, and appeared to be salivating. Jackson turned away and looked at Saul and Hector. The two just shrugged their shoulders and gave Jackson the look: What did you expect a maniac like Gal to say?

With the plans set, Saul, Jackson, and Hector went back to their hotel to pack up and head to the TT station. Gal gave them each a duffle bag that contained their uniforms and extra fire power. In Saul's bag there were also special eyeglass that had an integrated 3-D video and audio device that would enable him to patch right to Gal at any time. Gal wanted Saul to use the glasses whenever there was any action that he might be able to "help out" with. Saul understood. Loop Gal in anytime there may be a killing. A bit disgusting, but Saul knew Gal might come in handy if they found themselves in a tight spot and needed some extra help or money.

On the aero taxi ride back to the hotel, Hector looked into his bag and commented, "These duffle bags are pretty good size and sturdy. Gal left a lot of room for us to pack more into it."

Saul replied, "That's good because we're taking only one duffle bag each, so stuff whatever you need to into the bag Gal gave us. The rest we buy as we go. Gal gave me a bunch of credits to last us a while."

Jackson looked at his wrist "Hey, Gal didn't give me any credits."

Hector looked at his wrist ID as well with a frown on his face. "He didn't give me any either."

Saul looked at them with a smile. "Well then, you two, you'd better make sure I'm alive and well all the time. Looks like I'm your sugar daddy."

"Ugh" was all Jackson and Hector could say to Saul's smiling face. Hector said with a slight grin, "I guess just cutting off his arm wouldn't help us."

Saul replied, a bit quickly to squash any thoughts, "You know as well as I the credit chip dies with the user. Keep me alive, my friends, and all will be well." They all laughed.

As expected, the trio had little trouble at the Middle East ring-three TT station wearing their senior Authority uniforms. Each had a cabin to himself, a free upgrade provided by a nervous ticket attendant. They knew this was the easy part and took the time to enjoy a bit of luxury and peace. Each one was lost in his thoughts of what was yet to come.

The hours passed quickly, and they came back together when they met in Saul's cabin about half an hour before arriving at the South America ring-three station. Saul said to the two as they entered his cabin, "I hope you two got some nice rest and relaxation."

Jackson replied, as he took a seat on a small couch, "It was mighty nice of that young attendant to upgrade us for free. I'll have to put in a good word for him."

They all smiled at that remark. The poor attendant had been terrified when he saw the three high-ranking Authority officials standing before him. Huge Hector gave the man a frightfully mean look that got them the upgrade. Thinking about the scene a bit more, Jackson said, "Hector, if you came across any meaner, we might have gotten a super upgrade."

Hector replied with a smile, "It's all about attitude."

Saul interrupted the conversation, "Okay, you two. Make sure your duffle bags are secure and locked. I heard the thieves in the South America Ring are topnotch professionals. Have your blasters on full strength at your side. If we get into a rumble, we want to show everyone we mean business."

The two nodded. Hector said, "Gotcha, boss."

Saul continued, "Stay close together. I'll put on the eyeglasses so our friend Gal can get a glimpse of the area as we go through the South America rings. That's the least we can do for our new friend."

Walking through the Transit station was proving to be a breeze. Most people stayed as far away from the trio as possible. Walking side by side, they looked more like the old Wild West gunslingers moving through the middle of town while everyone ducked for cover as they passed by. As they exited the station, the air slapped them in the face. Hector remarked, "Whhooaa! What is that smell?" He wanted to hold his nose.

Jackson added, "And the heat and humidity!" He wanted to undo the tight collar of his uniform.

Saul said, "Now, now, you two. We are senior Authority officials, and this kind of stink is supposed to fill us with pleasure. Just think like our friend Gal. He would love this."

Hector replied, "Sure, Saul. He would probably shoot someone just because."

Saul said, "That's the spirit, Hector. Now you're into the role. Come on. Let's grab an aero taxi and get out of this soupy air."

Saul hailed a newer-model aero taxi, and they quickly sped away. The aero taxi driver looked a bit nervous due to his special quests. Jackson reminded Saul, "Saul, you forgot to put on the eyeglasses."

Saul replied, "You're right, Jackson." He fumbled through his pocket, pressed a button on the side of the glasses to activate the audio and video, slipped them on, and remarked, "Okay. We are live now." That was the cue not to say anything derogatory about Gal.

The aero taxi ride to the fifth ring was all that they had been dreading after seeing the virtual fly through. And it was all that Gal hoped it would be as they passed by miles and miles of crumbling old buildings, smoggy air, and a claustrophobically low dome ceiling. When they arrived at the Chinatown East Asian Mall with its sadly half-working sign announcing the entrance to the mall, the cabbie looked nervously back at his passengers and announced, "East Asian Mall, gentlemen. Uuhhh, are you sure this is the place you want to go to?" This was obviously not the place for three high-ranking officials.

Saul replied, clinking his arm to the driver's arm to transfer credits, "No worries. This is the place." Turning to Jackson and Hector, he said, "Lock and load." With that, they reached into their duffle bags and brought out the latest in high-technology blaster rifles. They slung them over their shoulders for show so that no one would mess with them. One blast could take out an entire aero car. It was a weapon meant to create significant collateral damage.

Now the cabbie was really worried; it was time to leave fast before the chaos started. He sped away leaving the three to themselves on the grimy, dirty street. Onlookers hanging out near the buildings looked at them curiously. Seeing their blasters, they immediately lost interest and turned away.

Saul said with a grimace, "Come on, guys, let's get this over with." He led his small team of two through the mall entrance. Once inside, he opened his clear screen device and tried to call the number Gal had given him, but there was no response, so it was on to plan B—find some security guards. It was lunchtime, and the mall was quite busy with people buying lunch and small goods in the open-air kiosk area of the mall, which had the feel of a grand bazaar—a bit chaotic with no real order. When they got to the center of the mall, they saw two men in uniform off to the side, and they headed that way. As they approached, the two guards noticed the trio with their guns and went on alert. Then, noticing their Authority uniforms, they immediately looked to make sure their uniforms were neat and proper. As the newcomers headed straight for them, the guards immediately stood at attention.

"Sirs!" One of the guards bellowed as the trio approached. Each man had his right arm pressed over his chest in a fist—the protocol when one greeted an officer. Saul and his team did not have to respond in kind. They just simply approached the guards.

Jackson addressed them: "Your names." The two guards recited their names immediately, and Jackson noted them in his hand-held device. A bad sign. If anything went wrong, the guards knew they would be blamed. As they were talking, a woman screamed near them, and they all turned to look. The woman was pointing and yelling at a young man who was running away from her fast carrying her purse. The man passed right by them, and the guards just looked at the scene with more curiosity than anything else. What struck them all was not the screaming woman or the man running away but the four young travelers who came along behind the frantic woman. They looked like adventure vacationers with their easy-to-carry backpacks and small duffle bags. It was the lady with the bright green eyes who seemed to mesmerize the group. Green Eyes looked at them and quickly turned away.

One of the guards explained, "Petty theft runs rampant around here. It's more of a nuisance for us than anything else."

What Saul, Hector, and Jackson noticed was that the young man who had stolen the woman's bag ran right by the guards without even diverting or without any hesitation. This place was obviously run by some crooked mafia.

Saul told the guards, "We are here to see Sir King."

One of the guards responded nervously, "What do you want with Sir King?"

Saul gave them the response code, "Quaero notitia." The guards looked at each other. They were toast if they didn't take them to Sir King, and if they did and Sir King wasn't happy, they were also doomed. There was only one good outcome—the guards reluctantly motioned the trio to follow as they headed toward the entrance to the mall.

Jackson asked, "Where are we going?"

One of the guards responded, "Sir King's office is quite far from here."

The guards' aero vehicle looked more like a flying tank, which said a lot for the area as well as who had all the money. It was the Wild West out there, and the ones with the guns ruled. Zooming away from Chinatown, the aero tank flew to a large area where all the buildings had been demolished. All that was left were the streets outlining derelict city blocks. There were miles of emptiness before them. After traveling for what seemed like forever, just on the hazy horizon, a single large building covering a whole square block came into view. It was about ten stories high and was surrounded by a high concrete wall with coils of old-fashioned barbed wire on top. Sometimes the old methods of protection were the best. At each corner of the wall there was an elevated tower with enormous guns sticking out. The compound was guarded in all directions with impressive fire power. The building itself was gleaming steel and glass—a modern structure in a wasteland.

Landing in the compound near a row of similar aero vehicles, the newcomers spotted enough firepower for a small army. One of the guards said, as they walked toward the building, "Come on, gentlemen. The boss is waiting for you. We will take your gear for you inside." Several other guards met them all at the building entrance. They were armed with the same high-powered blaster rifles that the trio had. Obviously, to see Sir King one needed to be completely unarmed. Saul hesitated for a second, but what choice did they have now? He nodded to Jackson and Hector, and they reluctantly gave the guards their duffle bags, sidearms, and their blaster rifles.

With guards walking in front of them and behind them, they were escorted into the gleaming building. Inside, a huge open atrium greeted them with high ceilings and open empty space. Sir King certainly believed in the concept of open space as a means of defense. From the isolated building location in a vast plain of nothingness that no one could approach without being seen, to an open-interior building where there was nowhere to hide an approaching force, Sir King knew what he was doing. As the trio walked through the building, a hidden door at the back of the atrium area opened as they approached. They never had to speed up or slow down. Everything was timed perfectly by watching eyes. On the other side of the secret door was a long, narrow corridor. They stepped from an open entry area into a confined corridor. The narrow hall and low ceiling made the hallway a shooting gallery of death for anyone trying to get through the building. Everything was set up for defense on a massive scale.

When they came to the end of the long corridor, another secret door in the wall opened. This time, they entered a warm and spacious room. It was like a very nice hotel lobby with couches, desks, and a bar on one side and an open kitchen area on the other. The lighting was soothing. The floor was covered in marble tiles, and exotic

Middle Eastern–looking rugs delineated the areas furnished with couches and lounge chairs. This was a pleasant change from the stark emptiness of what they had seen so far.

A man was sitting on one of the couches. Two other men sat opposite him on another couch with a low table in between. Hovering above the table was a holographic image of a strange-looking ring kingdom.

As they approached, the man sitting alone got up to greet the visitors. He was tall—well over six feet in height—and slim. He had wavy, dark hair and a dark complexion. His handsome facial features were enhanced by his dark-brown eyes. He was definitely a man with South American heritage.

"Welcome to the King residence. I am Mr. King."

As he shook hands, Saul introduced himself and then introduced Hector and Jackson. "Sir King, we appreciate your hospitality. And might we say you have done a superlative job on the defensive measures of your residence."

Sir King smiled and replied, "Coming from senior Authority officers, that is quite an honor. Call me Altair. Sir King is—how shall I describe it?—a stage name."

Jackson said with a neutral tone befitting an Authority official, "We have heard good things about you, Altair, and we have been told you can assist us in our quest."

Altair replied, "Yes, yes. Thank you, Mr. Jackson. The Authority is … er … how do you say? One of our biggest clients. We can supply anything in any location the South America Ring Kingdom."

Saul replied with the same tone. "We are not interested in goods, Altair."

Altair replied, not hesitating, "But of course. You seek information. Information is one of our biggest growth sectors." Altair was obviously a very keen businessman, always on the hunt for the next big thing. Altair waved his hands, "Come over here and see where you are headed next. Of course, as high officials, you probably know about the Venezuelan Post."

Saul said, "But of course." He spoke with a straight face, not letting on that he, Hector, and Jackson were baffled by the strange city hovering in front of them.

Hector jumped in. "What does that have to do with finding our two ... ah, people of interest?"

Pointing at the holographic image, Altair explained. "We have just learned that your two men traveled a few days ago to the Venezuelan Post via transport with the TT maintenance crew. Information is sketchy, but we are certain they checked into one of the three hotels in the post.

Saul and his crew of two were fascinated by the strange post that had just two rings, a small inner ring and one large outer ring that looked more like some mix of modern and medieval history with a lot of military-style structures scattered all over the place. Saul said, in an offhand way, "We have seen the Venezuelan Post image before, but of course we are tasked to oversee the Middle East Ring Kingdom and have little working knowledge of this particular post."

Altair said, "But of course. You three would not have known that your prey has gone there and not tapped into your data resources. Let me assure you that we can provide you with somewhat current working plans of the Venezuelan Post. And we have contacts there who can help you on the next leg of your pursuit."

Saul said with a stronger upbeat tone, "Thanks for the assistance. Make no mistake, your loyalty to the inner ring will not go unnoticed. There are many future endeavors like this that will require your services."

Altair just stared at the trio for a few seconds seemly lost in Saul's words of future contracts. Then he replied with a grin, "Well then, gentlemen. You've had a long journey. How about we show you to your rooms where you can freshen up and change. We will meet back here for dinner, and then we can plan your next moves."

Saul replied. "Excellent. Very excellent."

CHAPTER 24

Local Connections
(God's Quad Squad)

After their tense journey in the South America Ring Kingdom and meeting up with their Christian brothers and sisters in the East Asian Mall in ring-five Chinatown, the day was finally coming to an end. John, Matt, Sara, and Christie were worn out, yet excited at the same time. They felt safe in the hands of their new family, even more so knowing that they didn't have to do any more traveling for the day. They were happy to be tucked away at the safe house located in the back recesses of the East Asian Mall.

The tired foursome said good night to their host, Mr. Wang, and then Rui, their computer expert, led them to their rooms where they could shower and get a good night's sleep. Thankfully, Mr. Wang did not set a specific time for the next morning to start work on their next steps. The orders were to get a good night's sleep, wake up at no set time, and then, when they were all together, they would continue their planning.

Rest came easily for the four that night. It was John who got up first the next morning. Getting into the shower and turning up the hot water felt good and was a welcome bit of luxury. He reminded himself to cherish the moment because luxuries such as this would become few and far between as their quest continued. About twenty minutes later, refreshed from the shower and normal bathroom routines, John made his way to the small kitchen area. There were two small dining tables next to the kitchen, and Wang, Rui, and Young Mary were sitting at one of the tables. They had picked their plates clean and were just sitting and chatting. Wang was facing the kitchen and saw John first. "Good morning, John. How did you sleep, Brother?" Rui and young Mary turned their heads and said good morning to John as well.

John replied with a warm smile, "Thank you all for your great hospitality. I was so tired from the traveling and still full of that enormous lunch yesterday that I knocked out. But I am never fully awake and happy until my first cup of coffee." That got a laugh from the trio sitting down.

Young Mary smiled at John. "Well, then, for our sake you'd better get a big cup. We wouldn't want a grumpy John on our hands this morning."

John laughed. "Bless you, Mary. You already know me well." After pouring a steaming cup of black brew, John sat down with the three of them, and they talked about themselves, getting to know each other. About a half an hour later, Christie came dragging herself to the kitchen, and soon after that, Matt and Sara walked in, all of them seemingly drawn to the kitchen by the smells of coffee and breakfast sausages.

Rui remarked with a grin, "Well, I guess you all have a great sense of direction. Or is it a refined sense of smell that helps you track down coffee and breakfast?"

Sara said with a big smile, "You're right. You could blindfold me, and I would smell my way happily to the kitchen."

John jumped in clinking his mug with Sara, "I guess that makes you our map reader and navigator then. Just don't get down on us when you have to use your olfactory skills around the South America Ring and beyond."

Sara crinkled her nose. "Ugh" was all she could muster as a retort to John as she remembered the awful smells of the day before outside the mall.

As they ate breakfast, John and Sara took the lead in filling in Wang, Rui, and Young Mary about their adventurous trip to the morgue to examine the deceased body of the older Mary, downloading the data from a chip in Mary's wrist and finding that it was an actual artificial intelligence chip with a clone of Mary's knowledge.

John mused as he drank a cup of coffee, "Well, I tell you what—we seem to have two Marys now—Young Mary sitting with us here and our AI Mary. We'll need to give one of you a nickname."

After a few laughs, Young Mary spoke up. "How about you call me Maggie, after Mary Magdalene?"

John replied, from his limited newfound knowledge, "I like it. Right out of the Bible." Everyone nodded with smiles. It was a good name that fit her well.

John continued, "So Wang, Rui, and Maggie, would you like to speak with AI Mary?" Heads nodded in earnest as John tapped a few buttons on his wrist band. In the middle of the dining table, the image of AI Mary's head and shoulders appeared. Mary spoke with her soothing voice as she winked her right eye, "John, thank you for reviving me from my sleep. My, my! So good to see you four again and our new friends from the South America Ring Kingdom. Our Lord is truly so wonderful to bring us here and to tie us together in a bond of faith and love of our Lord Jesus."

A resounding "Amen!" came from everyone.

AI Mary continued, "Wang, Rui, and Maggie. How much do you know about the Bible?"

Wang answered for the three of them. "Mary, we have a few fragments of the New Testament. Some information came to us in electronic format and some from actual books that our underground has saved and passed on over the years. There are very few copies of anything. As you know, to be caught with religious items results in an automatic death sentence. Much of what we know has been handed down through oral stories."

AI Mary asked, "Do you know about the book of Revelation?"

Wang responded, "Not much—except that it foretells of our Lord returning to Earth."

Mary paused for a second then said, "Okay, then." She slipped into teaching mode and gave Wang, Rui, and Maggie an abbreviated lesson on what information she had on the book of Revelation. John, Sara, Matt, and Christie had heard the same and more from AI Mary before but soaked in her talk all the same because it was so fascinating—scary but fascinating.

Mary started off as she had before, describing the final book of the Bible, the book of Revelation—the Apocalypse of John—the writings of the apostle John about the end times of the world: "It will be a time when all the people of the world will be judged by God, will feel the wrath of heaven and hell brought down because of their evil ways. For the sins of humanity, God will let loose the evil one—the angel who turned away from heaven and was outcaste. The dark angel will manifest himself on Earth to rule the planet with an iron hand and devastate the world with his evil power. He will decimate all until the second coming of our Lord Jesus. God will do this not to punish us but to give people one final chance to repent and accept Jesus as their savior. He will do it to shock people into making the decision. It will be one final plea to get humanity to accept Jesus, have their sins washed away by the love of Jesus, or suffer eternal darkness. Make no mistake, the dark angel will persecute all Christians as he wants no one to go to be saved."

AI Mary continued her lecture: "The book of Revelation warns us and tells us what will happen in these end times. It will not happen all at once. The end will come through a series of events." Mary talked about the foretold end times and described the horrific events that were to plague the world by the seven seals. "From there we just have fragments of the rest of the book of Revelation. We have a small fragment that mentions seven trumpets, and later something about seven bowls." Everyone just sat there paying intense attention to AI Mary as they thought about the terrors of the seal prophecies and imagined what disasters would come from the trumpet and the bowl prophecies.

Mary continued. "We have a fragment from Revelation chapter thirteen that describes the rise of the Antichrist, the devil himself, the evil one, returning to earth." She went on to describe what little they knew about the Antichrist. He would miraculously heal from a fatal wound. He would have authority for forty-two months. He could be identified by his number, six-six-six.

Mary marched on, telling the group about the world's history. Nuclear world war had started around the year 2100. The sequence of events seemed to match perfectly with the description of the first six seals of calamity—war, starvation, massive waves of death throughout the world, and then the rise of the Antichrist—and how it fit so well with what happened after the nuclear war. The promise of peace by the newly crowned one-world leader in 2118, the so-called father of the world, Shoa Khad. He changed everything to a one-world government with a one-world currency, and he even reset the calendar to the year zero, the start of the Enlightened Era (EE). AI Mary described how he had almost died but miraculously recovered. As the newly crowned one-world leader, Shoa, abolished all religion as evil proclaiming that there is no heaven or hell. He burned all religious books and wiped all religious records. His campaign washed over the world as he conquered and slaughtered all who defied him. The new world leader brought the world's population down to 666,000,000 and declared that, from then on, the population would remain at that level to ensure the remaining resources would last. He instituted the "retirement" age of forty-four years and four months.

Mary went on to explain that Revelation stated that the evil one would rule for forty-two months. And she explained her thoughts that the actual time might be interpreted as 420 years, and not forty-two months. If she began her calculations with the beginning of the reign of Shoa Khad in 2118 (EE 0) and added 420 years, she arrived at the present day!

She then began to talk about recent activities. Over the last several years, the underground networks had noticed increasing unrest within the inner Middle East Ring Kingdom, the center of power for the ten ring kingdoms. There had been a big increase in persecutions and the purging of people. Feelings of paranoia and anxiousness was on the rise within the Authority leadership. Previously, death had been instant for those captured for religious activity. Recently, Mary related, the Authority personnel had been torturing the captured to force them to give up names and to promote more fear others. The aim was to keep people from practicing religion, especially Christianity.

Mary let those words sink in for a minute before continuing, "Every year, Shoa Khad gives a speech to all the people. It was thought that they were prerecorded messages or some form of artificial intelligence projection. But what if it really is him? Our inside contact says he lives! And he looks the same as he did in the EE year zero, four hundred twenty years ago! What if we are about to enter the second half of the forty-two months and that it will really be months, not years? What if we are about to enter the trumpet and bowl prophecies, and then witness the return of our Lord? To know the truth, the times that we live in, and what is to come next, the rest of the book of Revelation must be found." Hours passed as the group listened in rapt attention to Mary's lecture before they broke for a late lunch.

That day's fare was old-fashioned sandwiches with chips and iced tea. Everyone was hungry and, after a quick prayer, ate in silence lost in thoughts of Mary's words. It was John who spoke first after a few minutes of silence. "I've heard Mary speak those same words before. This time it seems even deeper, scarier, and very intimidating. If we are truly on the cusp of the next series of disasters—the final end times—I feel so small and unprepared."

Sara jumped in. "I feel the same way. Now that we are actually on a quest to find the rest of the book of the Revelation, Lord willing, we will find it. The depth and the magnitude of the times we are in is unimaginable."

Wang thought out loud: "Imagine that! The end of days and the return of Jesus may occur in our lifetime. He turned to his guests. "Your quest is so critical now. We must find out what is to happen next so we can prepare ourselves and the rest of the underground Christian community."

Rui asked, "Prepare for what? To continue hiding even more than we are now and to wait for Jesus to come for us?"

Wang replied, "Based on what we know, there will be even more suffering and devastation ahead. But perhaps also a reawaking of faith as millions come to Christ before he returns. It will be our time to mobilize the faithful to reach out to the lost and bring them back to Christ before it's too late."

Rui reached for her cup of iced tea. Her hands were shaky, and she drank a big gulp, spilling some on her clothes. With a little bit of a hoarse voice, she asked in a soft whisper, almost fearing what the response will be, "If it is time for us to come out from hiding and actively spread the gospel, how many of us will survive to see his glorious return?"

Wang looked at Maggie, Rui, and the others sitting at the table and was overcome with emotion. Old friends and new friends. Certainly, if these were the end times, not all those sitting there would see it through to the end. Some would be taken to the Kingdom earlier. He was not fearful for himself, but he was not able to imagine the others suffering. Wang put his hands on his face as he wept.

They all knew Wang's thoughts, and they all had tears in their eyes—tears of happiness at the prospect of seeing their Lord's return mixed in with tears of sadness over the hardships to come. All felt the fear for what would happen to themselves and their loved ones if they were captured.

It was Maggie who broke their silent tears. "I do not know how I will handle the future. All I know is that I am thankful to Jesus that he has sent you all to be in my life, and I am forever grateful to be a part of this family. Thank you, Lord. I pray that, come what may, we will all be together until His glorious return. And if not on this Earth, we will see each other in his kingdom in heaven."

A round of "Amen!" came from everyone around the table. Maggie's words lightened up the group and got them focused once again on the tasks at hand. They all chatted for the rest of the lunch period, leaving behind the heaviness of the end-of-times talk and focusing on everything that had to be done that day to get a copy of the book of the Revelation. Wang and his team did not know about the mission that John, Sara, Matt, and Christie were tasked to accomplish, so Matt explained to them their need to get to Bogotá, Columbia, to the The Wilborada 1047 bookstore, one of the last known remaining accessible and intact bookstore/libraries that might have copies of the complete Bible.

Wang whistled as Matt finished describing their task, "Whew, that is a big journey you are all on. From what little we heard over the years, the Venezuelan Post makes our South America fifth ring look like paradise." As they continued talking, the head of Mary appeared and filled in what information they had on the Venezuelan Post from their contacts last heard over fifty years ago. She mentioned a military presence that had been dispatched there to fight off something or some people that no one knew anything about.

Wang sat back in his chair and motioned to Rui, their in-house IT specialist. She walked to her desk and brought back her clear tablet. As she typed furiously for a minute, everyone waited with anticipation and curiosity. Rui finished her last screen tap with a grand sweep of her hand and set her tablet on the table. Moments later, a two-dimensional schematic of a city with only two rings appeared and hovered in front of everyone. The inner ring was very small, but the second ring was massive. The streets and buildings did not form a typical city grid pattern; it was more like an elaborate maze.

AI Mary said, with an impressed look, "We've never seen an image of the Venezuelan Post before."

Rui explained. "Just a few weeks ago, one of our underground members contacted us and handed us a chip that contained this information. For security purposes, we transfer information and communications the old-fashioned way—person-to-person via dead drops. We don't contact each other face to face or by video, text, or voice. In case anyone is caught, we can't give up another cell. It's very sad not to know our other brothers and sisters in Christ, but that is how we live here in the South America Ring Kingdom. Only very rarely do we risk reaching out in any way. The chip they gave us had the information you see now of the Venezuelan Post, and the data is very recent—within the past year. The chip also contained a message that there is a large Christian underground in that post. Why we got this information is a mystery to us—until just now, of course, learning of your mission."

John asked with an amazed look on his face, "And you knew nothing of our mission and no one else knows what we are attempting to do?"

Wang replied, "We knew nothing."

AI Mary added, "Just as Rui said, for security we have not told anyone about your mission. Only I knew of it, and one other. And that other would not say a word for fear of his life and the lives of everyone around him."

John exclaimed, "Then this information is a true miracle! Wang, when was the last time you had contact with the Venezuelan Post underground?"

Wang replied, "John, before we received this chip, we never had contact with anyone from the Venezuelan Post before." Maggie and Rui nodded their heads to affirm what Wang said. The impact of what they just heard washed over them. Jesus was at work guiding them on their mission! Opening doors where none existed! Wang stated as a matter of fact, "It is a miracle!" He added, "And there's more. Rui, please continue."

Rui beamed like a parent who had a great gift to give to her children and who had been given the green light to present it. "Along with the schematic on the chip was an encrypted message. It took me some time to decode it as it used words and symbols from the Aramaic language."

AI Mary nodded. "The language of Jesus."

Rui responded excitedly, "Yes!" She then digressed a bit and discussed how she had decoded the message with technical speak about her algorithms that she developed based on Christian history, languages, and symbology. Seeing the anxious faces looking at her, she begged forgiveness. "Oops. Sorry about the diversion." The only person who wanted to hear more about Rui's programming was Christie, who was an IT expert. Christie had a bit of a disappointed look on her face when Rui stopped her technical explanation. Rui continued, "So the decoded message reads, 'Friends, we have been praying for so long for our Savior to come and rescue us. Life here is as it was for the enslaved Jewish people during the time of the Pharaohs. The other day, we gathered in secret, and we were amazed to learn that we'd all had the same dream! We dreamed of an awaking of millions of people to the Word of God. We dreamed of apostles from the South America Ring Kingdom coming to us on a quest to release God's Word. We voted to take a risk to send over what information we have on the Venezuelan Post, and we prayed that you, our long-lost brothers and sisters in the South America Ring Kingdom, still use the old dead drop. We await you and will pray daily for you. If this is God's will, seek us out at the Horseshoe Market located in Blacksmith City. When you arrive at the Horseshoe Market, go to the Silver Horse Store and ask for Mo. Give Mo the chip for proof. May our Lord Jesus be with you. We await your coming.'"

Rui paused to let everyone take in what they just heard. Wang said, "And there is more. The other day we were contacted through a black-market cutout. The word is that there are two men who made some quick money transporting people from the South America Ring Kingdom to the Venezuelan Post, and they are carefully reaching out to the secret societies that they are for hire. For some reason, they reached out to one of our underground cells. How about that for timing? When we received that bit of information and the information on the chip, we had no idea what it all meant—until today. Now all the pieces are fitting together."

They all thought about it. Sara said it first: "Answered prayers."

CHAPTER 25

The Venezuelan Post
(The Detectives)

After Dom and Jack finished packing up their duffle bags and had changed into their Authority dark red military uniforms, Caeso and Ant inspected them both. "Whooeee!" Ant remarked, "Your major's bars and that Venezuelan circle patch with a VP and armored tank symbol makes you look mighty authentic. Yes indeed."

Caeso added, "Looking good! Close-cropped hair, shiny black boots, and side-arm blasters in a hip holster. We are about fifteen minutes from the end of the tube. Once we dock at the end, Ant will immediately take you two to the maintenance door. From there, follow the layout as we discussed. Once you're through the maintenance door, you two are on your own. Ant and I will immediately push off and head back to the South America Ring Kingdom." Dom and Jack nodded. There was no need for additional words. It was time to put their game faces on.

The *Nebuchadnezzar* slowed and stopped right at the docking area, and Dom and Jack shook hands quickly with Caeso. Ant led them out to the maintenance door. He keyed in the code, and the door opened swiftly. Ant gave them a quick farewell, "May the winds of good luck carry you on your journey."

Dom replied as they passed through the doorway, "We will see you and Caeso on our way back!"

Ant smiled, "Looking forward to seeing you again, my friends. And another payday!"

Dom and Jack moved quickly down the service corridor, noticing that it was just the way Ant and Caeso had described it. About twenty feet down a short corridor, there was an elevator and a door to an emergency stairway adjacent to the elevator. Dom and Jack took the stairway and went up two floors. They exited onto a large open area filled with massive amounts of large equipment that powered the magnetic levitating TT. The area hummed with the sound of the equipment. The power was so high, the electricity made them feel as if something was crawling all over their skin. Not wasting any time, the duo moved quickly to the end of the area, keeping close to the right wall as a reference. At the end, there was a door with a keypad. Dom punched in the numbers that Ant had given to him. But the door didn't open. Sweat began to pour down Dom's forehead. *Did I key it in wrong? Or did Ant double cross us?* When he keyed the numbers in again, he was thankful when a green light appeared. The door opened to a wider corridor with doors on either side leading to machine shops and other maintenance rooms. At the end of the corridor was a T-intersection. There was still no one around this early in the morning. Dom and Jack kept the pace up, not running but nearly so. At the T-intersection, they turned right. Then, in the middle of the corridor, they stopped at an elevator. After Dom punched in another code, the door opened, and they took the elevator to the ground level. Dom took a deep breath. "This is it, Jack. When the door opens, we'll be in the public area of the TT station." Jack just nodded, his face showing grim determination.

The door opened, and the silence of the last few minutes gave way to a throng of noises from everywhere. The duo had not been sure what to expect, but a scene of chaos had been far from their minds. Dom and Jack were now in the main hall area of the TT station, and there were soldiers everywhere. Everyone wore battle fatigues with full backpacks and were toting weapons. Soldiers were flowing out of two large openings in the center of the hall. The detectives assumed the area most likely led down to the train platform. As the soldiers formed up into their platoon, a sergeant was calling roll call. When all were accounted for, the unit would immediately move out. There were so many soldiers coming out at one time from the cavern below there was a lot of confusion and shouting by the sergeants trying to keep order. It was a good time to move through the crowds and out the TT station entrance. The way out was easy to follow as each gathered platoon all moved out in only one direction in a single line formation with the sergeant in the lead.

Dom whispered, "Let's roll." Wearing their major uniforms, Dom and Jack walked side by side, not looking at anyone in particular. They kept their posture straight and their strides in rhythm with one another. The soldiers parted to let the officers through; no one wanted to be close to them. No one wanted to make eye contact. Soldiers who passed close to the duo put their fisted right hands to their hearts and then made a thrusting motion, straightening out their arms with their hands stretched and fingers together just like the old Nazi salutes. Dom and Jack moved through them like a hot knife cutting through a block of butter. They quickly made their way out of the station.

As soon as Dom and Jack exited the station, the throngs of relatively organized soldiers gave way to a more generalized chaos. The air was filthy with the smell of burning coal and wood mixed in with an odor Dom and Jack had never smelled before. Jack crinkled his nose, "What is that stench in the air, Dom? Whew! Powerful stink!"

Dom replied in a whisper, "Keep the comments soft, Jack. Remember we are supposed to be regulars here. It's just another day in paradise." Just then an old familiar voice popped into their heads. Fast Eddie's live audio and video feed came back on once they cleared the station. Dom had recorded their Tube and TT station journey for Fast Eddie as promised for his later viewing pleasure.

Eddie's voice came alive in their heads, "Hoowee, gents! Thanks for recording and sending me those feeds from your time in the transit tube. I'll definitely watch the highlights later. For now, great to be with you, my friends, in real time! I just wish I could have all my senses alive with you too."

Dom whispered softly, "Believe me, Eddie, you definitely don't want to smell what we smell." The air was filled with smog just like the air in the South America Ring Kingdom.

The transit station building opened onto a large open concrete area that led to the street. The street itself was wide—at least four lanes each way. Buildings about five stories high lined the opposite side of the street in both directions as far as the eye could see. Jack whistled as they approached the busy street. "Whooa, Dom. Look at all those surface vehicles." Cars of every shape and size whizzed by. Big old busses carrying workers rumbled down the road belching black smoke out of their tail pipes. Smaller passenger vehicles, most of them beaten up and old, rattled passed them.

Dom took off his major's hat and scratched his head, "Hmm, Jack, maybe we won't be taking an aero taxi after all."

Jack looked at Dom incredulously. "What you mean? You want to take a surface vehicle cab? The way they drive we may never make it to the hotel."

Dom replied flatly, "I guess this is the part where our odds of survival go down Jack."

Eddie, the voice in their heads, began to narrate a bit of history. "Gents, my research shows that Venezuela had the most oil reserves in the world. So, it makes sense that they continued to use old carbon-burning vehicles. With no exports after the Great Conflict, they have enough oil for themselves to last for eternity."

Jack muttered, "That's just great, and we can inhale all the carbon smog we want."

A loud animal noise sounded: "Hheeyy hhhaawwww!" Dom and Jack jumped back from the curb just as a whole line of horse-drawn carriages rolled by them. They looked up to see a large number of people making their way along the street in between the cars on horseback! Dom said, "Jack, there's the source of your smells." Because they were in a dome, there were no rainstorms to wash the horse manure away, so the manure built up on the streets and was then smashed up by cars running over it. Eventually, the manure dried and was blown away in the circulating recycled air system.

"Fabulous sights!" exclaimed Eddie.

After a few more minutes of standing at the street curb and not seeing any aero taxis, Jack gave up hope and hailed a street cab. The cabbie stopped and looked a bit nervous as he looked at Dom's and Jack's uniforms. Everyone knew it did not pay to mess with the military, especially officers. Out of caution, Dom and Jack Loaded their gear in the backseat where they sat instead of the trunk. They had to squeeze into the cab with their duffle bags stuffed between their legs. Nervously, the cabbie looked back and asked, "Where to, sirs?"

Dom replied in a monotone voice, "Take us to the Roundup Hotel." There was no emotion in his voice. He sounded just like the cold and efficient military robots they were.

CHAPTER 26

The Venezuelan Post
(The Authority Three)

fter a long journey from the Middle East Ring Kingdom, Saul, Hector, and Jackson were able to rendezvous with their contact in the South America Ring Kingdom, Sir King, otherwise known as Altair. After brief introductions, the trio went to rest for a few hours before meeting up again for dinner at seven in the main dining hall at Altair's residence. Altair's home was more like a fortress sitting in the middle of nowhere in the South America Kingdom fifth ring, surrounded by high walls and open space for miles around so that any approaching intruders could be easily detected.

Saul, Jackson, and Hector were dressed in the uniforms of senior Authority officials because they were the guest of honors. The security guards escorted them from their rooms to the dining area. Altair was already at the dining table with the same two other men the detectives had met earlier in the day, who had been sitting with Altair reviewing the holographic image of the Venezuelan Post.

Seeing the three Authority officials approaching, Altair got up from his chair to greet his new friends, "Ahh, gentlemen! Come! Come and have a seat." Altair was dressed impeccably in a tailored charcoal-grey suit. The two men with him, Tech and Log, were dressed in dark-blue suits that looked more like uniforms. The dining table was large, with room for at least twenty or more people. Normally, a formal dining room was located at the exterior of a building with windows to bring light in and give a view of the outside. This room was a bit unusual as it was in the center of the house and had no windows. Instead, very nice artwork—classical oil paintings—hung on the walls. A modern chandelier hung from the high ceiling lighting up the dining table, and small wall lights spotlighted the paintings and gave the room a warm glow. Having the dining room in the center of the residence increased protection and was another safety precaution that Saul appreciated. Altair had thought of everything.

Altair asked, "I hope you don't mind if my two aides join us for dinner. I assure you they are very loyal and have the utmost discussion. For security measures, we have mission names for them. Tech will assist with all software and hardware requirements, and Log will assist with all logistics, mapping, permits, and routing for the mission."

Saul, Hector, and Jackson greeted Tech and Log again, shaking their hands. Saul turned to Altair, "A small but efficient team is what we need, Sir King. The Authority appreciates your help and discretion."

"Thank you, Saul. Please, let's not be so formal. Call me Altair."

Dinner was a sumptuous traditional Italian four-course dinner starting with a few appetizers, aperitivo style with small bites to eat including tasty prosciutto, *gambas ailo* (shrimp in oil), and a wide selection of cheese and breads. The second course was pasta with clams (*spaghetti vongole),* and then huge Tuscany-style steaks (T-bone steaks) for the main course, and a full platter of sweets for dessert.

During dinner, as they ate and drank red wine, Tech and Log went over their plan to catch up with the two fugitives, Dom and Jack. As senior Authority personnel, they would be able to take the TT along with the Authority soldiers to the Venezuelan Post. From there, their sources had found that the two detectives were staying at one of three hotels. If they could not pinpoint the hotel, Saul, Jackson, and Hector would have go to each hotel together or split up and each take a hotel.

Log spoke up. "Even as senior Authority officials, you are taking a huge risk going in without backup support. It would be far easier to enlist the support of the Authority military, but we understand the need for discretion on this mission. There are a lot of factions in the Venezuelan Post, and even senior military officials and the Authority are fair game for many who are not happy with the system."

Hector asked, "So, the thought of overpowering forces doesn't keep the population in check?"

Log replied, "Good question. Our sources tell us the Venezuelan Post as well as the other posts are completely different than the ring kingdoms. Brute force seems to make the underground all the angrier, and unlike the ring kingdoms, the posts appear to have many more underground forces that oppose the Authority. We can't get any more information than that."

Saul rubbed his forehead as he thought out loud: "Hmmm, then for protection, we'd better not split up. It may take longer, but we'll go together to each of the three hotels."

Log replied as he took another gulp of the fine red wine, "Mr. Saul, that was my thought as well."

Tech jumped into the conversation. "From what I saw, you three brought in enough firepower to make anyone pause before they try anything with you three."

Jackson replied with a smile, "It's the latest technology. On the high setting, it can take out an armored vehicle."

Tech whistled. "That is impressive! When this is over, we'd love to get our hands on a couple of those."

Jackson replied firmly, "That can be arranged." Tech smiled big back at Jackson at the thought of some new technology. No doubt he would take it apart and try to replicate it.

After dinner, Tech and Log gave them a run through of the new gear that now filled their duffle bags. Log gave them what maps they had and a list of local Venezuelan contacts should they need anything.

The next morning, Saul, Jackson, and Hector headed back out after a light breakfast. The TT to the Venezuelan Post was not in the same TT station as the trains that connected the ring kingdoms; it was in ring two. Log and Tech accompanied them on the ride over to the ring-three checkpoint to ring two to review their plans. Saul, Hector, and Jackson would have to walk through the checkpoint on foot because access to the inner rings was very restricted. At the other side, there would be an aero car waiting for them. They had a contact name and number to call for the pickup.

Log also mentioned that the intelligence his team had gathered was that the detectives were being helped by a local mafia gang in the Chinatown area. They had not found out yet where Dom and Jack were getting their money and support, but it was obviously someone with a lot of connections and money, most likely from the Middle East Ring Kingdom where the two detectives came from.

Saul, Hector, and Jackson already knew Dom and Jack's backing certainly came from the Middle East Ring Kingdom because they had traced the detectives to the warehouse belonging to the Middle Eastern Imports/Exports. But they only had the front name of the owner—Bin Laden— and did not know his real name. So they said nothing and let Altair and his team keep digging. Maybe they would find out more than they could.

With their duffle bags slung over their left shoulders and their blaster rifles over their right shoulders, and wearing their senior Authority all-black uniforms, Saul, Jackson, and Hector were a formidable looking force not to be trifled with by anyone. They walked into the heavily armed ring-two checkpoint area, scanned their identification codes, which were embedded in their right wrists, and kept walking through without acknowledging anyone. Everyone they passed stood at attention and did not say a word. Their ID chips classified them as Middle East ring one Authority officials, one of the highest ranks possible. Any misstep from anyone in the duo's vicinity would surely mean death.

As they entered ring two, Saul tapped his clear communicator device and called their contact. Exactly as planned, an aero car came and hovered in front of them as they approached the curb. The air was noticeably better in ring two but not as clean smelling as even the air in ring five in the Middle East Ring Kingdom, which said a lot for the overall condition of the South America Ring Kingdom. Not a good place at all to live. Even here in ring two, people survived more than they lived.

The ride to the TT station was uneventful, and the trio didn't say a word to the driver. As they got closer to the station, the more modern looking buildings gave way to a more industrial area. The driver came to a stop at a nondescript warehouse building area. The short, five-story buildings filled the blocks around the station. Not asking the driver if this was the right place, Saul, Hector, and Jackson kept their robot-like game faces on, just as would be expected of ring-one officials. Continuing their stony silence, they got out of the aero car, grabbed their gear, and headed to the entrance of the closest warehouse building with no emotion; they were all business. That served them well as they entered the building that looked nothing like a TT station.

A guard inside the building directed them to take off their gear and place everything through a scanner. Instead, without saying a word, the trio continued forward with their gear, approached the guard's ID chip scanner, scanned their wrists, and kept walking. Several soldiers took notice and started to approach. The guard at the scanner was about to shout at them when he looked down at his display, which showed them as ring-one Authority officials. The guard stood erect and gave them the traditional salute, fist to chest and then straight arm out. The approaching solders stopped in their tracks, noting that the security guard was letting the three. They also stood ramrod straight and tried not to look at the three passing their checkpoint. Obviously these three were not to be trifled with.

Passing through and walking slowly so they could recognize what Log had told them about how to get to the TT, Saul, Hector, and Jackson never stopped, estimating that the next train was departing in fifteen minutes. Unlike the regular TT stations, there was no ticket booth. Making their way down several escalators, they found the train as described. They went to the front of the train where the VIPs boarded. Another guard at the entrance to the forward train car scanned their wrists, and they got the same treatment as they entered—the big ramrod salute. The guard nervously escorted them to the first door. "Please, sirs. This is our finest cabin with full privacy." Without saying a word, the trio entered the cabin and shut the door.

After putting down their duffle bags and blasters, Saul used his clear pad device to scan for video or audio bugs. Seeing nothing, he said, "Okay, guys. The room is clean."

Hector spoke up, "Hey, Saul, I could get used to this super treatment being a ring-one official. Look at this cabin! We even have our own restroom."

Saul replied, "Well, take it while you can, Hector. From what Log told us, once we're at the Venezuelan Post, our senior status will just make us juicy targets for disgruntled underground people. Let's get some rest. Traveling at over seven hundred miles an hour, we'll be at the Venezuelan Post in about three hours."

CHAPTER 27

The Venezuelan Post
(God's Quad Squad)

T he full impact of the information before them was just sinking in. Wang, Rui, and Maggie knew nothing about the mission that John, Matt, Sara, and Christie were on. And yet, just within the last few days, they had received, through a very trusted contact, a chip from a previously unknown underground Christian group in the Venezuelan Post that contained schematics of the post as well as a coded message. The message detailed their struggles, their prayers, and a vision of apostles who would come from the South America Ring Kingdom to help revive an awakening of faith to millions. Part of their message read; "If this is God's will, seek us out at the Horseshoe Market located in the Blacksmith City. When you arrive at the Horseshoe Market, go to the Silver Horse Store and ask for Mo. Give Mo the chip for proof. May our Lord Jesus be with you. We await your coming."

And on top of that miracle of information, Wang and his team had just been contacted through another source about two guys who had made some quick money transporting people from the South America Ring Kingdom to the Venezuelan Post, and they were now carefully reaching out to the secret societies that they were for hire.

All the pieces of the puzzle were aligning. The quest of John, Matt, Sara, and Christie was to retrieve a copy of the Bible, which would contain the book of Revelation, otherwise known as the Apocalypse of John, from the Wilborada 1047 bookstore/library in Bogotá, Columbia. And their mission was coming together.

Wang breathed out a long whistle. "Wow! It all makes sense now. We had no idea what the information we received about the Venezuelan Post was about until you four showed up and told us of your mission."

John exclaimed, "The information, the potential passage to the Venezuelan Post, and the Venezuelan contacts are just what we needed, and we received them when we were most in need. Thank you so much for all the support, Wang!"

Wang replied, "Don't thank me or anyone here for all of that. We did nothing to reach out to get that set up. God's hand is surely at work here. Nothing else can explain it."

Wang and his team ran with the information they had received and reached out to their contacts to set up the travel to the Venezuelan Post for John, Matt, Christie, and Sara. It took a maddening amount of time to send the message, get a response, resend it, and then receive a confirmation. All in all, it was another two days before it was all arranged. John asked Wang how much it cost, but Wang wouldn't answer John. It was their privilege to help their fellow Christian brothers and sisters on such a quest. Besides, Wang noted with a smile, if it were true that the end time was near, what was the point in saving money? They should just use it now while the money could be used for the tasks at hand. What tomorrow would bring only the Lord could know.

John asked, as they all sat around the dining table having dinner, "Wang, please run through the plan again." The next day they were to restart their journey meeting up with their "ride" to the Venezuelan Post.

After finishing a bite of chicken, Wang wiped his mouth with a napkin. "Tomorrow morning, we leave here early, at about seven. We will travel through the main gates of ring five to ring four. And then from ring four, we'll advance to ring three using an old but active worker permit we have to service a power plant there. You will be dressed in utility worker uniforms. It's almost impossible to get from ring three to ring two. For that we will literally use our underground connection. There is an old, abandoned utility tunnel that is just big enough to crawl through that goes under the wall between rings three and two in the industrial area. It's a few hundred years old, and the current maps don't show it."

Christie asked a bit nervously, "How long is the tunnel? I am not entirely claustrophobic, but I don't like enclosed spaces."

Rui hit a couple of keys on her pad, and a holographic image appeared hovering in middle of the dining table. "It's about one thousand feet long." Before Christie could ask Rui responded, "The utility corridor is five feet wide and five feet tall, so you will have to bend over but not crawl." Christie felt better knowing they would not be crawling on their hands and knees. Rui continued, "Just to make sure, you will all have weatherproof clothing and respirators. No telling if there are any hazardous gases or enough oxygen in the old tunnel."

Sara asked, "Weatherproof clothing?"

Rui replied, "Just a precaution in case there is water or any other type of infiltration into the tunnel. Remember, it's hundreds of years old. In fact, your very movements within the tunnel could cause structural instability."

Matt replied nervously, "Structural instability? You mean a tunnel collapse?"

Wang shot Rui a look and then replied, "I don't think we can assess all the potential issues with the tunnel. We do know it was used some time ago in the past by our underground brothers and sisters. Rui was just pointing out that we have some equipment that may help you get through unforeseen conditions. The rest, my friends, is up to God."

An uncomfortable silence filled the room as the trio thought about the old tunnel. John broke the silence. "Wang, Rui, Maggie, thank you so much for all that you are doing for us. We are blessed that, through you, the Lord has provided us with the means to get to our next step in our journey to Bogotá. The timing of the information you received was a miracle. Surely this can only be from God." Everyone settled down on John's words of encouragement, and they came to terms with their next steps. They knew they could plan all they wanted, prepare all they could, but in the end, the Lord would guide them to their destination and the fulfillment of their quest.

A day later, reality finally arrived. The self-named God's Quad Squad—John, Sara, Christie, and Matt—were wearing their weatherproof, tan-colored, one-piece suits along with old-style miners' hard hats with lights attached in the front. They got through the checkpoint between rings four and three easily enough with their fake permit papers and identification chips. Now they stood—hunched over—in the cramped concrete utility tunnel. Water sloshed around their knees, and they thanked Wang for insisting that they also wore tall rubber boots. Each of them carried a small backpack, which made it even harder to bend over. They had opted for agility, choosing backpacks instead of duffle bags. They wanted to make it as easy as possible to maneuver and run in case of an emergency.

"Let's go." John motioned and led the way. Matt brought up the rear. After about twenty minutes of slow, hunched walking, they realized the waterproof clothing protected them from the water, mold, and other bad elements in the tunnel, but it also kept in all of their body heat making them sweat up a storm.

"Ugh! How much longer?" Matt asked.

John called back, "We're about halfway there. Let's keep going. Take it slow. You don't want to slip and fall in this soupy mess or get a cut on a sharp edge." Along the walls of the small utility tunnel hung old, rusty, broken piping. There was no way of knowing what was growing on them or what chemicals they used to transport.

Thirty minutes later, they came to another shaft. The tunnel kept on going, but this was their exit point. The shaft led upward into the basement of a building where they could change and leave the waterproof clothes for their return trip. Climbing up the thirty-foot, narrow shaft took time because they all had to go slowly. When they finally made it to the top of the shaft, John opened the grate, and they all collapsed onto the concrete floor of the empty room in the basement trying to cool off from the tortuous tunnel walk and climb. Sara and Christie were stretching as John and Matt looked for a place to hide their watertight clothes and boots. The basement room was small and empty with only a few old desks along the side wall. Thinking of everything, Wang had made sure the lights on their hardhats were extra bright and provided light in a wide area. And the lights were detachable so they could take them with them in their backpacks. John and Matt found that the desks had drawers just big enough to hold all the gear they would leave behind.

They took long drinks from their water bottles and had a light snack of nuts and dried fruit. John looked at his clear pad device. "Okay. It's seven p.m. now. Our contact is supposed to meet us at the entrance to this building in about thirty minutes. From here, it's a half-hour aero car ride to the station."

The next thirty minutes went by fast as they rechecked their gear to make sure nothing had been lost in the utility tunnel. They went over the plan and their code phrases.

Because the ring kingdoms were enclosed in domes, darkness always came right at seven in the evening to simulate the real world. The foursome were waiting inside the front entrance of the building at seven thirty. Matt cracked the door cracked open, stuck his head out, and looked for the aero car. About ten minutes later, they heard a low rumble as a large vehicle hovered toward them. It was much larger than a typical aero car. It was an aero utility truck about thirty feet long and fifteen feet wide; it looked like a flying rectangular box. After the vehicle settled down in front of the building, two men stepped out and walked toward the door where the squad was concealed. "This is it," Matt whispered, and the four of them walked out to greet their ride.

Introductions were quick. The two newcomers were Caeso and
Ant. Caeso was of medium height and had jet black hair, a slim
physique, and the typical Brazilin brown skin. Definitely a native.
Ant, on the other hand, did not do justice to his name. He was a
huge, fair-skinned Eastern European who stood well over six feet
tall, and was all muscle.

The four climbed into the back hatch-like door of the large
aero utility vehicle. The interior was a reflection of the outward
appearance: a large rectangular box. There was room to move
around, and there were lots of tools and gear attached to the walls.
There was a worktable in the center surrounded by chairs that were
secured to the floor. The four adventurers sat down for their ride
to the station. Ant passed out dark-red service coveralls, each with
appropriate Authority badges. They were one-piece coveralls that
could be slipped on over street clothes.

Ant explained, "If anyone tries to talk to you or ask you any
questions, don't answer. Caeso and I will do the talking. You four
are trainees, and your badges will support that if they are scanned."

John replied as he was slipping on the utility coverall, "That's
good work, Mr. Ant."

"We aim to please. It's for all our protection. Remember, one
slip-up and we are all dead." With that somber note, Ant returned
to the front of the aero vehicle.

Caeso and Ant had planned their timing well and arrived at the
small ring-two TT station during a shift change when things were a
bit chaotic and many workers were badging in and out. The crew of
six walked purposefully through the back corridors and accessed the
maintenance door to the area between the inner tube that housed the
train and the larger structural outer tube. All the power, life support,
ventilation, and other systems that supported the train system were
located in this space. Ant quickly hustled Matt, John, Christie, and Sara
onto their maintenance vehicle, the *Nebuchadnezzar*, as Caeso powered
up the system and got them under way. Everything was going smoothly;
everyone started to relax as they felt relieved of the weight of pressure.

Once the *Nebuchadnezzar* was underway, Caeso came back to the kitchen area where John, Matt, Sara, and Christie were sitting at the small dining table. Caeso spoke, "I see you all found the best spot on our little ship."

"We leave it up to John." Matt remarked. "He has natural an unusual ability to find coffee."

John smiled as he took a sip of the hot, black brew. "Hmmfff. It's just one of my special powers. So, what is the plan, Mr. Caeso?"

"Glad you asked. Our normal speed is about one hundred fifty miles an hour. That enables us to check the systems as we travel to our scheduled repair point. That would take about eighteen hours to get you to the Venezuelan Post. But, to reduce risk, we want to get you four in and out as fast as we can, so we're making a speed run to the post. Then we'll perform the repair and make a slow return to the South America Ring Kingdom. Get a bit of rest. We are traveling at over six hundred miles an hour now and will have you at your destination in just under four hours. We have some snacks and food, so help yourself. There are bunk beds on the upper level. Take the stairs in that far corner. Our ship is your ship."

With that update, Caeso quickly turned and went back to the front of the ship where Ant was monitoring their journey. Caeso and Ant had decided to take on a bit more extra work to supplement the big payday they had earned by transporting Dom and Jack, but they had also decided it would be best not to get too close to their passengers. The less they knew, the better.

The few hours went by quickly, and fifteen minutes before they would arrive at their destination, Caeso and Ant came back to the kitchen area to see how their passengers were doing. They were pleasantly surprised to see them wearing completely different clothes—one-piece, dark-brown worker uniforms with the Venezuelan Post patch on their left arms and dark brown hats with the same emblem on the front. They were now disguised as low-level common workers who performed miscellaneous cleaning and small repairs. They were nonentities—essentially ghosts that no one paid attention to.

Caeso smiled. "Very smart. Whoever you are working for certainly has up-to-date information on the Venezuelan Post, which is extremely difficult to get."

Ant nodded in confirmation. "Yes, those are the same types of worker clothes that Caeso and I saw in the Venezuelan Post TT station. You all should have an easy time blending in except …"

"What's wrong?" Christie asked. "Is there something wrong with our clothes?"

Ant pointed at Sara. "It's her."

Caeso looked at Sara. "You're right, Ant." He turned to Sara. "Your bright green eyes and white skin will attract too much attention from the soldiers. You need to do something about that." A bit embarrassed about her beauty being called out, Sara blushed, but there was also concern in her expression.

Caeso turned. "Ant, get the kit." Ant moved to a small utility storage room and came back with a small briefcase, which he handed to Sara. "It's a disguise kit with cream to change your skin color and a pill that will temporarily change your eye color. The effect of the pill will last a week. Take several of them with you for your mission."

John looked with appreciation at the kit. "Thanks, gents. You two think of everything."

Caeso put his hand on John's shoulder. "Think nothing of it. It's all part of our service to keep you—and us—safe."

Caeso and Ant went back to their driving seats in the command pilot station, and they started to slow the *Nebuchadnezzar* down and prepare for docking. Caeso clicked the intercom "Five minutes. Get ready."

God's Quad Squad got up from their chairs and made a small circle. John, Matt, Sara, and Christie held hands as John led them in prayer: "Jesus, we thank you for this opportunity to be of service to our fellow brothers and sisters. Lord, we pray you cover us with safety as we go forward not knowing what the day will bring us. Lord, we are in your hands today, tomorrow, and always. Give us strength, Lord, to do your will. Give us wisdom, Lord, to know your will. Give us perseverance, Lord, to fulfill your will." In the next few minutes, each said a brief prayer for what was to come. And they ended with a resounding, "Amen."

John looked at each of his friends. They all looked at each other and then to John. John whispered in a low but steady voice "We are ready. Let's go."

SCENES FROM APOCALYPSE
BOOK 2: THE CALLING

About an hour later, the cabbie announced, "We're getting close to the Roundup Hotel. We should be there in five minutes. It's straight down this street."

The voice in Dom's and Jack's heads came to life. "Yes! I have five hundred thousand credits on the line that you two will make it. Looks like I actually may make money on your adventure."

Jack was about to make a remark when the cabbie's dashboard lit up suddenly. A huge red word began flashing, and an alarm buzzer sounded. The cabbie yelled, "Oh my! We have been target-locked! Hold on!" The cabbie quickly swerved between lanes trying to speed ahead to get in between two large transport trucks for cover.

Just as Dom yelled, "What's going on?" A flash of light appeared in the front of their cab. Then there was a huge explosion as a rocket-propelled grenade (RPG) hit the front of the cab. The entire car lifted off the ground about ten feet and then flipped over.

The cabbie was killed instantly. Dom and Jack were barely conscious in the backseat. After a minute, Dom began to move around—slowly at first, hands on his head from the pain. And then he quickly made a check of his body. No big injuries. Looking over at Jack, who was also moving around, but just a bit slower, Dom called out, "Jack! Are you all right?"

Jack responded weakly. "Yeah. Feels like no broken bones."

Dom responded, "We need to get out fast! This car may blow, and whoever targeted us is sure to be here soon to finish the job!"

The voice of Eddie in their heads urged them on, seeing his 500,000 credits evaporating quickly. But more than that, he liked Dom and Jack. "Guys! Get out of there now!"

Dom replied, "You don't have to tell us, Eddie. We are out of here!"

Scrambling through the broken car window, Dom and Jack made it out with their duffle bags and ran, weaving through the stopped cars. Everyone was running and screaming around them. The rocket blast had created a lot of collateral damage. A few other cars were also on fire, and bodies lay in the street. Injured people were screaming. It was chaos.

Jack pointed ahead and yelled, "Incoming!" Another old-fashioned rocket-propelled grenade streaked toward them, passing just over their heads. It exploded into a stopped car about twenty feet behind them. Dom and Jack were thrown forward by the explosion.

Shaking off the blast, Dom yelled as he pointed up and to the right, "It came from that building to the right! Open window about five stories up near the top!" Jack and Dom dug out their rifle blasters. They both aimed and unloaded multiple rounds into the building at full blaster setting. It was overkill, but there was no time to think their attack through. The entire corner face of the building exploded.

ABOUT THE AUTHOR

It has been a blessing to spend a lifetime living and working in the USA, Europe, Middle East, and Asia as an engineer. Over the years I had the honor to meet and serve with many full-time missionaries; gaining an appreciation of the joy, challenges, and hardships they face on a day-to-day basis. Brothers and sisters in Christ who have dedicated their lives to spreading the Good News of Jesus and serving others physically and spiritually.

The Apocalypse series is a labor of love as it combines Christian faith with my joy of science fiction. I pray you enjoy this first book in the Apocalypse series, the Quest, as much as I had in writing it.

ABOUT THE COVER ARTIST (JU OSHIRO)

Ju Oshiro is a renowned artist whose work has been accepted and showcased in local, regional, and international competitions, as well as at national and international art academies. Her major accomplishments include being placed as a finalist in the International Art Renewal Center (ARC) Salon competition and the Portrait Society of America members-only competition. Ju is a multi-cultural Mission Painter, Representational Oil Painter, and Commissioned Portrait Artist with a unique style and flair. Originally born in South Korea, Ju's world perspective comes alive in her works having lived around the globe during the past two decades in; Spain, Turkey, Italy, UAE, and her current home, in the USA.

See Ju's art at:
juoshiroart.com

Printed in the United States
by Baker & Taylor Publisher Services